EXIT 22

Safe travels!

P. M. terrell

EXIT 22

by p.m.terrell

Published by
Drake Valley Press
USA

ISBN 0-9728186-6-9; 978-0-9728186-6-7 (Soft cover)

Library of Congress Cataloging-in-Publication Data applied for

Printed in the United States of America

10 9 8 7 6 5 4 3 2 1

Author's website: www.pmterrell.com

OTHER BOOKS BY
p.m.terrell

KICKBACK (2002)

THE CHINA CONSPIRACY (2003)

RICOCHET (2006)

**TAKE THE MYSTERY OUT OF
PROMOTING YOUR BOOK** (2006)

SONGBIRDS ARE FREE (2007)

SPECIAL THANKS

The technical accuracy of this book would not have been possible without the assistance and input of many people who were gracious enough to lend their time and efforts to this project. I'd like to thank the following people for providing technical expertise: *Dr. Bob Andrews*, Robeson County, North Carolina's first Medical Examiner; *James Bourque*, Retired Assistant Chief of Police, Chesterfield, Virginia; *Scott Hyatt*, Chief of Police, Town of Lake Waccamaw, North Carolina; *John W. Neelley*, Sr., Federal Bureau of Investigation Special Agent, Retired; *G. Mitchell (Mick) Reed*, Chief of Police, Washington, North Carolina; *John C. Rozier, MD*, Obstetrics & Gynecology; and *T. Randy Stevens*, Chairman of the Board and CEO, First Farmers and Merchants Bank, Columbia, Tennessee.

I'd also like to offer special thanks to the following individuals for assistance in place settings and knowledge of Lumberton, Robeson County and Lake Waccamaw, North Carolina: *Martha and Frank Averitt; Mary Ann Masters*, O.D.; and *Farleigh Rozier.*

And to the following individuals for permission to use their names in the book to lend authenticity: *Zach Neelley* and *Danny and Mary Pittman.*

And to the following individuals for editorial comments and suggestions to help make this book the best it could be: *Pamela June Kimmell*, author of *The Mystery of David's Bridge*; *Karen Luffred*, thriller expert; *Georgia Richardson*, author of *A Funny Thing Happened on the Way to the Throne*; *Don Terrell*; and *Pat Thompson.*

1

Friday evening

It rarely snows in the Coastal Plain, but tonight Joseph was relying on the impending forecast to cover his tracks.

Dinnertime was barely approaching but the sky was already the color of pitch. He switched off his headlights once he turned off the main road, though the gravel road on which he found himself was difficult to see in the darkness. He slowed the truck to a crawl and relied on his memory of the straight, narrow drive lined on both sides by perfectly flat tobacco fields. Set back a quarter mile from the road was an old clapboard farmhouse, the windows glowing from the lights within and the pleasant aroma of burning wood wafting from its chimney.

As he passed by, he came upon an old tobacco barn that appeared to be one gust away from toppling onto its side. He knew immediately past the barn was a narrow dirt driveway. He turned onto it, edging the battered pickup alongside the barn until the dilapidated structure blocked the farmhouse from view.

He turned off the engine and focused his attention on a newer home to his left at the end of a long gravel driveway, nestled inside a semi-circle of thick woods.

About a half acre around the home had been cleared and from the looks of the fresh, small plantings around the foundation, he determined the brick and vinyl sided structure was fairly new. A set of dim solar lights lined a path from the driveway to the front door.

His eyes wandered from one window to the next. The upstairs consisted of three dormer-style windows. The one furthest from him was cast in a diffused yellow glow and as he watched, a young man wandered past the window. A moment later, the light was turned off, replaced by a soft one in the center window. He watched as the man moved past it, his head slowly lowering as if he were walking down a flight of stairs.

He followed his movements as he reached the first floor and turned on a light in the entrance hall, throwing the stained glass in the front door into a radiant mosaic.

Joseph's eyes wandered a few yards from the house, where the pine trees provided privacy from the old farmhouse, now off to his right behind the barn.

He opened a box containing latex surgical gloves. Methodically, he removed his leather gloves and donned the others. When he was finished, he clasped his hands together and flexed the fingers. They might soon cause his hands to sweat, but he didn't intend to wear them for more than a few minutes.

With his eyes set on the newer house, he opened another box and slipped a pair of black rubber overshoes over his Italian loafers.

His breath was beginning to fog the windows when he dipped his hand between the seats and retrieved a Smith & Wesson Model 351PD Revolver. He knew without checking that seven bullets were in the cylinder, though he didn't expect to use more than two. About six inches in length, the weapon was surprisingly light. He knew others who used silencers, but he didn't care for them. They reduced the accuracy and were more difficult to conceal, as they added length and bulk. He slipped the weapon into the deep pocket of his trench coat, absent-mindedly fingering the metal as he continued to stare at the house.

He cautiously opened the truck door. The interior light did not come on; he'd made sure it wouldn't after he'd stolen the vehicle. He left the door open. He walked to the edge of the truck and looked back at the road. He could barely see it in the darkness. And with the truck pulled close to the barn, it would not be noticeable from the roadway.

He glanced farther down the gravel road. There was nothing else there. No other homes, no businesses. Just these two houses set back amidst tobacco fields. The air was cold and crisp, with the unmistakable feel of an impending snowstorm in the air.

Once he passed the barn, he walked in a steady gait to a line of trees. He stopped briefly when he reached them and studied the old farmhouse. Its lights were still visible in the darkness, but even if someone were to peer outside, he knew he was sufficiently concealed. He remained close to the trees as he neared the new house.

He ignored the pathway from the driveway to the front door, opting instead to move around the house toward the back. There were three windows on the side of the house; through the gossamer curtains in the first window, he could see a formal living room from ambient lighting in the entrance hall. The second window was set high and didn't open; he assumed it was in a bathroom. The third window was the same size as the first. He stopped when he reached it.

The curtains were open here, revealing a breakfast nook. An Early American-style pedestal table was surrounded by four chairs with blue and white cushions secured with bows. Through this room, he could clearly view the kitchen. The cabinets appeared to be light oak. Along the left wall was a refrigerator and countertops obscured by mounds of papers and half-empty food containers. Along the right wall was the door leading outside. There was a security chain dangling on the wall beside it. A window in the door was framed in ruffled curtains. Stepping forward and peering through the window, he narrowed his eyes. The door was unlocked, just as he'd been told it would be.

   Directly across from him against the far wall was another set of cabinets, a kitchen counter, a sink and a stove and oven combination. And in front of the stove with his back to Joseph, was the young man.

Joseph remained at the window for a couple of minutes. His eyes wandered briefly to an open can on the counter.

He moved toward the back of the house. A detached garage was located just beyond the house with two doors facing the road. There was a new white Ford F-250 with a crew cab parked in the driveway just outside one of the doors.

He moved up several steps onto a deck. He stopped at another window that was located opposite the refrigerator. The young man remained at the stove, stirring the contents of the pot. The flame was high, as if he intended to bring the food to a boil.

He moved to the door. He watched the young man's profile.

The telephone rang and Joseph remained perfectly still, but the man turned his back to the door and hurried into the hallway. Joseph grasped the door knob. It turned easily.

He opened the door and slipped inside softly closing it behind him. He could hear the man's voice in the hallway. Joseph noticed the food was bubbling. The aroma of chili spices wafted toward his nostrils. He reached to the stove and turned it off.

"Okay," the young man was saying. "Yeah, we can talk about it after church on Sunday."

Joseph stood beside the refrigerator. Pictures were plastered all over it with the kind of magnets sold in tourist traps.

"Okay, bye," the man said.

He listened to the sound of footsteps approaching the kitchen. The man entered, turning immediately toward the stove. "Huh," he said, bending down to look at the extinguished flame.

Joseph took a step forward.

The man whirled around, coming face to face with the revolver. Joseph was no more than two feet away when he fired one shot directly into the man's left eye. He had already sunk to the floor before blood began to ooze out. There was no need to check his pulse. Joseph knew he was dead.

He was returning the weapon to his pocket when he heard a faint click. He cocked his head and listened. The house was silent.

He stepped over the body into the hallway. He stopped near the foot of the stairs and listened again. It had sounded like a door closing. He glanced up the stairs. The heater kicked on, and he let out an inaudible sigh. Probably the heater, he thought. There wasn't supposed to be anyone else here.

A light shone through the living room window, briefly brushing over him, and he instinctively recoiled. Someone was coming up the driveway.

He moved to the shadows, and made his way around the living room toward the window. Standing to the side, he watched as a deep blue sports car drove past the side of the house. The automatic garage door opened and the vehicle pulled past the truck and parked inside. A moment later, the driver side door opened. Under the glare of the garage's ceiling lights, he could clearly see a flash of long, lean legs before an attractive young woman stepped out and pulled a long coat around her. Then the car door was shut and she hurried from the garage to the house, using a remote to close the garage door behind her.

Joseph swore under his breath. She wasn't supposed to be here, he thought with growing irritation.

The back door opened and she screamed. He glanced around the living room, his eyes resting on an open doorway that led down a short hall to the breakfast nook. Silently, he moved into the hall and past a half bath to the breakfast table.

The woman was crouched over the man, cradling his head and trying to awaken him. She began to scream for help.

Joseph pursed his lips. This would never do.

He stepped toward the kitchen, but the woman heard his movement and swung around. He raised the weapon, pointing it directly at her head.

She screamed and tried to come to her feet but she slipped in the blood that now pooled on the floor. Continuing to scream, she half-crawled, half-raced behind the refrigerator into the hallway. He heard the telephone as it was knocked off the hall table, the bell emitting a short burst as it hit the floor. He heard another, louder, thump.

He calmly stepped over the man and followed the woman into the hall. There was a noticeable trail of blood across the floor, leading from the dead man to the woman. She had fallen again. Her coat was soaked in blood. One arm had flailed at a banister, leaving fresh red prints all over the white paint. She had retrieved the telephone and was frantically trying to punch the buttons for 9-1-1 but her fingers were all over the keypad.

He raised his weapon.

She grabbed for the banister, hauling herself upward as she screamed again. The phone dropped to the floor as the shot rang out, striking her in the face. She keeled backward, her head ricocheting off the newel post before she slumped to the floor.

He tried to step around the blood that she'd dragged from the kitchen into the hallway. He picked up the phone and listened for a dial tone. Her call had not gone through.

He heard a moan and he turned to study her. She had beautiful brunette hair that flowed down her back. He looked at the arch in her back and her three inch heels. He surveyed the blood splattered across the floor, the walls, and the telephone table. It was sloppy work. It should never have gone down like this, but there was no helping it now.

He retreated down the hallway and stepped over the young man. He glanced into the pan and sniffed the chili. It was a good night for chili, he thought as he moved past. Then he opened the back door and eased onto the back deck. He reached back inside and set the lock before pulling it shut. He checked to make certain it was secure.

Then he was heading back to the truck along the reverse route he had taken a few minutes before. He glanced at his watch. Only twelve minutes had passed since he'd exited the truck. That was about twice as long as it should have taken.

As he climbed into the driver's seat, a heavy, wet snow began to fall. He smiled as he started the truck, backed down the driveway beside the barn, and headed back toward Lumberton.

The silence grew oppressive in the house. Once the crunch of the gravel could be heard under the truck's tires heralding its departure from the house, the door softly opened to the upstairs guest room.

2

Christopher Sandige was so tired he could no longer muster the energy to remain irritated.

It had been a horrible day after a long and grueling political campaign. For weeks, he'd looked forward to this day. Win or lose, incumbent Congressman Willo would leave for the Bahamas, and he would take a break from his duties as campaign strategist. He'd been scheduled to leave Reagan National for the Florida Keys early this morning, but shortly after the Congressman's flight left, all of the remaining planes were grounded. Ice half an inch thick soon coated the entire Washington region.

After sitting in the airport for more than an hour, he'd decided to drive. After all, it was a straight shot down Interstate 95, even if it would take two days to drive it. He was in dire need of a break from life inside the Beltway, and even the drive had the potential to be relaxing. At least, that was the theory.

Traffic had been dicey all the way from Washington to Richmond, with accidents littering the shoulders and occasionally the lanes. As he passed Petersburg, the traffic thinned and the ice turned to snow flurries and then to freezing rain.

Now it was after dark and he hadn't yet reached South Carolina. He glanced in his rear-view mirror, catching a glimpse of his own eyes staring back at him. They were light brown under dark brows; a single wrinkle between them bespoke of years of furrowing them in deep concentration. Absent-mindedly, he rubbed his face, feeling the day's stubble, the deep dimple in his firm chin, and the slightly loose skin on his cheeks that his occasional dates seemed compelled to want to pinch. His thick hair was warm brown with just a hint of premature silver at one temple. He was taller than most, his head almost touching the ceiling in his vehicle. And he was lean, blessed with the type of high metabolism that instantly converted food to energy.

He averted his eyes from the rear-view mirror and concentrated again on the road. At this rate, he thought, it would take him four days to reach the Keys—just in time to catch a flight back to Washington.

His cell phone rang incessantly. At the beginning of his trip, he had answered it. There was nothing else to do, he had reasoned, except stare at the bumper in front of him. But as traffic picked up, he found himself gripping the steering wheel with both hands as he tried to avoid sliding on black ice. The calls were all work-related; his profession had forced him to give up on any type of meaningful personal life.

But then he'd become irritated; after all, this was his vacation, even if he did intend to spend it alone. So he'd tossed the cell phone into the passenger seat after he thought he'd powered it down—only to have it begin ringing again a couple of minutes later.

Now it alternately beeped to alert him of voice messages and rang with additional calls.

He glanced in his mirror. There wasn't another vehicle in sight. He held onto the steering wheel with his left hand as he groped beside him with his right. He was going to stop that blasted phone from ringing, even if he had to pull the battery.

He had just started to wrap his fingers around the device when it slipped from his grasp. He glanced over to see where it had fallen, but the seat was hidden in shadows. As he barreled down the interstate, the only illumination was from occasional highway lights, which cast a momentary beam across the seat that disappeared in the next instant. He reached for the interior light switch when a movement out of the corner of his eye caught his attention.

His head whipped to the left just as a large tan dog raced across the interstate in front of him. He jerked the wheel in an attempt to avoid it, but the Lincoln quickly careened out of control. The airbag deployed instantly, breaking through the steering wheel hub and coming at him like a beach ball out of control. It pushed his hands off the wheel, cutting off his wind before settling into place, a bobbing mass of fabric, his face involuntarily sinking into it.

Blinded by the airbag, he sensed the car turning sideways, traversing the highway so fast that he felt as if he were on a wild carnival ride. He was pummeled from left to right and back again before he had the sensation of becoming airborne. Then the wind was knocked out of him as it slammed into the ground. He shifted forward as the rear of the car rose behind him and almost above him before settling rudely into an embankment alongside the highway.

He heard himself moan, the sound loud and forceful in the car's close interior. A few seconds later, the bag began to hiss as the gas escaped.

His eyes burned with a fine powder that floated through the air and landed on everything in sight. He rubbed his eyes and tried to check for injuries. He flipped down the visor and peered at himself in the mirror. No blood. Just his bloodshot eyes staring back at him, wide and incredulous.

He unbuckled his seatbelt and opened the door. He didn't remember turning off the engine but when he stepped outside, it was no longer running. Steam was filling the air, and he opened the rear door and retrieved what he could grab quickly before backing away from the car.

After a few moments, he determined it would not catch fire. As he slipped and slid around the dark sedan, he surveyed the damage. The engine compartment was buckled, and the radiator had no doubt been severely damaged.

He turned his back to the interstate and studied his location. Robeson Community College loomed a short distance from the roadway. Just beyond it, he could see a service station, its bright lights serving as a beacon in the darkness. Closer to him was a sign alongside the interstate that read "Welcome to Lumberton, an All-America City."

He glanced back at the interstate. Not a single car was in sight.

When he turned back, he spotted the dog as it raced across the college parking lot. It ran with the same abandon and glee he would have expected if he were chasing a rabbit.

He sighed, his breath sending up a cloud in the moisture-laden air, and went back to the car. He could still hear the cell phone ringing, but he no longer bothered to locate it. Instead, he grabbed his suitcase and started walking toward Exit 22.

3

Joseph parked the late model Lexus beside the hotel and turned off the ignition. He pulled his cell phone from his coat pocket and dialed a number. The phone was answered on the first ring.

"Yeah?"

"One target down," Joseph said. "Collateral damage."

"How many?"

"One."

"And the next target?"

"Tonight."

The line went dead.

Joseph scrolled through his list of recent calls and cleared the last entry. Then he returned the phone to his pocket and grabbed the Wendy's bag on the seat beside him.

The parking lot was slick with a heavy, wet snow as he crossed to the hotel entrance. As the automatic doors opened, he strolled in, nodding to the young woman behind the registration desk.

"Good ev'nin', Mr. Gabucci," said the young lady who had checked him into his room only two hours earlier.

"Hello, Dear," he answered.

"You go out?"

He held up the bag. "Chili," he said. "Mind if I eat it down here?"

"No, sir," she said pleasantly. "How're the roads?"

"Slick. I hope you're not planning to drive anytime soon."

She glanced at the wall clock. "I'll be here another four and a half hours," she moaned.

He passed the desk and entered a lounge area. He stopped at the counter and poured a cup of coffee. Then he sat at a table, removed his coat and leather gloves, and carefully pulled the container of chili from the bag.

When he was finished eating, he helped himself to two chocolate chip cookies from a platter near the coffee. Then he tossed his trash into the can, peeled off two paper towels, and returned to his table and cleaned it of non-existent food crumbs. He tossed the paper towels into the can on his way to the elevator.

He returned about five minutes later with a tweed knitting bag. He settled into a comfortable chair and pulled a pair of half-glasses from his shirt pocket. After carefully situating them on the end of his nose, he pulled a tiny pink square of the finest Merino wool from the bag and began to knit.

"What're you makin'?" the young lady asked a few minutes later.

"Booties," he said, "for my granddaughter."

He remained in the lounge for several hours, finishing one tiny bootie and starting on another. It was quiet in the lobby, except for the occasional phone call. No one else checked in and no one else came downstairs. Through the front windows, he could see the snow turning to sleet and freezing rain.

4

Chris sat in a corner of the darkened restaurant and took a long sip of his merlot. Once it traveled down his throat and he felt its warmth, he let out a barely audible sigh in a vain attempt to rid himself of tension.

As luck would have it, once he'd reached the service station, he could see a sign to a Lincoln-Mercury dealer along the service road. It took the better part of an hour for a tow truck to pick him up at the station, get out to the interstate and load his car, and deposit it in the dealer's parking lot.

The service department was closed and wouldn't reopen until Monday morning. The tow truck driver was amiable and accommodating, offering to drive him anywhere he needed to go—as long as it was in Lumberton. Chris had asked for a ride to a hotel with a full-service restaurant within walking distance. So here he sat.

He took another long sip. The alcohol warmed his throat and cast the chill of the weather from him. Despite his ordeal, he began to feel the first inkling of relaxation. He might not have made it to Florida but he was far enough from Washington—and a world removed—to find some enjoyment in the free weekend he'd worked so hard for.

He leaned back in his chair, swirled the liquid in the glass, and surveyed the dining room.

Candlelight flickered romantically on each of the twenty-odd tables. A young lady with a sultry voice stood in the opposite corner and sang slow melodies that transported him back to the days of Joan Baez, Joni Mitchell, and Dan Fogelberg. His mind wandered to his college years when he was majoring in political science, of the tumultuous but invigorating days filled with anti-war protests and pro-civil rights rallies. He was going to set the world on fire one moment and save it the next. Where had his idealism gone? He wondered. When had it left him? When the singer began to croon *Key Largo*, her voice became both haunting and mesmerizing, and despite himself, he felt something tugging at his heart. For the first time in months, he felt an emptiness welling up inside him, and he wished he was not alone.

It was easy to forgo a relationship when his life consisted of hitting the ground running long before dawn, and continued hours after the sun had set. It was easy to come home to an empty refrigerator when most days included Washington power-lunches, or during an election year, pizza in the campaign war room. It was easy to say his life was too busy for dating, much less a serious romance, when every evening consisted of analyzing news reports, combing government documents, and strategizing. But when those things fell away, the vacuum that was left was almost unbearable.

Two tables away, the restaurant manager and the waiter converged at a front window overlooking the parking lot, parting the heavy drapes and watching the mixture of sleet and freezing rain pelt the pavement outside. They murmured something but Chris couldn't quite make out the words; he imagined they were blaming the empty restaurant on the inclement weather.

His eyes wandered around the room. Only one other table was occupied. The young lady must have arrived shortly before he did; when the waiter brought his drink, he had also deposited a glass of white wine at her table. She sat with her back against the wall, watching the doorway with veiled eyes. She wore a newsboy cap that reminded him of *The Great Gatsby*, and he found himself staring at her features—a slightly wide, upturned nose, high cheekbones, deep dimples beside full lips, and gently arching brows. One brow was slightly higher than the other, a feature that intrigued him. Though the room was warm, she wore a trench coat, the navy color accentuating her pale skin. As he watched, she lifted the glass and downed what liquid was left in it. As she tilted her head back, several strands of hair came loose from under the cap and cascaded across her shoulder.

He felt hypnotized by her hair. He took another sip of his wine as he studied it. The candlelight caught it just right, revealing copper hues that curled gently over her shoulder and reached down her back. He found himself wishing she would remove the cap and allow her hair to tumble freely.

He hadn't realized the waiter had left the window until he returned with two salad plates and two bread baskets, depositing one at the woman's table and the other at his. Chris tore a slice of bread from the half-loaf, his eyes still riveted on her. She had petite ears from which small pearl drop earrings hung coquettishly.

The singer was softly singing Roy Orbison's *Crying*.

Chris pushed his chair away from the table and stepped to her table. As he approached, she looked up from her salad. She leaned back, her face partially shrouded in the shadows.

"Excuse me," Chris said, "I noticed we're both alone, and I thought you might enjoy a dinner companion?"

She looked at him for a moment before turning her attention to his table. She held the fork just above her salad. Her nails were manicured. She wore a broad silver filigreed band on her right hand. Her left hand remained in her lap.

"It's just dinner," he said awkwardly. "I'm passing through town, and, well…"

"Sure," she said, setting down her fork and pushing her chair back.

"No," Chris hurriedly added, "don't move. Stay where you are, and I'll be right back."

"I'll move everything for you," the waiter said, quickly moving to his table. "More wine?"

"Yes," she said before Chris could respond.

With the waiter busily retrieving the items from his table, Chris held out his hand. His throat had become dry as he said, "My name's Chris. Chris Sandige."

She shook it. Her hand was as soft as a baby's skin, but the shake was firm.

"Your name…?"

"Brenda," she said.

"Brenda…?"

She peered out from under the cap's bill, her chin slightly tilted upward. "It's just dinner."

He downed the rest of his wine and ordered another glass.

By the time he had finished his steak, he still knew nothing more than her name. She had barely touched her salad, had eaten none of her bread, and only a couple of forkfuls of a seafood dish. She'd kept her eyes gently moving from the doorway to a window, watching as an occasional car passed by.

He'd repositioned the candle when the entrees had come, and now he could see that her eyes were so light a shade of brown they appeared to be amber. He had never seen eyes that color, and he found himself following their movement, and the slight shift of those long strands of copper hair as she tilted her head.

"So what do you do?" she asked, raising her wine to her lips. Her voice was husky, he thought, the kind of voice a woman wakes up with but is gone before her lipstick is on.

"I work for a congressman," he said. "In Washington."

One brow lifted slightly. "Oh?" Then her attention returned to her food.

He felt a strange mixture of sensations. Normally, when he announced he worked for a congressman, the reaction was predictable: the women were suitably impressed, their eyes wide and starry, and their defenses immediately vanished. The reaction was magnified the farther he got from the nation's capital. But he might have told her he was a window washer or a shoe salesman from her disinterested reaction, and his heart sank. At the same time, he felt flushed and breathless. He pushed his wine glass away from his plate and took a deep swallow of water instead.

"I've been working on a reelection campaign," he continued.

Her eyes locked on his. "So did she win?"

"He. Yes."

"Congratulations."

"Thank you."

He ordered coffee and dessert. It was too late for caffeine and he never ate dessert, but he couldn't think of another way to prolong the evening. He breathed a sigh of relief when she also ordered coffee. She passed on dessert. When it came, he considered offering her a taste of his, but he thought better of the idea. He felt as if an invisible arm was stretched out between them, holding him back.

"So what are you doing here?" she asked, stirring some cream into her coffee.

"I had an accident," he said. "On the interstate."

Her eyes brushed over him. "Were you hurt?"

"No. Just ran off the road."

She nodded. Another strand of hair escaped from her cap. "Bad road conditions."

"Yes. Bad road conditions."

She continued looking at him. He thought he should turn his attention to his dessert, but he couldn't tear his eyes from hers.

"The dealer won't reopen until Monday," he said, his voice sounding far away. "I'm kind of stuck here until then."

"What will you do?"

"I know what I'd like to do."

She tilted her chin up. Her lips were full, he noted, but they weren't smiling.

He cleared his throat. "I'd like to be on my way to Florida," he said. "That's where I was headed when I ran off the road." He shrugged. "But that's not going to happen."

He didn't know when the singer stopped singing, packed up and left the restaurant. He only knew that his coffee had grown cold and his dessert had grown warm, and still he didn't want the evening to end. But finally, he provided his room number to the waiter and signed the check to add the meals to his room bill, waving off her attempt to pay for her own meal.

Then he rose and helped her out of her seat. They strolled through the restaurant; she walked just far enough ahead of him to enable him to examine her figure in the navy trench coat, the broad belt accentuating her slender waist. She was taller than she'd appeared when seated; he figured she must have been about five foot eight. He found himself standing straighter, though he was a good four inches taller.

They stopped outside the restaurant, in the lobby of the hotel.

"Are you staying here?" he asked.

"No."

After an awkward moment of silence, he pointed toward the end of the hall. "I take the elevator upstairs."

She nodded. After another moment, she turned her head and looked down the hallway. "I'll take the back door to my car," she said. "Less walking outside."

He motioned for her to go first. He thought he should say something more, ask her to spend more time with him, but he had no idea what he could say. He had no car, didn't know his way around town, and had no clue where they could go.

They reached the elevator and he pushed the button.

She held out her hand. "It was nice meeting you, Chris Sandige," she said. "And thank you for dinner."

He grasped her hand. Behind her, at the end of the hallway, he glimpsed two police officers approaching the door from outside. A blast of cold air reached the pair as they opened the door. He said, "It was nice meeting you, Brenda... Brenda?"

She gently but firmly pulled her hand from his grasp as the elevator door opened.

"Tell me your last name," he whispered.

"Your elevator is here," she said.

He stepped inside the elevator but he didn't punch a button. His eyes were glued to her face, at her slightly parted lips and eyes that appeared somewhat saddened. As the door began to shut, she turned to go.

He watched the wide door glide in front of him as a feeling of emptiness washed over him. Despite the urgency to leave Washington and escape his work, even if it were only for a weekend, he now dreaded the thought of an empty hotel room, with the furniture and sanitized odors exactly like a hundred others… Reluctantly, he reached forward. He was just about to punch the button for his floor when an arm in a blue trench coat shot inside, causing the door to jerk open.

Then she was inside, frantically pushing the buttons. "Close, close, close," she said as the door shut behind her.

5

It was after midnight when Joseph turned south on Elm Street. The air in the Ford Taurus was cold from having sat on the rental car lot, and though he had the heat cranked up high, he didn't expect it to take away the chill before he had arrived at her house.

He drove past it slowly. The town was quiet, its inhabitants still sleeping. He glanced in the rearview mirror. The tires left two slushy impressions all the way down the street. That would dissipate, he thought, once the sun rose.

It was a small house. There was a front door adorned with a grapevine wreath swathed in autumn colors that opened onto a tiny roofless stoop. One ground floor window faced the road. The blinds were drawn, but Joseph knew the door opened directly into the living room.

He stopped at the corner and turned, driving past the side of the house. There were three windows on the ground floor. They would be to the living room, the dining room and the kitchen, he reminded himself. Upstairs, there were two windows—one for each bedroom. There was a full bath upstairs, accessible from either bedroom, and a half bath downstairs off the kitchen and laundry area. There was no garage but a short gravel driveway just long enough for one car. And there it was: her sand-colored Toyota Highlander.

His headlights bathed two figures in their harsh white light. He turned his head as he passed a tall, thin woman walking a Jack Russell terrier. He nodded. She did not return his nod, but watched him as he drove past. He drove two more blocks, scrutinizing her in the rearview mirror. She continued watching him, her figure visible from a streetlight.

He turned onto Pine Street, drove a few blocks, and then circled back toward Elm. As he neared her house for the second time, a dim light in an upstairs bedroom was turned on. He drove past it this time, continuing for another block before turning down a side street and parking.

He could see the house clearly. He shut off the ignition and turned off the headlights. He opened a new package of latex gloves and slipped them on. He surveyed the block between them; the sidewalk beside neatly trimmed centipede grass that had turned brown in the cold weather, the darkened houses between his car and her house, and the trees that reached over the road like giant spiders.

Turning toward his side mirror, he spotted the woman and the dog walking up the side street. They were still a full house away from him, but the woman was peering at his license plate.

He started the engine and pulled away from the curb, calmly driving several blocks before turning. This time, he retreated to downtown Lumberton, pulling into a church parking lot. He felt his breath grow shallower. In a few hours, the sun would begin to rise and his window of opportunity would have closed.

He waited ten minutes and then circled the houses in the quaint, quiet neighborhood. Somewhere in the distance, a dog howled.

He drove along the side road, coming up behind her house. Now the entire second floor was bathed in a bright bluish-white light.

He stopped at the end of the driveway. He watched for a shadow crossing in front of the blinds, but he saw none. He was unable to determine which bedroom she was in.

A light came on downstairs in the back of the house, followed immediately by a light in front. It had been too rapid for her to have crossed from one room to another, he thought. Could she have company?

He spotted the woman with the dog across the street. She had one hand on her hip and was talking on a cell phone. She was facing him.

He pulled the car away from the curb and drove past her. It was the wrong time. There would be another opportunity. There would have to be, if he were to accomplish his assignment and get back to Washington.

6

Saturday morning

Lieutenant Alec Brodie of the Robeson County Sheriff's
Department drove slowly north on Chestnut Street.
He liked this time of day, before the sun rose and the people
were out and about. It was peaceful now, the streetlights
casting an idyllic glow over the wet streets.

In another hour, the wet pavement would begin to dry
as the sun made its appearance and the temperature rose.
The snow had lasted for less than an hour, just long enough
to create a slippery mess the previous night. It was followed
by several hours of sleet and freezing rain, prompting more
than one fender-bender in the county but nothing serious.

Alec didn't work those calls but simply listened to the
radio traffic as they were dispatched. He was new in the
Department, having retired from the Baltimore, Maryland
Police Department just last summer. He'd been a homicide
detective there for more years than he cared to think about
until he'd finally had enough and decided to return to North
Carolina. He'd been born and raised in nearby Scotland
County, as generations of his family had been before him.
He met his wife Cherie at the state fair, and when she

wanted to return to her home state of Maryland to be closer to her parents, he was more than happy to accommodate her. She had been the love of his life, his everything... But that was before. Now he was back in North Carolina, though he was a county over and starting all over again.

A pickup whizzed past him and he watched it until it was out of sight. He caught a glimpse of himself in his rear-view mirror but tried not to dwell on his gray-green eyes. There were bags forming under them and they seemed to droop more distinctly at the outer corners. A hang-dog look is what his father would have called it. His forehead was etched as if he'd spent a lifetime in the sun; sometimes a stray lock of his sandy hair fell onto his thick brows. He'd been handsome once, or so he'd been told, but he'd come to the conclusion that those days were over. His middle was thicker than it had ever been, although it wasn't hanging over his belt like a lot of men he'd known; he hoped he'd never let himself get that far out of shape even though he didn't have the motivation to halt its advance.

He passed Trinity Episcopal Church and started to slow even more, eventually stopping in front of a well-kept house with purple pansies encapsulated in thin sheets of ice. He tapped his horn and waited.

A woman appeared at the window next door, her gray hair disheveled. Alec waved but the woman grasped her housecoat at her neck as if protecting her dignity and ducked away from the window but not quite out of sight.

He turned his attention back to the first house. Usually, Martin Malleck opened the front door and offered a brief but courteous half-wave, half-salute, but this morning the door remained closed.

As he continued watching, a calico cat jumped onto the window ledge in the living room and began meticulously grooming itself. He knew it to be one of four, unless his partner Dani had learned of others in need of rescue and a warm home. Just in the past two weeks, Dani had rescued two litters of kittens and found them all good homes within twenty-four hours.

The front door opened a moment later and a woman stepped outside, balancing a coffee cup in her palm while she closed and locked the door behind her. She made her way down a couple of slippery steps and a short sidewalk before coming around to the passenger side of the vehicle. She was dressed in dark blue dress slacks above short black heels; a matching blue blazer and white blouse peeked from the neckline of a jacket with the Robeson County Sheriff's Department insignia emblazoned on it.

Alec reached across the seat and opened the door for her. She slid in, still balancing the plastic cup. She wrapped both her hands around it for warmth.

"Good morning," Alec said.

"Morning," she answered.

Alec glanced back at the neighbor's house, where the woman had returned to the window and was watching them. Alec waved again. She didn't respond but after a moment, she stepped away.

"Where's Martin?" Alec asked as he started to drive.

"Out of town. Business trip. He'll be back tomorrow night."

He stole a sideways glance at her. When he'd been told his partner's name, he assumed it was *Danny* Malleck, a male. He still remembered how surprised he'd been when he discovered the name was *Dani* Malleck, and she was a knock-out female. He supposed she was in her mid thirties. He'd never seen her hair down, and wondered how long it was; it was always pulled into a proper bun on the back of her head. Not a wisp was ever out of place. It was jet black against flawless olive skin. When she looked at him with her crystal blue eyes, she appeared exotic, like a Mediterranean fantasy. As thick as he was becoming, she appeared to be getting thinner. She was as tall as he was; and after seeing her UNC track awards displayed on her credenza, he knew she could outrun him. Their first time at the firing range, he discovered she could outshoot him as well.

She'd worked for the Sheriff's Office for almost fifteen years and had just become the department's first female homicide detective. She seemed very much aware that she'd broken through a tough glass ceiling; her high degree of professionalism told him she took the title very seriously. Sometimes too seriously.

They were partnering until she had enough experience to work on her own and he had learned how things were done in this outfit. The others in the office called them Alec and Malleck, something neither was fond of hearing. She was as smart as a whip, and Alec didn't think it would take her long to fly solo.

The radio crackled to life. She responded.

"Got a double homicide for you," the dispatcher said.

They listened as the address was given. Alec turned right at the next cross-street and hurried to Pine Street, where he turned left and headed to the north side of town.

"The farm's out past Meadow Road?" Dani was saying to the dispatcher. "That's Jerry Landon's place, isn't it?"

"It's Jerry's son, Nate, and his wife Peggy Lynn. The house next door," the dispatcher answered. Alec thought he detected her voice cracking. "Jerry'll be waiting for you."

7

The gravel road in front of the farmhouse was packed with people, though the sunrise was just beginning to peek over the horizon. Alec rolled down his window and politely asked them to move to the other side of the road so he could get by. By the time he parked at the end of the driveway, they were back, surrounding his car and asking questions.

"Where did all these folks come from?" he said to Dani under his breath.

"Jerry Landon's a big name in these parts," Dani answered. "Word travels fast."

A deputy was rounding the side of the house as they approached. He waved them toward the back. "They're in there," he said, pointing toward the back door. Alec thought his face appeared ashen. "I went to church with 'em," he said, shaking his head.

Before Alec could respond, the deputy was halfway to the street. "Didn't I ask y'all to stay back aways?" he called out. "We won't know anything for awhile; y'all just go on."

Alec stopped when he reached the deck at the back of the house.

"What is it?" Dani asked.

"Footprints," he said, nodding toward the garage.

"Female," Dani said, leaning down to study them. Their eyes followed the petite set of footprints as they meandered from the closed garage door to the back deck, where they were obliterated by the slush from more recent shoes.

"Get somebody out here to photograph that line before everything melts," Alec said.

"Already on it," she responded as she radioed for crime scene techs.

Alec pointed in another direction. "Those too," he said, "Looks like they lead to the barn."

They were met at the back door by a slight young deputy with a bulbous nose more suited to a larger man. "Alec and Malleck are here," he announced to the people behind him.

"Tyler, did you follow those prints?" Alec asked, pointing to the second set of footprints.

"Well, no," Tyler said, scratching his head. "I didn't notice them. I was too busy inside with Mr. Landon—"

"Do me a favor; check them out?"

"Yeah, yeah, I will."

They watched as Tyler walked a reasonable distance from the soggy prints, following their direction. As he neared the barn, he fingered his revolver in its holster. Tyler was young and he was honest and hard-working but he had a lot to learn, Alec thought.

Alec turned around and stepped into the kitchen. The body of a young man was sprawled across the kitchen tile. The amount of blood was astonishing; he'd bled out across the floor, running almost to the back door. A smeared set of prints and a swirl was near his body, almost like someone had run a mop through the blood.

He knelt beside the victim. He hoped his own face wasn't as pale and clammy as it felt. The room began to spin, and he forced himself to concentrate. There was a single gunshot wound to the man's eye. He knew from the brain matter on the floor that the exit wound was much larger at the back of his head. As he stared at the man's face, the hair seemed to morph into his wife's long brown hair; his one open eye becoming hers. It all threatened to rush back to him in an instant: finding his wife on the bedroom floor, the self-inflicted gunshot wound to her head, the stilled pulse and unseeing eyes. But Cherie had been shot in the temple, not the eye; and as he had stared into her face on that nightmarish day, both eyes had stared back at him. She was the reason he'd left Baltimore, why he'd never spent another night in the home they'd built together, and why he was back home again in North Carolina.

Dani cleared her throat, and he glanced up. "Close range," he said. "Probably killed instantly." He came to his feet. "Evidence techs on their way?"

"Should be here any minute," Dani answered.

"Who found him?"

Dani nodded toward the dining table, and Alec followed her eyes as they came to rest on a deputy sitting next to a man slumped at the table. As he approached, Deputy Gus Howard stood up.

"Jerry," he said to the man, "this is Lieutenant Alec Brodie."

The man barely looked up. He was silver-haired; the thinning top was unkempt as he ran his trembling fingers through it. His silvery blue eyes protruded slightly and his face was twisted in anguish; from the appearance of his puffy cheeks and plump red nose, he'd been crying. His shoulders were slumped and his back bent.

"Mr. Landon," Alec said, kneeling beside him, "I'm sorry for your loss. I take it that Nate is your son?"

The man nodded. "My only child," he managed to say before his body was wracked with sobs.

Alec waited a moment before continuing. "I know this is hard for you right now, but we want to catch whoever did this. Can you tell me when you found him?"

"We were going deer hunting," he said. "He was supposed to be at my house at dawn, and when he didn't show…" His shoulders shook as he burst into fresh tears.

Alec waited patiently. "So you came over here," he said, "and was the door open?"

"No. It was locked. It's never locked," he added as if in a daze. "Had to go back home and get a key. I let myself in. And there he was—"

Alec rose and studied Nate's body. "You came through the back door?" he asked.

Jerry Landon nodded.

"What did you do when you saw him?"

"I ran to him, of course," he said. "I tried to help him, but—but, he was already—" Unable to finish the sentence, his body shook with a fresh onslaught of tears.

Alec took a few steps toward the body. "Did you try to clean up?"

"Clean up?" He looked up.

"Clean up the blood."

"No," he said, his lower lip trembling. He turned to Dani. "Was I supposed to clean up?"

"No, sir," she said, grasping his hand. "It's just… we're wondering about that swirl in the blood."

Everyone's eyes were on the blood, following it as it led toward the opposite door in the kitchen. Alec stepped toward it but then he stopped abruptly. His eyes roamed over the counter, where a bowl sat adjacent to the stove. It was empty, except for a splash of blood. His eyes moved to the top of the stove, where chili sat congealing in a small pot. "Did you turn off the stove?" he asked without turning around.

"No. Was it on?"

Alec didn't answer. Instead, he turned to Dani. "He was cooking dinner. Maybe he shut off the stove, turned around and there was the intruder." They stood a few feet from the body.

"And right here," Dani finished, "at point-blank range, he was shot and killed."

He motioned for Gus. When the deputy joined him, he asked, "Were there any signs of forced entry?"

"None. Every window and door was closed and locked."

"So whoever it was had a key," Dani offered.

Gus shrugged. "You ain't seen nothin' yet."

Alec followed his pointed nod toward the door. He stepped around the body. The swirl disappeared in the doorway, but as he stepped into the hallway, he felt a chill sweep over him. The floor was covered in blood. It stretched all the way down the hall, past a table that had been turned over, the base of a phone strung from the power cord halfway across the hall. A short distance away, he found the handset. The keys were smeared with blood. There were bloody fingerprints spreading like tentacles across the wall and the banister, as though the victim had tried to claw her way out of the room. And as he continued to the end of the hallway, he stopped at a slumped body at the bottom of the stairs.

Her hair was long and full and brunette, judging from the ends; but the area at the back of her head was drenched in rich, thick red blood. He knelt beside her, his eyes taking in the winter coat and the purse strap hanging precariously from one shoulder and disappearing beneath her body. One hand grabbed the hardwood floor like a claw, the manicured nails digging into the wood. As the sunlight peered through the stained glass in the front door, it danced across her hand.

"That's one hell of a rock," he commented as he nodded toward her hand. "Two carat. At least."

Her eyes met his. "It wasn't robbery… And I'll bet all her money and credit cards are still in her purse."

"Techs are here," Gus announced from the kitchen doorway.

Alec looked up as Kate Lockheart entered the hall. She was a buxom woman with honey skin and short, prematurely gray hair. She had an eye for detail and a no-nonsense attitude.

"Over here," Alec said, coming to his feet. "Did you get those prints outside?"

"We photographed them, but we'll have to come back and do the plaster. The ground is pretty muddy. Lots of water in the prints."

Alec stroked his chin thoughtfully. "Let me know when you're done with this body. I want to check out that purse under her."

As he backed away to allow Kate the room she needed, his eyes took in the scene around him. There was no evidence she'd left this hallway; no blood trailing into the adjacent living room. She hadn't reached the front door. He followed the blood on the banister, visualizing her final, fatal attempt to flee her attacker. Then his eyes rested on the banister rail.

Slowly, he stepped around the blood pooled on the floor and climbed a few steps up the staircase. He stopped and held his hand up, then placed it a few inches above the banister where he held it in mid-air.

"What are you doing?" Dani asked.

"There's a thumbprint here."

"There are prints here, too," she pointed out. "Peggy Lynn obviously was trying to get away—"

"No. This one's different."

Dani climbed the stairs behind him. Alec continued holding his hand above the banister. "Look at this print," he said. "The person was facing downward, toward the hallway."

"There's no blood on the steps—" she said.

"—which means this print isn't hers," Alec finished. He turned to the technician below. "Kate, make sure you get this print here," he said, pointing. "See if you can get an i.d. on it."

"Will do."

Alec turned to face the bottom of the staircase. "Look at that," he said to Dani.

She followed his pointing finger, her eyes coming to rest on a single shoe print in the blood.

"Belongs to a woman," he continued.

Dani picked up his train of thought. "She came down the stairs," she said, slowly descending the staircase as she spoke. "She reached the bottom and stepped directly into the blood."

Alec joined her. "She walked around the body," he said, pointing to other prints that grew fainter as they circled the victim.

"We find the woman wearing that shoe—" Dani began, her eyes meeting Alec's.

"—and we'll have solved these murders," he finished.

8

Chris could feel the slow heat from the light penetrating his eyelids. He moaned softly, his own voice startling him. He began to roll over when he realized he was close to sliding off. Then in a state somewhere between sleep and wakefulness, he realized it wasn't soft linen beneath him that rubbed his cheek, but the coarse fabric of the couch. He was fully dressed except for his shoes, and it wasn't the sunlight penetrating his skin but the harsh glare of the light bulb from the floor lamp beside the sofa.

He opened his eyes and slowly raised his stiffened body to a seated position. He ran his hands through his hair as he pieced together his circumstances.

The coffee table in front of him was littered with a half dozen empty soft drink cans and an ice bucket that was half-full with melting ice. Two disposable plastic cups sat across from each other in pools of condensation. The one closest to him was empty. The one at the opposite side of the table had some watered down soft drink in it.

His eyes wandered from the cup with the deep pink lipstick imprinted on its rim, to the chair opposite the couch. It was empty. The beautiful woman who had perched in it during the night, her knees drawn up to her chest and her bare feet with the red toenail polish staring at him, was gone.

He stretched his neck and peered above the half-wall that separated the sitting area from the bed. It was empty, the pillows exactly as they had been when he checked in, the bedspread still tight and neat.

He sighed.

How was it possible for him to spend half the night with a woman and still know barely more than her first name? One moment, she was saying good-bye and the next, she was in the elevator with him and accompanying him to his room.

Startled, he rose quickly and glanced at the dresser. His wallet was there, the keys to his car beside it, the change from his pants pocket untouched. Still, he crossed to the dresser in two short steps, opened his wallet, and flipped through it. His credit cards and all his money appeared exactly as it had the night before. What an idiot, he thought. *She could have rolled me and I'd be stranded here without a penny.*

He turned back to the room. The bathroom door was slightly ajar. Brenda stood at the sink, using his comb to run through her dampened hair. She'd removed her cap some time during the night as they'd talked, and her hair had cascaded past her shoulders in thick copper waves that prompted him to wonder how it had all fit under the cap. She spotted him in the mirror and opened the door, stepping into the small hallway.

"Good morning," she said.

"Good morning," he answered. His voice sounded raspy to him, and he cleared his throat.

"I made some coffee," she said.

His eyes followed her to the wet bar, where she poured coffee into two ivory cups.

"You take it black."

"Yes."

She crossed the room and handed it to him.

He returned to the couch and sat down, cupping his coffee between his hands.

She returned to the chair opposite him.

"I know you're wondering why I'm here," she said.

"The thought occurred to me."

"I mean, I've learned so much about you—you work in Washington, never been married, politics is your whole life ... A workaholic, I think you called yourself? Only child, parents live in New Jersey... And this was your first vacation in six years. Did I get all that right?"

He nodded. He felt himself sit a bit straighter and could feel a warm flush in his cheeks. She had actually been listening to him, he thought, and she'd remembered. He gazed across the coffee table. He thought he detected a sparkle in her eyes.

"And yet you don't know anything about me," she said coyly.

"I'd like to change that." He took a sip of his coffee, but kept his eyes locked on hers. "For starters, what are you running from?"

She narrowed her eyes and cocked her head. "What makes you think I'm running?"

He chose his words carefully. "I wasn't born yesterday. You needed to lay low last night, and this was the perfect place to do it."

She hesitated, taking a sip of her coffee and studying the carpet. "Yes."

"What did you do?"

She glanced up quickly. "Nothing."

He shrugged. "If you come clean, maybe I can help you."

She laughed, the laughter sounding like a gentle wind chime. "Thanks for the offer, but I didn't do anything."

She paused. "I have a friend who was in trouble—"

"Your friend," Chris said. He realized as he said it how sarcastic his voice sounded.

Her eyes remained fixed on his. "Yes, a friend."

There was a period of silence as he waited for her to continue, but she didn't. Finally, he said, "So because your friend was in trouble, you came here. Help me out here; I don't see how that could help."

"Look, I really don't know how to explain this to you—"

"Why don't you try telling me the truth?"

She leaned forward in her chair. She stared at his hands for so long that he felt compelled to move them.

"Someone was upset with my friend and me," she said at last. "I knew they were going to confront him, and… I wanted to stay away from home, in case they also wanted to confront me."

He remained silent.

"So, there. You have it."

He sipped his coffee. The drapes were not pulled completely together, and a muted ray of sunshine began to penetrate the room.

"He," he said, his voice sounding strained. "Your husband?"

"No," she said firmly. "I've never been married."

"Live-in boyfriend?"

She shook her head. "Nothing like that."

He waited for her to elaborate, but she didn't. "So, what happens now?"

She hesitated. Her eyes wandered to the window. Then she glanced at her watch. "Do you mind giving me a lift?"

"I'd love to. But my car is wrecked, remember?"

She nodded.

"I thought you drove to this place last night… How did you get here?"

She smiled wryly. "I walked."

"From where?"

She shrugged. "It was only a couple of miles."

He didn't respond.

"From my friend's house. I live across town."

"I see."

"I'll help you get a rental car, if you'll drop me off afterward."

"What makes you think I was getting a rental car?"

"Were you planning on staying in this room all day?"

He finished his coffee and set the cup on the table. He felt her eyes on him as he opened a suitcase. Inside were several sets of new clothes; a gift to himself after all the months of wearing dark suits and white shirts. He removed a pair of khaki dress slacks with the tag still on it. He clipped off the tag and laid it on the bed. A freshly pressed shirt with a buttoned-down collar joined it, along with an expensive mohair sweater. They were the best clothes from the best clothier in Washington, but if she was impressed, she didn't show it.

He unpacked a pair of Santoni dress shoes; they might have been a bit dressy, but it was either the dress shoes or the running shoes, and the latter was definitely too casual… He was being ridiculous. He left the clothes and shoes on the bed and poured himself another cup of coffee. Then he left it on the counter and went into the bathroom.

A few minutes later, he was showered and shaved, all the time alternately chastising himself and fighting an excitement he hadn't felt in years. He half-expected her to be gone when he emerged with a towel wrapped around him, but she was still there, still sitting in the chair, patiently waiting.

"So, what do you say?" she asked.

9

The slush was melted and the sun rising higher by the time Alec left the house by the back door. Kate and her assistant were busy processing the house—dusting for fingerprints, taking photographs, and sketching the crime scene. Dani was still inside, interviewing Nate's father, Jerry, with what would certainly be considered a more empathetic approach than his own.

Alec was trying to quit smoking, but the urge was coming on strong. He'd only had one this morning, right before he left home to pick up Dani. He felt a twinge of guilt as he searched his pocket for his cigarettes, but the feeling was soon replaced with satisfaction when he took his first puff.

He'd performed his initial examination of the crime scene, and now as he stood on the back deck and stared toward the barn at the edge of the field, he mentally pieced it together. Tyler was emerging from the barn. At the sight of Alec, he began making his way toward the house. They met halfway.

"Find anything?"

"Just a couple of horses," he said.

Alec nodded. "I think I'll take a quick look."

Tyler continued to the house as Alec followed the footprints toward the barn. Though the mud was distorting the prints, they appeared to have been made by small feet, possibly by the same shoe pattern he'd seen in the blood at the foot of the staircase. They were undoubtedly a woman's print. He imagined her moving quickly; by the time she reached the barn, she might have been running.

He stopped at the entrance. The barn looked to be about thirty feet long by twenty feet wide. Some of the wood was old and weathered, but new golden planks were scattered throughout, as if someone had taken care to maintain it. Dutch doors, now closed, led into the barn. There were no women's shoe prints leading away from it, only a couple of hoof prints.

Carefully, he opened one of the doors and allowed his eyes to adjust to the dim light. He heard a soft nicker from a nearby horse. Quietly, he made his way to the first stall and stroked the horse's long white-starred nose. "What did you see, fella?" he whispered.

He wandered around the barn, using his flashlight to illuminate the dirt floor and examine darkened corners. There were stalls on either side, separated by a wide center aisle. There was one horse in each of two stalls, located adjacent to one another. On the opposite side were two empty stalls, though manure in one of them appeared to be fresh.

He climbed a ladder to the loft, which was empty. His shoes left prints in the dust, as did another, larger set of shoes that he deduced belonged to Tyler. He stopped at a hayloft door, opening it just wide enough to peer outside. The sun was burning through the early morning haze. Soon the bad weather of the previous night would be only a memory.

Tobacco fields stretched almost as far as he could see, broken every now and again by a cluster of trees. He knew he was standing above the doorway, and he stared at the area where the woman's footprints had been, as if they would be made clearer to him. There was only one entrance to the barn, and if she wasn't here, how would she have escaped? As he stared at the ground and the fields beyond, it suddenly hit him. Quickly, he scampered down the ladder and returned to the barn door. He stepped outside and studied the ground. There were several hoof prints leading away from the barn, down a slope and into the field. She'd left by horse.

He had started toward the field when he heard someone calling his name. He turned to face a short, stout woman breathing heavily as she crossed the lot behind the house. Her hair was strawberry blond, the roots white, and lay in tight little curls about her head.

"Lieutenant Brodie?" she asked as she drew near.

"Yes, ma'am."

"I am Caroline Rauch Taft." She stopped a couple of feet from him and raised her chin high, as if waiting for a response.

"Yes, ma'am," he said again. He knew the name well; her family had owned several retail businesses in these parts, and though she was the last of the line and no longer working, she continued to be a formidable presence in town.

"Do you have a suspect?" she demanded.

"I'm not at liberty to discuss the case," Alec began.

"Well, of course you are; don't be ridiculous."

When he didn't respond, she continued, "You need to be aware of something. Now, I'm not one to go blabbing about other people's private business, you understand, but, well, two people have died, I'm told, and Jerry is a good man. I've known his family for years, and was with his wife Betsy Anne when she passed. Jerry's father went to school with my father, Harold Rauch, that's Harold H.

Rauch, not Harold M. Rauch, who was his father before him—"

"Yes, ma'am," he said, glancing back toward the trail of hoof prints. "I'm a bit busy right now."

"You're not too busy to hear me out." He saw a movement out of the corner of his eye and wondered if she'd stomped her foot. Her heavy brows were knit tightly together over pale gray eyes. "Nate Landon was having an affair. And it had turned ugly, very ugly indeed."

"How do you know that?"

"I see a lot of things happening around here that folks don't know I see," she said, jabbing her finger toward his chest. "And just the other day, I was sitting in that nice restaurant, the one with the wonderful French onion soup, right by the potted plants in the center, you know where they are?"

A series of restaurants flashed through his mind, but she didn't wait for his answer before she continued.

"Well, I was waiting for Miss Beatrice Nevin, over in Fairmont, and she was running late because her toilet had overflowed that morning and the sewage water went everywhere!"

"Yes, ma'am," Alec interjected.

"And I heard these voices on the other side of the plants, while I'm sitting there, sipping my iced tea, minding my own business, don't you know. And the woman said, 'Don't tell your wife anything, I'm begging you. She doesn't need to know.' And then a man piped up, and I recognized his voice, it was Nate, don't you know, and he was saying how guilty he felt and he couldn't keep deceiving her—meaning Peggy Lynn, what a beautiful girl, she'd lived down the street from me once, when she was just a child, in the old Sawyer house, you know where that is?"

"Yes, ma'am."

"And they just got into the most heated exchange, and the woman was telling him if he told his wife anything, his life would be in danger—"

"She threatened him?"

"Like I told you. And he said he didn't care, he would have to come clean, and she got downright ugly with him, don't you know. And they sat there, just a'arguing back and forth, and when Beatrice Nevin arrived from Fairmont, she sat right there with me and we just sipped our tea and listened to the whole exchange, we did."

"Do you know who the woman was?"

"Well, of course, I know who she was. I know everybody comes to this town, one way or t'other. It was Brenda Carnegie." She straightened her back and stared into his eyes.

"Brenda Carnegie," he repeated. She'd said it as if he should have recognized it, but he didn't.

"Well, you know who Brenda Carnegie is!"

"Why don't you tell me?"

"Why, she grew up in this county. Moved away right after high school. Some say she went to college and others say she most certainly did not, she never got an education higher than twelfth grade, but when she moved back, she was a wealthy woman, so I hear. No man in her life, and I don't have the faintest where she might have gotten all that money, but first thing she did was go straight down to the bank and open up a great big account with it, and their eyes nearly popped out of their heads when they saw how much she had, don't you know, and then she moved right downtown, paid cash for the house, so I hear from the realtor who sold it to her—"

"Do you know the address?" Alec said, removing a note pad from his jacket pocket.

She rattled off the exact address. "You know, the Kinley-Gabe house, the one Widow Gabe lived in, the one they called Widow Gabby, 'cause she couldn't stop talking, but she died 'bout ten years ago, and the house set empty for a spell, but then Miss Brenda Carnegie, she moved in and never did a lick of work. Not a bit. Course, she had all that money that nobody knows where she got it—could'a been drug money, don't you know, and sometimes I'd see her working in a flower garden but often as not I'd catch a glimpse of her in an upstairs window, 'cept when she drew the blinds, which she always did when Nate came a'calling—"

"So Nate went to her home?"

"Parked a block away, not in the driveway, like any self-respecting man would do, if he was visiting her for a reputable reason." She clasped her hands together and rested them on her ample chest.

Alec spotted Dani emerging from the house, and he waved at her. Catching sight of him, she started down the deck stairs toward them.

"Do you know how long they knew each other?" Alec prodded. "Did they go to school together?"

"No, they met when she opened that bank account. Nate was working in the bank, on account of the tobacco money isn't what it used to be, and poor Jerry thought Nate would live the rest of his days doing tobacco farming just like he did and his daddy before him, but things have changed and it just isn't bringing in what it used to, don't you know. So Nate went to work for the bank, though Jerry told him he'd never have to work anywhere else, 'cause he had enough saved to pass on, but Nate didn't want to hear none of that, and poor Betsy Anne, she was just beside herself when Nate went to work, what would the neighbors think, for goodness' sake? That he couldn't earn a decent living on the farm with his daddy? It was scandalous, I tell you—"

"So they met at the bank?"

"The day she opened that account. And the folks there tell me, she had her eyes set on him from the very beginning, she did, and it didn't matter to her that he was a married man, not at all, and there she was, single and with no man in her life, and what kind of life is that, don't you know? I was married for 67 years, I was, and would still be married today if my husband, Mister Tobias Taft, my Toby, I called him, hadn't passed away, God rest his soul—"

"Mrs. Taft."

The older woman stopped in mid-sentence and turned to greet Dani. Over her head, Alec rolled his eyes.

"I'm sorry to interrupt," Dani said, "but I need to pull Detective Brodie away for just a moment."

"That's quite all right. I was just telling him that I bet Miss Brenda Carnegie did it, I just know she did, she was having an affair with Nate, and normally I wouldn't mention it, because I don't repeat gossip, don't you know, but two people have died, and to think they were so happy, Nate and Peggy Lynn, and expecting their very first child—"

"What did you say?" Alec stepped forward.

"Young man, haven't you been listening to me? Honestly!"

Alec shook his head as if to clear it. "Did you say they were expecting a child?"

"Well, of course I did. Didn't you notice? She was seven months pregnant, actually seven-and-a-half, I reckon, and I hear it was a little girl, and don't you know Miss Brenda Carnegie was upset at that news, seeing as how she must have thought Nate would leave his wife and run off with her—"

She stopped abruptly as Alec sprinted toward the house, Dani right on his heels. He yelled at Tyler as he neared the house. "Get an ambulance!"

"What—? Who?"

"Just get an ambulance!"

He burst into the house and rushed down the hallway. Peggy Lynn was still lying in the same position as he'd left her. He flipped her onto her back and yanked the coat apart, sending buttons flying.

"Alec, what are you doing?" Tyler demanded.

"She's pregnant," Alec said, placing his ear against her belly. "I don't know if the baby is still alive!"

"Lord," Tyler said as he radioed for an ambulance.

He could hear a heartbeat, but his own heart was thumping so wildly that he wasn't sure if it was the baby's he heard or his own. He glanced at Peggy Lynn's face, at the strain around the mouth and the brows that appeared permanently furrowed. He quickly looked away. He would be paying a young woman across town a visit, he thought as he squared his jaw, but right now, he might have a baby to save.

10

Chris took a bite out of his cheese Danish as he stared at a family of four entering the restaurant in their pajamas. Amazed, he watched as they filled their Styrofoam plates with items from the breakfast bar. Balancing the plates and cups filled with coffee and juice, they made their way back through the restaurant toward the elevators. Their hair was disheveled from a night's sleep, and one of them was in danger of having his pajama pants slide a bit too low.

He turned toward Brenda to say something about the absurdity, but she was watching the television with what appeared to be intense interest. He found himself studying her; her angular face with a delightful dimple, though her face was in repose; her amber eyes under long curled lashes riveted toward the corner of the room. He heard the noise from the news program, but that's all it was to him: noise. He wanted everything else around him to fade away, leaving only himself and this beautiful, mysterious woman.

She turned to him, and her eyes widened slightly. He wondered if his face had revealed his thoughts. Before he could speak, she said, "More than a hundred dollars a barrel."

"What?"

"Oil. It's going up."

He shrugged. "What else is new?"

"Gasoline will top four dollars a gallon."

"It won't be the first time," he said, finishing off the Danish. "And I'm sure it won't be the last."

She sipped her orange juice. Chris noticed she wasn't eating. Other than the coffee she'd had in their room, she'd only consumed a bit of juice. "You don't seem alarmed."

"Why should I be?"

She shrugged. "Maybe you shouldn't."

"For decades, the rest of the world has been paying a lot more than Americans," he said. "Even at four bucks a gallon, it's a steal."

"Is it now?"

Before he could respond, she started to rise from the table. "There he is!"

He followed her gaze to a white four-door truck that had just pulled in front of the hotel. As she grabbed her orange juice, he quickly cleared the table and tossed the trash into the can. She was already through the door and standing on the sidewalk when he joined her. She reached for him, clasping his hand in hers as she opened the passenger side door with her free hand.

"Hey, Zach," she said to the driver.

"Hey, Brenda," he answered pleasantly.

Chris knew the young man's eyes were wandering from Brenda to him, but he was still focused on her hand grasping his.

"This is my friend Chris," she said. "He's the one who needs the car."

Zach nodded. "Nice to meet you. Welcome to Lumberton."

"I'll ride up front," Brenda said.

Chris reluctantly released her hand as she got in. He closed the door behind her and quickly climbed into the back seat. His door was barely closed before they took off.

"Thanks for picking us up," Brenda said.

Chris studied them from his vantage point behind them. The driver appeared young, perhaps in his early twenties. He was thin as a rail. His hair was wavy and of medium length, the light brown curls brushing his jacket collar. He wore a camouflage hunting cap that matched his jacket. There was a decent distance between them, he noted, and Brenda appeared to be focused on the road ahead. Despite himself, he let out a sigh of relief. He caught a glimpse of the driver's eyes in the rearview mirror. They were hazel and almond shaped.

"Where's your car, Brenda?" he was asking.

"You know what? It wouldn't start."

"Is that right?" he said, his brows furrowing. "That's a new car, ain't it? Did you run down the battery?"

"I don't know what's wrong with it," she said smoothly. "Would you mind towing it to your shop and checking it out?"

"No problem."

"The spare key's—"

"Not still in that magnet holder under the bumper, I hope."

"What's wrong with that?"

Zach shook his head. "You're gonna hit a bump someday and that key'll be layin' in the middle of the road."

"You'll keep it in the garage, right?" She asked, ignoring his comment. "Not on the lot, where it can be vandalized?"

"Like I always do. Don't want nothin' bad to happen to your car. You still want the rental?" His eyes met Chris' in the mirror.

Brenda half-turned toward Chris. "I'm sure he does," she said before he could answer. "He might not want to be stuck with me all weekend."

"Oh, I can think of worse things now," Zach answered. His eyes were riveted on Chris for so long that he wondered why the truck didn't wander into the next lane.

Chris remained silent as they drove down a five-lane road. They passed a variety of fast food restaurants that were just beginning to come to life. Two pharmacies on opposite corners already had a few vehicles in their parking lots, but it was *The Robesonian* newspaper building that appeared to be hopping, judging from the vehicles along the side.

Zach turned into a combination used car lot and rental car business. He pulled directly in front of the door. As he turned off the engine, he said, "Business don't open for another couple hours. Might be cold in there."

"I'll wait here until you get the door open," Brenda said. "I've got a chill I can't shake."

Chris hesitated.

"You go ahead," she said, turning to him. "I'll be along."

Zach was already out of the truck and had the door open when Chris joined him. "Give me a sec to turn off the alarm," he said before disappearing toward the back. It was only a moment before he returned. "Come on back."

Chris followed him down a short hallway. Zach gestured him inside a small office. "Let's get that rental car for you."

Less than ten minutes later, Zach was handing over a set of keys to a white Honda Accord. As they made their way toward the front, Chris was surprised to see Brenda sitting in the main showroom behind a partition. "You okay?" he asked.

"Fine. You got what you needed?"

He held up the keys. "Thanks to your friend Zach here."

Zach walked to the front door and pointed across the lot. "It's that car right over there," he said. Then he stopped short. "That's weird."

"Something wrong?" Chris asked.

"Could have sworn I parked a minivan right there," Zach murmured, gesturing toward an empty spot. "Maybe Josh brought it home last night." He turned toward Chris. "Well, thanks for your business. You have a good weekend."

Chris shook his hand and turned toward Brenda.

"I just need to duck in here," she said, motioning toward the rest room. "I'll join you outside."

As she disappeared behind the ladies' room door, Chris made his way to the rental car. He had it warmed up and waiting by the front door when Brenda emerged. Her hair was underneath the newsboy cap, as it had been when he'd first laid eyes on her the night before. As she directed him to turn left out of the parking lot, he glanced at her out of the corner of his eye. Her hair was already beginning to escape, one tantalizing wisp at a time. He fought the impulse to reach across the front seat and kiss her. They would soon be at her house, he reminded himself, where he hoped they'd get to know one another much better.

11

Joseph drove slowly down North Walnut Street in a white minivan. He'd already been back to the rental car lot, returned the Taurus to its original parking spot and hotwired an aging minivan.

He spotted a woman in a dressy coat and heels hurrying to a corner house with a beagle by her side. She stopped at the side gate to a chain link fence, detached the leash from the dog's collar, and slipped him inside the back yard. She clipped the leash to the fence and scurried to a car that idled in the driveway. As Joseph came to a stop at the intersection, she backed out and sped off.

Late for work, Joseph thought as he watched her taillights disappear around a bend.

The rest of the neighborhood was quiet. He pulled the van alongside the house and quickly got out. He reached the fence in four steps, had the leash in one hand and the gate opened with the other. The dog was upon him immediately, wagging its tail. Joseph stooped and picked him up, cradling him against his coat. The dog felt cold and its paws were muddy.

He returned to the van and set the dog on the front seat. Then he quickly pulled away from the curb and headed back toward downtown, glancing at the clock on the dash. He had been stopped for less than sixty seconds.

He stopped at a parking lot framed by two churches, just two blocks from his destination on Elm Street. He pulled into an ambiguous corner spot, where it wouldn't be clear to a passerby which church he was presumably visiting.

He clipped the leash onto the dog's collar and slipped out of the van, gently placing him onto the sidewalk. He watched the beagle for a moment as it sniffed the grass beside the walk. He had been very affectionate on the drive, crawling into his lap and licking his chin. It reminded him of a dog he'd owned long ago.

He pulled his collar around his neck. The wind was beginning to pick up, though the temperature had begun to climb. The streets were wet now but no longer slushy. He wondered briefly if the night's precipitation had adequately covered his tracks at the farmhouse. It wouldn't matter; he would be long gone before the bodies were discovered.

He began walking slowly, allowing the dog to rush here and there at the end of the six-foot lead, stopping dutifully to allow it to sniff every hydrant and tree along their path. A flatbed truck pulled alongside a house. He watched as several men jumped out of the extended truck cab and began unloading heavy bundles of roof shingles, hitting the ground with heavy thumps as they piled them near the house.

In another block, he was able to see the house on the corner, *her* house.

The lights were off in the upstairs rooms now, but the kitchen light and another light near the front door were still on. The occasional car passed him as he walked, but he knew he was above suspicion, tethered as he was to the adorable pup at his feet. He allowed the dog to check out the terrain to its heart's content as Joseph concentrated on the house. Slowly, they approached it.

The front yard was small and the front door was too close to the road. He would be spotted by any passerby or anyone happening to glance out of their windows. But the back door was less visible. He turned down the side street and gave the pup a chance to relieve himself as he studied it. The Toyota Highlander was still parked in the driveway. Between the car and the back door was a row of mature red shrubs. The door was visible at the top of a short set of steps, but the door knob itself was hidden by the bushes.

He carefully surveyed the surrounding houses. Most remained dark except for the occasional light behind shades or blinds. He could hear the shouts from the nearby workers; he presumed they were now on the roof, though they were concealed behind mature evergreens.

He quickly turned and walked the dog up the driveway and up three wooden steps to a small landing. He slid the leash to his left hand. With his right, he reached to an inside pocket and retrieved a carpenter's pry bar. Timing his movements with the sounds of the nearby construction, he pried the back door away from the flimsy dead bolt. With one final jerk, he was in.

A cordless phone sat in a charger on the kitchen counter, and he grabbed it immediately and hit the "talk" button. There was only dial tone. The sound continued to reach his ears until he slipped the phone inside the uppermost drawer before pushing the back door closed. He detached the leash from the dog's collar and allowed him to run freely through the downstairs, his muddy paw prints leaving a trail on the varnished wood floors.

The kitchen was warm, the heat radiating from floor vents. It was clean and neat, the counters completely clear of crumbs, the floor gleaming, and the stark white modern appliances free of smudges. Beside the stove were a jar of pasta sauce and a package of wheat spaghetti. There were no signs of breakfast—no telltale sausage or bacon odor, no dishes in the sink, not even a coffee aroma. He spotted a teapot on the stove, and he placed his gloved hand on it. His glove was thick, and he could feel no warmth emanating from the pot.

At the corner of the kitchen was a small entry to a pantry, a laundry area, and a tiny half bath.

He retraced his steps to the kitchen and stopped at the doorway to the dining room. There was a round, light oak table in the center of the room, surrounded by four chairs. It was mission style, very plain and very simple. There were no pictures on the walls, no stack of bills or papers on the table. No evidence that it was anything more than a room in a model home.

He strode through the dining room to an open double doorway into the living room. Here he found a rattan loveseat and two matching chairs. There was a neat stack of magazines on the coffee table. He reached down and nudged the top magazine. Beneath the copy of *Good Housekeeping* was a stack of *Offshore Magazine.*

An enlarged, framed photograph hugged the wall above the loveseat and he stepped closer. At first glance, it depicted the serenity of a beach at sunset, the water lapping at the shores; the type of photograph one could envision in a beach cottage. But upon closer inspection, the sunset was offset from the water, meaning the photographer was facing south and not west. He stared at the horizon in the picture. It wasn't his imagination: there were two refinery spires barely visible, two seemingly inconsequential blips on the horizon, miles from shore, and he knew why she had this photograph in her living room.

A grandfather clock ticked loudly and he returned to the present.

He stopped at the foot of the steps and listened. There was no movement upstairs. The dog remained in the living room. It had found a tattered sneaker and was beginning to chew on it. He did not see the sneaker's mate.

Joseph began the ascent to the upstairs bedrooms. In the quiet of the house, he could hear the grandfather clock continuing to tick.

He stopped when he reached the top step. He found himself in a small hallway. Directly across from him was a bathroom. The door was open and the shower curtain was pulled all the way back. The room was empty. A bedroom was situated at each end of the hallway. Both doors were open.

He chose the front bedroom, and quietly, methodically, made his way to the door. One window overlooked the street in front of the house while the other window faced the side street. Both had sheer curtains that allowed him to view the outside surroundings. Inside the room were a simple desk and a desk chair. Against the opposite wall was a bookshelf. There was no bed.

He stepped toward the desk where a laptop hummed away, a green light blinking intermittently. He moved a gloved finger over the touch pad and the system came to life.

A sound behind him seized his attention and he whirled around, his hand instantly drawing the gun that had rested in his pocket. It was only the pup, running up the stairs and into the second bedroom.

He relaxed his grip and followed.

The bed was neatly made, the dresser bare except for a simple hand mirror. On the chest was a jewelry box. One photograph looked down upon the room. It was of two figures atop camels, riding through a desolate desert, a swath of fabric covering every inch of their bodies except for their fingers and eyes. And just beyond the figures rose a gleaming city of glass high-rise buildings and neon signs amidst palm trees. The contradiction was startling.

He doubted if she had been home all night.

He opened the closet door, abruptly moving the clothes so he could view the floor space. There was nothing inside except a set of luggage and one pair of shoes under a half-dozen slacks, blouses and a single cardigan.

He returned to the other bedroom and opened the closet door. It had been converted to shelf space. The shelves were filled with office products—envelopes, printer paper, blank CDs, scissors, pens, and tape.

He returned to the desk and unplugged the laptop. He stuffed the cord in his pocket. Then he tucked the laptop under one arm and proceeded back down the hall toward the stairs. The pup followed him, its tail wagging as they descended. It was clearly enjoying the field trip.

He clipped the leash onto the dog and retraced his steps through the kitchen to the back door, where he quietly let himself out.

12

Alec drove south on Fayetteville Road, seemingly unaware of the heavy traffic that flowed on one of the most heavily traveled roads through Lumberton.

"You shouldn't be beating yourself up," Dani was saying. "How were we to know she was still alive?"

"We should have checked," Alec responded. "She was lying there, barely alive, all that time…"

"But Tyler said he checked her pulse. It was an honest mistake."

"Yeah. Right." They stopped at a red light. Alec watched a mother with a young child exit the Walgreen's on the corner. "It was a stupid mistake, an amateur mistake."

"Look, Alec, you might have saved her life. And the baby's. There's that, you know."

He sighed deeply. "I hope so. God, I hope so."

The light changed and he drove several more blocks before crossing over to Elm Street. He barely heard Dani report to Dispatch where they were headed, but when the dispatcher told Dani that Peggy Lynn was in surgery, he perked up. They were performing a Cesarean.

"There's that," Dani said.

Alec nodded. "She laid there God knows how long…"

"Don't do that to yourself. Anyway, there it is."

He pulled in front of the small corner house and turned off the engine. "Yep. There it is." He opened his car door. "Let's go pay Miss Carnegie a visit."

The sidewalk was still wet, the slush having turned to water. Alec noticed the lawn was covered in aged pecans from two old trees that draped the front yard. As they approached the house, it appeared as though a light was turned off upstairs.

They reached the small stoop and he rang the bell. He heard it reverberate. He listened for the sound of footsteps, but heard none. After a moment, he rang again. The light upstairs began to gnaw at him; the lack of sound within, of the door still closed tight.

"I'm going around back," he announced.

While Dani took a position at the front door, he walked around the corner of the house. A Toyota Highlander sat in the driveway, the windshield covered with a fine mist. He looked at the windows—three downstairs and two up. They were all closed. He retraced his footsteps across the front lawn to the other side. There was a small octagonal window near the front of the house, and a larger window toward the back. There were no windows upstairs on this side. He quietly made his way down the side of the house to the back.

The back yard was surrounded with bushes in dire need of trimming. He was almost at the back door before he could even glimpse the vehicle that still sat in the driveway. He climbed the steps to the back door and pounded on it.

The door swung open, a broken hasp dangling from the door jam. Pieces of wood lay across the threshold; one glance at the door knob and he could clearly see where it had been forced open.

He reached for his radio. "Forced entry at the back door, Dani," he said. "I'm going in."

There were muddy paw prints across the floor; he could see at a glance they hadn't been there long. They were still wet and thick. But as he made his way from one small room to the next, there was no sign of a dog. He reached the living room and took in the chewed shoe at the base of the stairs. The rooms were sparsely furnished and there was no place for someone to hide down there, he reasoned as he stopped at the staircase.

He could hear Dani just outside the door radioing for backup. He reached forward and opened the front door for her.

The light upstairs still weighed on his mind as he began to ascend the stairs. It was eerily silent. Though he didn't look down, he could sense Dani moving back through the house, reversing the path he had just taken, as he moved quietly, cautiously upward. In his mind's eye, he could see the front of the house and the light turning off, and when he reached the top of the staircase, he instinctively moved toward the front of the house. He took in the bathroom, with the door wide open, the shower curtain pulled completely back.

He made his way into the front room, his eyes sweeping all four walls. He looked behind the door before making his way toward the closet. He stood back while he quickly swung the door wide. But there was no one there, just a set of shelves filled with office supplies.

He took a step back and looked around the room again. It was stark; the table was empty except for a disconnected printer cable and a computer mouse. The printer rested on a stand nearby, but there was no sign of a CPU.

He stepped back through the room and alongside the open stairwell. He glanced down to see Dani moving through the hallway. Her eyes met his as she looked upward.

He motioned toward the back room. As Dani ascended the stairs, he made his way stealthily down the hallway to the opposite bedroom. The door was open, and as he crossed the threshold his eyes swept the room, in a swift moment taking in the position of the bed, the dresser, the nightstand. There was no master bath, and one closet. The closet door was open, the clothes pulled apart from the middle, as if someone had been there, or someone else had looked there. He looked under the bed, but it was empty except for the mate to the chewed shoe downstairs.

He turned as Dani made her way into the room.

"It's empty," he said.

She nodded.

"Did you see a light turn off when we approached?"

"I didn't notice it."

"Must have been my imagination."

"Unless she ran out the back door before you went around back."

He heard a car door slam, and he crossed to the front room and looked out the window. "It's Gus." As the deputy reached the front door, he called down to him to come in. "She's gone," Alec said as he entered.

Alec stopped in the front yard and lit a cigarette. Maybe this wasn't a good time to quit smoking, he thought. Cigarettes calmed him down and gave his hands something to do. He would quit once this case was solved, he told himself.

"Hello, there!"

The voice was deep and when Alec turned around, he expected to see a man. Instead, he found himself looking into the deep-set eyes of a tall, thin woman. Her face was almost skeletal, the skull smaller than he would have imagined for her height and frame. At her feet was a Jack

Russell terrier. As still as the woman stood, the dog was just the opposite, jumping from one side to the other, testing the boundaries of the long leash.

"Ma'am."

"Something wrong?"

"Do you know Miss Carnegie?"

She eyed his cigarette. When she spoke again, he realized her voice was raspy from years of smoking. "Who doesn't?"

"Have you seen her today?"

"Early this morning."

"Oh?" Alec removed his small notebook from his jacket pocket. "And you are—?"

"McElroy. Edna McElroy."

He wrote down the name and then motioned toward the house. "Any idea where she might be right now?"

Edna shrugged so slightly that Alec wondered if he'd imagined it. "She got up same time she always does. I see her every morning when I walk my dog, Jackie."

"That when she walks her dog?"

She chuckled. "She doesn't have a dog."

Alec found himself looking at the Jack Russell's paws. They weren't muddy, but there would have been time for her to have cleaned the dog. "She doesn't have a dog. You sure about that?"

"One hundred percent. I know every dog owner in this neighborhood. And half of the next."

"You friends with Miss Carnegie?"

She chuckled again and he thought he caught a gleam in her eye. "You're kidding, right? She doesn't have any friends."

"None?"

"No women friends. Might have a male friend."

"You know who that is?"

"Sure I do. Manages one of the banks around here. Nate Landon."

Neighbors were beginning to gather along the sidewalk and a third patrol car pulled in front of the house, followed by a small white car. Alec watched as the driver emerged; it was Patsy Jonsen, a reporter from the local newspaper. He turned back to Edna. "What time did you see her this morning?"

"I saw her twice. She gets up around midnight—she works nights. I get home 'bout that time. Last night was no different."

"And you saw her—what, through the windows?"

"That's right. She works in that room right there," she said, motioning toward the front bedroom window upstairs. "Comes downstairs, gets something to eat, I guess, I see her through the kitchen window. Makes her way back up… She works until early morning. Then the lights go out and I reckon she sleeps during the day. Except when *he* comes calling."

"Nate Landon."

"Is this related to the homicide?"

The voice caught him off guard, and he turned. Patsy was busy scribbling in a notebook.

"What homicide?" Edna asked.

"Nate Landon. Found dead this morning," Patsy said without looking up.

"No."

"They thought Peggy Lynn was dead, too, but turned out she was still alive but just barely—"

"Do you mind?" Alec interjected. "I'm busy here."

"Is Brenda Carnegie a suspect?" Patsy asked.

Alec hesitated. "She's a person of interest."

"Meaning she's a suspect."

"Meaning I'm interested in speaking with her."

"Uh-huh." Patsy continued scribbling.

Alec turned back to Edna. "So last night was no different, you say? She got up around midnight and worked all night?"

"That's right."

"And she never left?"

"I didn't say that. After I take Jackie for her walk, I hit the sack myself. Got up around six, like I always do, and the lights were still on. They just started going out shortly before you got here."

"Is that right?" Alec murmured. He turned back toward the house, his eyes roaming from the front door to the window upstairs. "Better check the crawl space," he called out to Gus as he emerged from the house. He finished his cigarette and started on another. This was going to be a long day.

13

Chris was feeling pretty good as he turned off Roberts Avenue and headed toward downtown Lumberton. Twenty-four hours ago, he was sitting at the airport listening to one delay after another. And today he was two states away with a beautiful woman seated next to him. Life was definitely looking up.

He stole a glance at her out of the corner of his eye. God, she drove him crazy. He didn't know why—maybe it was the warm amber color of her eyes, the tantalizingly long copper hair, or her tall, slender figure. Or maybe it was her relative silence, her mysterious air, the adventure that seemed to surround her.

This time yesterday, he wouldn't have believed he would spend the night with a woman he didn't even know, just sitting and talking. And that he would be here now, on his way to her house.

He thought of his cell phone and realized how free he felt now that he wasn't constantly interrupted. His mind wandered to Congressman Willo, the reelection campaign, and briefly, to all the work that awaited him when he returned to Washington. For a moment, he felt weighted, his stomach sinking, as he thought of the non-stop workload. He had ignored his personal needs for far too long, he reasoned. This weekend was his, and his alone. The work—and the congressman—would wait.

"Make a right at the next light," Brenda said quietly.

He turned as directed, and followed her instructions as he crossed two blocks and turned left onto Elm Street. It was a beautiful street, and he found himself driving more slowly, taking in the gorgeous antebellum homes, the tree-lined street, and the sidewalks that spoke of days gone by, days when people knew their neighbors, days when they could walk to a vibrant downtown area, days when the grocer and the banker and the pharmacist knew their names… He'd grown up in a small town; though it had been in New Jersey, it was surprisingly a lot like Lumberton. He'd been anxious to leave it, but now nostalgia set in and he remembered the excruciatingly slow Sunday afternoons when the blue laws kept everything closed and locked except for the churches, where everyone seemed to congregate for the day. He remembered the small town atmosphere, and of mowing lawns for neighbors in the summer to earn extra money.

He remembered his sister playing hopscotch on the sidewalk, of walking to the corner Italian bakery to buy a fresh baked loaf of bread, his mutt dog following him. He missed his dog. He didn't have time for one now, he realized. His travel schedule was far too hectic, his hours long. And when he did get home, his house in northwest Washington seemed cold and empty. He remembered his mother's kitchen pantry, the rows of baking goods, the fresh vegetables that were always laid out across the butcher block table. They were always fresh, always tasty. Now he could buy a single head of lettuce and it would turn before he had a chance to use it.

"Penny for your thoughts," Brenda said softly.

"Oh, it's nothing," he said. His voice sounded softer to him for some reason. "This town just brings back memories."

"Oh?" She raised one eyebrow. "Looks like New Jersey, huh? Well, that's a first."

"I left there at 18, went to college in DC... and never looked back." He smiled wryly. "Until now."

"Well, it's a special town, Lumberton, that is. There are some real good folks here, friendly folks, people who go out of their way to be helpful."

"Like Zach," he said.

"Yes. Like Zach."

A car was stopped in the roadway, and Chris pulled behind it and stopped as well. "Traffic jam?"

Brenda laughed. "Not in Lumberton. They probably saw somebody they know, and stopped to chat. See if you can go around them?"

He started to pull across the center line, but pulled back in. "Several cars are stopped up there."

She settled into the seat. "I'm sure it's nothing."

"Are you from around here?" he asked tentatively. "Originally, I mean."

She glanced at him, her eyes wandering across his face and down to his shoulders and then his arms. They stopped when they reached his hands on the steering wheel, but Chris almost felt as though she wasn't seeing him at all. Her eyes had a far-away look to them, and he longed to have known her as she was growing up, to have spent time with her...

"I grew up here," she said. "Went to college in Massachusetts. Got into programming."

"Oh, so you're a programmer?" Funny; he wouldn't have guessed that profession for her.

The vehicle in front of them began to creep forward, but it stopped after moving only a car-length. Chris would normally have grown impatient, perhaps blowing the horn or trying to veer into the street to see around the car in front of him. But he was in no hurry to move. He was perfectly content to remain right there, his right hand resting on the armrest just inches from hers, listening to her soft voice.

He sensed the car in front of him moving, but he was still looking at her face, still waiting for her to continue talking. She was peering straight ahead, her eyes growing narrower as if she were trying to focus.

"Turn right," she said hoarsely.

"At the next street—?"

"No. Turn right *now*."

"That looks like someone's driveway—"

She ducked, her face touching the dash. "*Please*. Turn *now*."

Out of the corner of his eye, he realized the car was no longer in front of him, and he instinctively turned to look ahead. Two houses down, a crowd had formed in front of a small corner house. A deputy stood in the front yard, talking to a tall, thin woman with a tiny dog yapping at her feet. Another deputy was trying vainly to keep the cars moving as they stopped to sate their curiosity. He glanced at Brenda, her head ever lower but turned slightly to the side where her eyes could meet his. Her lips were forming the word, *"Please."*

He turned right and found himself driving along an alleyway. Two houses down, the road emptied into a larger road and he stopped to wait for a car to pass.

"Where to?" he said.

"The hotel."

He turned toward her. "Give me one good reason—one *really* good reason—why I shouldn't turn around and go right back to those deputies."

She remained with her head down. He could see her hands grasping her knees, the knuckles pale.

"That was your house, wasn't it?"

"Take me back to the hotel, and I'll tell you everything."

14

Chris knew what he must do before they stepped off the elevator. He had but one choice: he must turn her in. They'd been quiet on the short drive back to the hotel, and as they'd gotten closer to their destination, he had been overcome with a sense of dread.

He could not, would not, be an accomplice. And though he still did not know what crime she had committed, and what or who she was running from, he could not compromise his own career and his future by helping her.

When the doors to the elevator opened, he stepped back and motioned for her to exit. She did so without a word. Silently, they made their way down the hushed hallway to the room. The plush carpet took on a new significance as he watched her feet moving lightly across it, and as they neared the door, he knew his time with her was almost over.

He unlocked the door and held it open for her. She brushed past him, but the bill of her cap sheltered her eyes. He stepped inside behind her. With a heaviness that seemed ready to engulf him, he turned and closed the door. Out of habit, he locked the deadbolt.

He had just turned around to face the room when she was upon him. Startled, he almost fended her off when he realized she was wrapping her arms around him and burying her face against his chest. He felt the wetness of her tears through his shirt, and he wanted to place his arms around her and hold her close to him, but his instincts told him it was a trap. And so he stood with his arms not quite at his side but not touching her either, wondering what to do as his heart pounded in his chest.

Finally, she looked up at him, her cap slightly askew, her eyes clouded and her cheeks wet. "You don't know what to think of me," she said with a touch of sadness.

"It's what I think that scares me," he answered.

Her eyes wandered across his face. He became acutely aware of his heavy breathing as she studied his nose, and of his burning cheeks as her eyes encompassed them. By the time they reached his lips, he felt as if he'd been laid bare.

"No," he said firmly.

But the word was drowned out by her full, moist lips on his. Her body pinned him against the door. As her upturned face pressed against his, and her trembling lips moved ever so gently over his, he knew he could not allow this to happen. It was the oldest trick in the book—feminine wiles, that's what it was. And it angered him to think she considered him so basic that he would fall for it. He tried to steel himself against her tears and he tightened his grip on her shoulders, knowing in another moment he would push her away. Then her lips parted and she sobbed. And then his hands were moving upward and removing her cap, and as her hair tumbled over her shoulders, he grabbed it in one hand and then both. And then he was pressing his lips against hers and wrapping one hand around her neck and then feeling the angular shape of her jaw, pulling her ever closer.

He had to stop this, he thought. He had to turn her away and turn her in. Her hair smelled like honeysuckle after a spring rain, and her lips were soft and full as they slightly parted and moved toward the corner of his mouth and down to his chin. His own face was wet with her tears and with each sob that escaped from her, he held her more tightly until he was losing himself in her embrace.

His lips brushed her hair, and then he wrapped his arms like a vise around her and spun her around, so she was now standing with her back against the door and he was pushing against her.

I'll turn her in, he told himself, but a few more minutes won't matter.

He pulled the sheet away from her body and lay on his side, resting his elbow on his pillow and running his hand through his hair as he studied her. In the small of her back was an angel tattoo. He felt himself drawn to it and as he followed the curve of her back to her legs, his eyes rested on a petite dragonfly tattooed on one ankle.

She rolled over and faced him, her lips turning up slightly before she grew serious. "I don't know why the cops were at my house," she said in a voice barely above a whisper.

He waited a long moment before answering. Then he reached toward her, picked up a lock of her hair as it cascaded over her shoulder and studied it. "When I put myself in your position," he said finally, "I know if I was on my way home and I saw police in my front yard, I'd stop. And I'd find out why they were there."

She nodded.

After a long silence, he continued, "And I wonder, under what circumstances, I'd feel compelled to hide from them." His eyes met hers.

"And what do you think those circumstances would be?" she whispered.

He hesitated before answering. "If your husband mistreated you—if he beat you, if you had to defend yourself—"

Her eyes widened and she placed a finger against his lips. "It's nothing like that."

The heater kicked on and they grew silent as they listened to the constant hum. He waited for her to continue but when she didn't, he said, "Then why don't you tell me what you did?"

Her lips parted as if to speak, but she closed them and shook her head.

"I might be able to help you. You'll never know, unless you confide in me."

She sighed and lay on her back. She stared at the ceiling for a long time before answering. "I run an Internet business."

He watched her face but could detect no emotion. "You run a scam."

She looked at him. "No. I run a business. A legitimate business."

He waited for her to elaborate. When she didn't, he asked, "You're not in politics, are you?"

Her eyes grew wide. "Why on earth would you ask that?"

"Because I'm asking you direct questions, and you're not telling me a thing." He could hear the hard edge in his voice. "I've been around politicians my whole life. I'd hoped you were... different."

She swallowed. "I had an associate—a business associate, nothing else—who was," she stared into his eyes for a moment before continuing, "killed."

"Did you kill him?"

"No."

"Then why did you run from the police?"

She shook her head. "I don't know," she moaned in anguish.

He leaned back, resting his head in the soft pillow while he studied the ceiling. It was stippled and there was a water sprinkler directly over the bed. He stared at it for a long time. "Did he die at your house?"

"No. I don't know why they were there."

"How did he die?"

"Shot."

He nodded. "Why?"

"Does it matter?" she whispered. She rolled toward him and draped her arm over him. When he reluctantly moved his eyes from the ceiling to her face, she said, "It wasn't about me."

He brushed a stray hair away from her eyes. "I want to believe you," he said. "God, how I want to believe you."

"Then—"

"But you're running from the law—"

She sought out his hand and ran her fingers over his. She studied them, one finger tracing his ring finger. "I don't trust the cops," she said.

"If you can't trust the cops, who can you trust?"

Her eyes met his. "Can I trust you, Chris?"

He opened his mouth but astonished himself when he didn't answer.

She moved her face closer to his, her eyes imploring. "Can I trust you?"

When he spoke, his voice was firm. "Yes. You can trust me."

She stared into his eyes for a long time. Hers were puffy and red from crying, but when she spoke, her voice was level. "My laptop is at my house. I have to get it."

His heart began to pound. "Are we going back? You're going to talk to the police?"

"I can't talk to them, not yet. But I've got to get that laptop."

15

Joseph sat quietly in the Italian restaurant. The only sounds were from a muffled conversation a few tables over and the light melody of background music. It was not yet noon and the lunch crowd, if there was to be one, had not yet arrived. It was the perfect time for clearing one's mind and enjoying a delicious meal. As he expertly swirled the spaghetti around his fork, he smiled inwardly. This is what he had come here for.

He sat in the corner nearest the window, where he could observe the entire dining room of twenty-odd tables, and still see the parking lot through the open vertical blinds. The lot opened onto an access road, which ran parallel to the Interstate. Now that the weather had improved, cars whizzed past en route to New York or Miami or points in between.

The little dog, full from a fresh sausage and egg croissant, was again secure in its own yard and the leash was clipped to the same area of the fence as he'd found it. The minivan was returned, just a few spaces down from the truck he'd borrowed the night before. After he'd walked

to a nearby restaurant and picked up his Lexus with the
New York plates, he'd driven past the rental car lot. The
Taurus was sitting alongside the other vehicles. Only the
absence of condensation on the windows was evidence
that it had been used. He glanced out the window. With
the sun higher in the sky and the temperatures warming,
the condensation on all of the vehicles would be gone now,
and no one would be the wiser.

He neatly folded the weekend copy of *USA Today* and
carefully removed his reading glasses. He meticulously
cleaned them with a soft cloth before returning them to an
eyeglass case. He wore a pullover sweater of solid gray on
top of a plaid shirt with a button-down collar; in the
absence of a pocket, he leaned to the seat beside him and
deposited the eyeglass case in a deep coat pocket.

He sipped his water and checked his watch. In ten
minutes, at precisely twelve o'clock, he knew his cell phone
would ring. With a few carefully chosen words, he would
provide his report. It would not be what they expected, or
what they would want to hear. He had not completed his
assignment. He must find her and eliminate her quickly,
before she could harm the operation.

But time was getting short. By the time the bodies were
discovered, he must be back in Washington and the Lexus
must have already been passed off to a driver who would
return it to New York.

He watched the traffic pass by as he placed each forkful
of spaghetti in his mouth, savoring the tart flavor of the
marinara sauce. Two people stepped outside the hotel
connected to the restaurant and stood on the sidewalk. He
watched them absent-mindedly. They were both above
average height. The man was wearing a coat that reminded
Joseph of the business attire he often saw on Capitol Hill;
it was black and fit his shoulders perfectly and from its
drape, he knew it was expensive. The man's hair was cut

short in a typical business style; it was warm brown but even from this short distance, he could see the subtlest swath of silver. His eyes followed the man's movements as he motioned toward the parking lot. He placed one hand on the small of the woman's back.

The woman was slender; the broad belt of the navy blue trench coat accentuating a slim waist. The coat fell just below her knees, where it joined crisp denims and ankle-high leather fashion boots. Her head was covered with a newsboy cap.

A gust of wind caught them, blowing the cap off the woman's head. The man was swift in recovering it, returning it to her as they braced against the wind. Copper hair billowed over her shoulders.

Joseph sucked in his breath. It was her.

The couple swiftly walked across the parking lot as Joseph grappled for his cell phone. By the time they reached a white Honda Accord he had taken a photograph of them, and another of the license plate.

"Can I get you anything else, sir?"

Joseph realized he was standing. The waiter was an arms-length away with a pitcher of water and ice. He shook his head and turned back to watch the car pull out of the parking spot. Inside, the woman was adjusting her hair and returning the cap to her head.

"I know that couple," Joseph said. "I think they used to live in my old neighborhood."

"Not both of them," the waiter laughed as he refilled his water glass. "They just met last night, right here in this restaurant."

"Is that so?" Joseph allowed himself to sink back into his chair. "Are you sure?"

The waiter nodded toward the parking lot. "That man was sitting right where you are," he said. "The woman was over there. They came in separately but they left together, if you know what I mean."

"Oh. Oh, I see." He watched them turn east on the access road.

The waiter leaned in close. "The man is staying here in this hotel. And from the looks of things," he cackled, "she stayed the night, too. If I could only be so lucky, my friend!"

"You didn't happen to catch their names? I—I still think I know the man; I just can't place him."

"Never got their names, but the front desk would know. He put their meals on his room bill. Room 201," he whispered. "I never forget those things."

Joseph had finished his spaghetti and was buttering his bread when his cell phone vibrated.

"Yes?" he whispered. He glanced around the room, which was beginning to fill up.

"Well?" came the one-word response.

"I'm still shopping," he said.

There was a slight pause but no response.

"I'll be home shortly," Joseph said.

There was a click on the line. Joseph cleared the call list from his phone and returned it to his belt clip. Then he turned the bill over, counted out the necessary amount and a generous tip, and left the payment on the table. Then he rose, slipped on his coat, and strode through the restaurant. Once past the restaurant door, he turned down the center hallway of the adjoining hotel. Just a short distance later, he located the elevator, which he took to the second floor. At the end of the hallway, two maids were talking non-stop over their cleaning cart. He approached a vending machine and watched out of the corner of his eye as one knocked on a door. Hearing no response, she used the pass key to open it. She then returned to the cart, slipped the pass key into a canvas pouch which hung on the side, and gathered an armload of linens. They were still discussing her previous night's amorous adventure when they both disappeared into the room.

Joseph was at the cleaning cart in seconds. He slipped his hand into the pouch, retrieved the pass key, and was back down the hall at Room 201 before they had reemerged. Silently, he let himself in and closed the door behind him.

It was a typical hotel room, the kind that is called a suite but was in reality just a larger room with a sofa and coffee table a few feet from the bed. He moved quickly.

His first stop was the closet, where a man's suit hung beside several more casual clothes. None of them were women's clothing.

He stepped to the bathroom door. It smelled like hotel soap and chlorinated water. One toothbrush stood in a cup. A man's shaving kit lay beside it. He rifled through it, finding toothpaste, after shave, an electric razor, and a few other items. Nothing was out of the ordinary. And nothing was feminine.

He returned to the bedroom. The bed was unmade, and the sheet and bedspread pulled toward the foot. The pillows on both sides contained heavy indentations. Next, he opened the dresser drawers. A handful of clothes were meticulously laid inside—t-shirts, underwear, two belts. Several pairs of shorts. One dress shirt amidst several casual pullovers. Many of the clothes had price tags still attached to them.

He glanced around the room. There was no laptop. His eyes rested on two expensive-looking suitcases. Quickly, he was upon them. He tossed the smaller one on the bed and turned it so the handle faced him. And there, just as he had hoped, was an identification card affixed to the handle. He held it an arms-length away, where his eyes could focus.

Christopher Sandige, he mouthed. The name was not familiar. But the address caused his blood to run cold. He sat on the edge of the bed and stared at it. Foxhall Road. It was in one of the most prestigious residential areas in Washington, DC, where homes routinely sold for three million or more.

There was only one reason for this man to be here. *She* had summoned him. Her plan was to double-cross them, and in so doing, she was compromising the entire operation. He didn't know precisely who this Christopher Sandige was, but he had no doubt that he would find out in short order. And he sensed his assignment had just doubled. Not only would he have to take care of the woman; once his superiors knew about her accomplice, he would be told to eliminate him as well. He knew the way they operated; all weak links must be terminated.

Quickly, he dialed a number on his cell phone.

"Yes?" the male voice answered.

"Another bird's in the nest," he said calmly.

There was a slight hesitation. The seconds ticked past. "What breed?"

"I believe it's the same."

"Exterminate."

The line went dead, and Joseph clicked off the phone and returned it to his pocket. He would soon be a little richer.

The sound of voices interrupted his thoughts, and he quickly crossed to the door. Through the peephole, he saw the two maids scurrying toward the elevator. They were arguing, one very loudly complaining that the other had violated rules and now she expected that they both would be fired.

He waited until the sound of the elevator signaled the door opening. Then the voices faded as the heavy door slid shut. He slipped back to the bed, returned the luggage to the floor beside the other suitcase, and exited the room. He took the stairs, his mind racing as he neared the ground floor.

There were no women's clothes in the room. That meant they would be returning to the house on Elm Street; she might be able to wear the same clothes twice in a row, but no woman he'd ever known could survive a day without her toiletries. He would go back to the house and look for another opportunity. And, he thought as he left the building, if there was none there, he would revisit the hotel room, where he would be waiting for them when they returned.

16

Joseph pulled away from the mall parking lot, having temporarily swapped his Lexus with a 1977 Oldsmobile Cutlass. He glanced at his watch. It was not yet 12:30 and with any luck at all, he will have completed his mission, returned the car to the mall, and would be on his way to Washington in less than an hour. For an assignment that should have taken him a very short time, things were beginning to get complicated. And he didn't like complications.

He wore a dark trench coat and his shoes were encased in a new pair of black rubber overshoes, a different brand from the one he'd worn the night before. That pair was resting at the bottom of a dumpster at the edge of a mobile home park. On the seat beside him was a fresh set of surgical gloves, which he would slip on after he'd parked the car. They would probably find their way into a dumpster outside a local dentist's office, joining the pair left the night before. With the vast number of disposable gloves a dentist's office must use each day, he knew one more pair would not raise suspicion.

He drove south on Pine Street and turned onto a side road. He would drive past the side of her house at a normal speed, continue for a block or two, and then double back. This time, he would know to watch for the rental vehicle. He would have to work quickly, while they were still in the house. He would ask questions later about her new accomplice.

Before he'd reached the stop sign a block from her house, he spotted the cars, but they were not the Toyota Highlander and Honda Accord that he'd anticipated. Instead, he found himself staring at two sedans with *Robeson County Sheriff's Department* emblazoned on the sides. They sat at an angle to the house and one protruded into the road.

He continued straight, driving slowly past the house, carefully negotiating around the vehicles. The back door was standing open. When he reached the corner on which her house stood, he had to wait while a car filled with onlookers drove past the house. Neighbors had come out of their homes and were milling about on the sidewalk. The woman who'd been walking the Jack Russell terrier early that morning was speaking to a deputy in the front yard.

He turned and drove past them at a steady speed. Once he was out of sight, he cursed under his breath.

A short time later, Joseph parked in front of the hotel and got out. As he passed in front of his Lexus, he noticed a smudge on the hood and he stopped to clean it. That was the trouble with dark cars, he thought, they were so difficult to keep clean.

He strolled into the lobby and went directly to the front desk. "A room, please," he said.

"Yes, sir," said the pleasant young woman behind the desk. "Do you have a reservation?"

"I'm afraid not," he said. "Do you have any vacancies?"

"Yes, sir."

He leaned toward her and smiled pleasantly. "You don't happen to have Room 202 available, do you? It's my lucky number."

He laid his suitcase on the end of the bed and flipped it open. He removed the Smith & Wesson Model 351PD Revolver. This time he removed the silencer. He assembled it onto the end of the revolver before slipping it into one of his deep coat pockets. He retrieved a set of screwdrivers from a suitcase pocket and crossed to the door. He studied the bolt that swung across the hotel room door and carefully selected the right screwdriver. Then he placed his ear against the door, listened for a moment, and hearing nothing, opened it. The hallway was clear.

He was across the hall in two steps, the master pass swiping the door in record time. When the green light flashed, he opened it, stepped inside, and closed the door behind him.

The room was just as he'd left it. He quickly unscrewed the bolt from the door and then lightly screwed it back in. A firm shove on the door would send the bolt flying across the room.

Again, he listened at the door and hearing nothing, he opened it and re-crossed the hallway. When he was back in his room with the door closed, he checked his watch. Ninety seconds had passed.

He returned the screwdrivers to the same suitcase pocket, neatly arranging them by size. Then he pulled a chair into the hallway of the room, just outside the bathroom and near the door.

He strolled through the bedroom and stopped at the window. The heavy drapes were pulled apart but sheers partially protected his privacy, though it was unlikely anyone passing by on the Interstate below would pay the least bit of attention to him. He turned off the heat in the room, eliminating the constant buzz from the unit. Then he pulled out his cell phone and dialed a number.

"Yeah?" came a thick voice on the other end of the line.

"Is this Bo's Automotive?" he asked.

"You have the wrong number, Pal."

"Sorry," he said before clicking the *off* button.

Still holding the phone in his right hand, he fumbled for a second cell phone in his left coat pocket. He had barely pulled it out when it began to ring.

"Yes?" he said, his voice barely more than a whisper.

"Bo here," came a low voice.

"Christopher Sandige," Joseph said. He spelled the last name.

"Got it."

Joseph clicked off the phone and returned it to his pocket. Then he removed his coat and laid it neatly on the bed beside his luggage. He picked up the tweed knitting bag he'd brought with him along with the revolver and returned to the chair beside the door. He peered through the peephole at the door to Room 201. Everything was perfect. All he had to do was wait.

He made himself comfortable in the chair, placing the revolver on the floor beside him. He pulled the pair of glasses from another coat pocket, wiped them carefully, and perched them on the end of his nose. Then he pulled out his knitting and went to work finishing a second pair of baby booties.

17

A dozen miles north of Lumberton, Chris parallel parked the rental car along a shady side street in a small but vibrant downtown area. Just around the corner was their destination: a cyber café.

The café was long and narrow, the thick walls with crackled paint belying its age. They passed one empty booth after another as Chris followed Brenda toward the back of the establishment. He noticed the floor was tiled in the red and white motif popular from the 50's and the ceiling was comprised of tin tiles. They passed booths with high wooden backs that provided plenty of privacy between them, while along one wall was a long bar reminiscent of the ice cream parlors he remembered from his boyhood. Just beyond that was an open kitchen. The aroma of fried potatoes and onions and grilled ham sandwiches reached his nostrils and he realized it had been a long time since the Danish he'd consumed that morning.

They stopped at the last booth, which was situated beside a short row of computer carts that faced the wall. Oddly out of place with the old fashioned ambiance, each cart contained a laptop with a small printer mounted at knee level below.

"How you doin', Brenda?"

Chris settled into the last booth as a server neared them. She was bone thin and a dowager's hump was beginning to protrude. Her hair was black over gaunt, pale skin. She wrapped her yellow sweater closer about her as she approached, as if to ward off the cold air that had entered the restaurant with them.

"Hi, Jeanette," Brenda said, pulling out the chair to the cart closest to the booth.

"You want your usual iced tea?"

"Yes; thanks."

"And you, Baby?"

Chris felt the color in his cheeks rising as she faced him. "Hot tea, please."

"All righty then," she said as she retreated toward the kitchen.

Chris pulled out two menus from the alligator clip atop the end of the table. Though he laid one where he anticipated Brenda to sit across from him, she did not turn around from the laptop. Jeanette brought a glass of iced tea and deposited it alongside Brenda's menu, and set a small stainless steel teapot and a china cup and saucer in front of Chris. As he steeped his tea, he kept one eye on Brenda. Though her back obscured most of the screen, he recognized the screen format of the Internet Explorer and he squinted in an effort to decipher the text.

She entered a series of numbers and waited for the domain to pop up. After a long moment, an error message appeared. She sighed heavily, stared at the numeric address, and reentered it. Again, the error message appeared. She leaned back in the chair and crossed her arms.

Chris glanced through the menu, becoming hungrier as the seconds ticked past. He watched as Brenda tried repeatedly to access a particular web site, to no avail. When Jeanette returned to take their order, Brenda ordered a turkey sandwich on rye with melted provolone without turning around.

"The meatloaf any good?" Chris asked.

"Best you'll ever have," Jeanette answered.

"Then I'll try it," Chris said with a smile.

"What vegetables you want with that? You get two."

"What do you recommend?" he asked gamely.

"Fried okra's good. So's the turnip greens."

Chris looked at the menu. "I'll take the mashed potatoes and green beans, please."

"Corn fritters or buttermilk biscuits?"

"Do you have wheat toast?"

"Yeah, Baby. That what you want?"

"Please."

He returned the menus to the alligator clip and then sipped his tea while he watched Brenda's long, slender fingers fly over the keyboard. Though he couldn't see her face, he sensed that she was becoming increasingly frustrated. When their food arrived, she remained at the computer for a few more minutes before turning around. Her brows were furrowed and she sighed again. Then she slipped from the computer chair to the booth without looking at Chris.

She took one bite of her sandwich and half-turned toward the laptop. She pursed her mouth as if deep in thought.

"I'm just going to take a stab in the dark here," Chris said, "that you're trying to access your Internet business?"

She looked back at him as if realizing for the first time that she was not alone. She took another bite and chewed it thoughtfully before answering. "That's right."

He waited for her to continue but when she didn't, he said, "So, what's the problem? Why isn't it coming up?"

She shook her head. "It's on my laptop at home. It's either turned off…"

"Or it was taken," Chris interjected.

Her head jerked slightly and she lowered her eyes immediately.

"Why would the sheriff's department want your laptop?" Chris asked.

She shook her head. "I don't know."

"Want some dessert, Baby?" Jeanette said as she approached the table and topped off Brenda's glass of iced tea, though she'd barely touched it.

"No, thanks," Brenda said. She returned her half-eaten sandwich to her plate and pushed it away.

Chris shook his head but he eagerly consumed the plate of meatloaf, mashed potatoes, and green beans. He'd never had green beans with bits of real ham in it, and in addition to the wheat toast, the server had brought something that looked like coarse pancakes. He tasted it. "Not bad," he said as much to himself as to Brenda.

When he finished eating, he realized Brenda appeared deep in thought. Her eyes kept wandering to the laptop, the screen now darkened. He wiped his mouth and pushed his plate away.

Her eyes met his. "I have to get into my house."

"That might be a tall order."

She nodded. "I know. But I have to know what happened to my laptop—if it's still there, if it was unplugged…"

"And what will you do if it's gone?"

"I know this sounds crazy," she said, "but I can't let my Internet business stop running. Not even for a weekend. If my laptop is gone, I have a backup. It's an external hard drive, and I keep it in my house. I have to get my hands on it."

He sipped his tea, but it was cold now. "Do you really think you can drive right up, walk right in, and waltz out with your laptop and the backup?"

She appeared pensive as she traced her finger over her tea glass. "We wait until dark," she said finally. "Until then, what do you say we go back to the hotel?"

18

Alec rounded the corner in the hospital corridor and abruptly stopped. A few feet away, Dani stood on the outside of a plate glass window. As he watched, a single tear made its way down her cheek but she did not wipe it away.

He quietly joined her at the window and followed her eyes.

Behind the glass were roughly three dozen nursery beds, of which perhaps half were occupied. Some of the babies were peacefully sleeping; some were awake and alert, their eyes searching their tiny environment; and an occasional one stirred and cried, resulting in a nurse appearing promptly at their side. And toward the back of the nursery was an incubator with a tiny, frail occupant: a little girl on a respirator, her hands in warm yellow mittens, and her petite head warmed by a yellow knit cap.

She stirred and they watched silently as an attractive young nurse responded. Alec found himself drawn into the scene unfolding before him, of the young lady with her long blond hair pulled back from her face, opening the incubator and pulling a polythene blanket over the tiny body, checking the tubes, and then closing the incubator. She checked the oxygen levels and temperature, and then she stood there for a long moment, just watching the baby girl breathing. Alec found himself wanting nothing more than to walk into that room, take that baby into his arms and protect her for the rest of her life.

"I knew Peggy Lynn my whole life," Dani said, breaking the silence. Her eyes were riveted on the little girl. "The doctor said she'd been shot in the brain. Everything else— her heart, her lungs—continued to function."

Alec thought of his wife raising his police revolver to her temple and firing it. With one shot, she'd ended her life. What would his life have been like if he'd found her still alive? Might he have been able to save her?

"They said she lay dying," Dani continued, "and they think she was brain dead, that she didn't feel anything, didn't know anything…" She stared at the incubator. "And in those final hours, she kept that little girl alive."

Alec softly squeezed her shoulder. "We'll find who did it."

She turned to face him, her olive skin now pale and taut. "They couldn't save her," she said. "She'd lost too much blood. Both her parents died recently… Her mama had cancer and her daddy died of a heart attack when he was just sixty. It was Nate's father, Jerry, who had to decide whether to try to save her life or the baby's." Her eyes began to water. "The doctors said even if they saved her, she'd have been on life support the rest of her life."

Alec wrapped his arm around her shoulder. "You can't dwell on it," he said quietly. "Jerry did the right thing, saving the baby. I'm sure that's the choice Peggy Lynn would have wanted him to make."

Dani nodded and visibly tried to fight back tears. "They don't know yet how the baby might have been affected.

They don't know if there was brain damage—"

Her words were choked off, and Alec squeezed her tightly, drawing her to him. He patted her back while he searched for the right words. He thought of the line of people at his wife's funeral service, of all the things they said, all the sentiments they expressed, and he realized not a single one did anything to ease his pain. He pulled her face away from him and looked into eyes the color of the Caribbean. Silently, he wiped away her tears with his thumb.

Her eyes moved slowly away from his and came to rest at a point beyond his shoulder. In an instant, her face became immobile, her eyes dry and sharp. Alec felt her body tense beneath his arm.

He half-turned to face a heavyset woman with white hair so over-permed that she appeared to be wearing a giant cotton ball. Momentarily startled, he took a step back. She bit her thin lower lip as she glared at Dani, her large nostrils beginning to flare.

Dani opened her mouth to speak but the woman turned on her heels and exited as quickly as she had appeared.

They stood in silence for a moment.

"Who was that?" Alec said flatly.

Dani shook her head. "You don't want to know," she said. "Anyway, it's time I got back home. I need to feed my cats. Give me a lift?"

Alec drove slowly past Brenda's darkened house, his eyes encompassing the crime scene tape draped around its perimeter. He had just driven Dani home after an unscheduled stop along a busy road to rescue yet another gaunt abandoned cat. He pictured Dani now providing it the best meal it had probably ever had and acclimating it to her growing brood, and now he was reluctant to return to his own empty house.

He parked in front of Brenda's home for a moment and watched as the sun began to set behind it. It was too early for nightfall, he thought. It was one of the things he hated most about the winter months.

With a heavy sigh, he slipped the car back into gear and made his way the few short blocks to his home. He parked in the driveway beside the house, as he always did. He wandered up the sidewalk from the driveway, and stopped on the front porch. He checked his mail, but it was mostly advertisements, so when he unlocked the front door, he tossed it on the table just inside as he brushed past it.

The house was dark and drafty. He checked the thermostat, and though he turned it up a few notches, it did nothing to take the chill from the air. He wandered into the kitchen and opened the refrigerator. There was an unopened bottle of milk on the top shelf, but the expiration date had already passed. He inspected the rest of the refrigerator's contents but found nothing else except a few half-empty condiments.

He opened the freezer and pulled out a frozen pizza. He set the oven temperature and removed the food from its plastic wrapper. He slid it onto a worn cookie sheet and slipped it into the oven. Only then did he remove his overcoat. He carried it into the living area, where he tossed it across a futon. He sat down beside it, shivered for a moment, and then draped himself with the overcoat. He sat there in the darkness and began to doze until the oven timer awakened him.

19

Unlike the last time Chris and Brenda entered the hotel elevator, Chris was feeling very sure of himself. Brenda had determined that their window of opportunity for entering her house would be between eleven o'clock and midnight—a time when most of her neighbors would be asleep. That gave them five or six hours to kill, and Chris was eager to get started.

He caught a glimpse of Brenda's profile mirrored in the chrome walls of the elevator. She couldn't be guilty of anything, he reasoned. She was a victim. And it was destiny that brought him to Lumberton; providence that led him to the restaurant where he would meet this beautiful woman.

The elevator ground to a halt and the bell sounded as the doors opened. Brenda stepped into the corridor first with Chris a half-step behind her. The hallway was empty but for newspapers placed neatly at each door. He felt his heart begin to quicken when he saw them; a conditioned response, he reasoned, from the months of an arduous political campaign. He wondered briefly how Congressman Willo was doing in the Bahamas and whether he was enjoying his vacation. He thought of the staff in

Washington and the work that awaited him, and he considered getting his cell phone out of his car at the car dealership's service department, in case they needed to reach him. But as they neared their room and he stared at the svelte back in front of him, he decided the cell phone would have to wait. So would Washington and Congressman Willo.

Brenda reached the door first and picked up the newspaper. As she read the headlines, Chris leaned past her and inserted his key in the door. When the light shone green, he pushed the door open and stood back for her to enter first.

Her head was downcast as she crossed the threshold, seemingly absorbed in the news. As Chris entered, he instinctively turned to push the door shut and lock it. With the deadbolt in place, he reached for the occupant bolt.

"That's odd," he murmured as much to himself as to Brenda.

"What is it?" Her voice seemed disproportionately on edge to him.

"This bolt," he mused.

She pushed past him, taking in the loose screws in the bolt in mere seconds. Then she flipped the deadbolt. "Get out of here," she ordered as she threw the door open.

They tumbled out of the hallway just as the door directly across the hall opened. An older man emerged with thinning salt and pepper hair. He ran headlong into him as Brenda pushed him from behind. "Excuse—" Chris began, but he was stopped cold by the man's eyes. They were the oddest shade of blue he had ever seen; so cold that the effect was not one of gazing into another human being's eyes but rather of staring headlong into a soulless body.

"Run!" Brenda screamed, shoving Chris toward the elevator.

As he started to move past the man, his hand brushed against his coat. He felt a hard metal that completely filled the man's coat pocket, a long, tubular object that could only be one thing. Before he could react, the man had his hand on the grip. In another instant, the pistol was in full view.

Chris grabbed his wrist with both hands and slammed him against the wall. The older man was surprisingly strong and they wrestled fiercely for the pistol. Chris banged his forearm against the wall in a desperate attempt to dislodge the weapon from his grasp, but the man held firmly onto it. He banged it again and again, and heard a distinctive shot ring out, almost like the sound of a cap pistol as a bullet spun through the silencer. Somewhere in the back of his mind, he could hear Brenda rushing down the hallway, throwing open the door to the stairwell and disappearing.

Chris knew he was in a fight for his life. With both hands on the man's wrist and forearm, he continued to slam him against the wall, but then the man was shoving back, pushing him across the hallway and against the opposite wall. And then Chris's left hand was on the barrel, and he was pointing it toward the ceiling as another shot rang out.

The elevator bell sounded and the doors opened. A man and woman stepped into the hallway; then the woman screamed and they both retreated back into the elevator. As the doors closed and it began to move again, Chris heard the woman's screams echoing through the shaft.

He redoubled his efforts, pushing the man back against the other wall. Again and again, he pummeled him. Blood was beginning to fly across the wallpaper, but whether it was his or the man's, Chris did not know. He only knew he had to expend every bullet in the chamber—however many were left—or he would die right there, in a hotel hallway more than three hundred miles from home, and none of his family, friends or coworkers knew where he was.

He could hear the man grunting under his blows, but he was unrelenting; for every shove Chris inflicted, he returned it with equal force, until they were both battered and bruised and bleeding. They had fought their way halfway down the hallway, farther and farther from the elevator and the stairs Brenda had taken. And Chris was desperately wondering why no one else surfaced, why no one opened their room doors to investigate, why the woman's screams had faded, and why no one was coming to his rescue. He couldn't hold on much longer. The man's hands and arms were like steel.

Frantically, he continued to bang the gun against the wall. He heard another shot and then another that seemed to ricochet through the close confines. Then the gun was flying through the air and landing near his feet. As the older man bent to retrieve it, Chris kicked it down the hallway, but the roughness of the carpet kept it from sailing yards away as he had intended. As the man moved farther away from him to recover it, Chris turned in the opposite direction.

He raced down the hallway toward the far stairwell. As he neared a fire alarm, he managed to pull the lever as he sped past. As the deafening sound of the alarm filled the hotel, he threw open the stairwell door as a bullet soared past and lodged in the door just inches from his head.

He took the stairs two at a time, rounding the first landing as the door above him flew open and the man raced into the stairwell, firing down on him. The bullet seemed to whiz past him but then Chris felt a searing pain in his left bicep. Instinctively, he grabbed his arm. His hand was filled with warm fluid.

Then he was at the ground floor, bursting into the hallway amid people emerging from their rooms. He could hear the frantic voice of the woman from the elevator as she described the fierce battle to the front desk, and the sound of the security officer as he made his way toward the elevator.

He turned and ran away from the lobby, down the hallway and through a room with an indoor swimming pool, past a family who stopped and stared at the blood oozing through his sleeve. He surged through the door leading to the outdoor pool and raced around the wrought iron fence until he reached the gate. Slinging it open, he rushed onto the sidewalk and into the parking lot.

At the far end of the lot with a view of both the side and front doors, the white rental car sat, the engine idling. As he stumbled toward it, he heard it move into gear and then it careened toward him, stopping just inches away. The passenger door was slung open, and without hesitation, he jumped inside. He barely had time to close the door before they were racing away from the hotel and toward the interstate.

20

Before Chris opened his eyes, he heard the low hum of a ceiling fan and the soft murmur of a television set. The moan that escaped from him was met instantly with firm, capable hands that pushed him back into soft sofa cushions.

"Try not to move," came Brenda's gentle, almost whispered voice.

He stared groggily at the sloped ceiling, at the blades of the fan turning slowly, and at the concerned eyes that came blurrily into view. "Where am I?"

"Lake Waccamaw," she answered.

"Where?"

She smiled. "About an hour from Lumberton."

He tried to place his arm across his eyes to block the harsh light from the lamp near his head, but his arm erupted in a scorching pain, and he instinctively grabbed it with his other hand and moaned.

"You'll be okay," Brenda said.

"Promise?" He vaguely remembered a car ride that felt as though it would never end, where every bump in the road jarred his arm until he thought it would fall off at the shoulder. And then he must have passed out; when he awakened, the car was stopped and Brenda was trying to half-carry, half-walk him into a small cabin at the edge of a lake. Then she was forcing him to swallow whiskey straight out of a bottle while she tore the sleeve to his new shirt away from his skin. He remembered the glaring beam from the kitchen's overhead lights, the rattling of utensils and a stack of towels on the table while he bled on the tablecloth. And now waking up on the sofa with Brenda leaning over him.

Against her protests, he painstakingly pulled himself to a half-seated position on the sofa and looked around. "Where are we?" he asked again.

"A friend's house." She hurriedly added, "We're alone. It's her vacation home; I know where she hides the key."

He looked around the small room. All of the furniture faced the back wall, which was comprised entirely of glass. Beyond that, he could see the moon reflected in a calm lake, the tranquility of the scene in stark contrast to the turmoil and pain he felt. He studied it for a moment, hoping it would slow his quickening heart but it didn't. Then he turned his attention back to the room and to Brenda, who perched on the edge of the sofa, anxiously watching him, and to his arm.

His shirt had been removed and a thick layer of white gauze had been wrapped securely around his upper arm.

As if in answer to his unasked questions, she said, "The bullet grazed you."

"All the blood—"

"I stopped it from bleeding. The skin was kind of pulled apart, so I taped it back together."

"You taped it."

She nodded. "Duct tape. It won't come apart. Unless you get into another fight." She leaned down, placing her hand against the side of his neck and pressing her cheek against his. "I'm sorry I got you into this," she whispered.

He wrapped his good hand through her hair and caressed the back of her neck. "Did you know that man?"

Her lips brushed his cheek as she pulled back far enough to look into his eyes. "I'd met him before, yes."

"Who is he?"

She sighed. She looked at his chest and then her eyes locked onto his. "A businessman. Part of a special interest group."

He laughed, but he realized it sounded forced. "I've known a lot of special interest groups, but I've never known any of them to pack a silencer."

"I don't know what to say."

"Why don't you start by telling me why he wants us dead?"

The muffled sound of the television set filled the small cabin, and Chris became acutely aware of a clock ticking in the next room.

Brenda laid her head on his chest. After a long moment, she spoke. "He doesn't want *you* dead; he wants *me* dead."

"Why?"

She pulled herself away from him, and he found himself trying to hold onto her long, wavy hair as she extricated herself from his grasp and crossed the room. When she returned, she carried a newspaper. She tossed it onto his lap. He was aware of her eyes boring into him as he lifted it, but the liquor and the pain blurred the pages. He slid his legs off the couch and came to a seated position while he held the paper close enough to focus.

The photograph above the fold came into view before he could decipher the words. It was a black and white picture of a slightly younger woman with her hair pulled away from her face. The facial features were unmistakable. He stared into the eyes and then looked up to find the same eyes staring back into his.

"What—?" He looked again at the newspaper as the headline jumped out at him: *Wanted in Connection with Double Homicide.*

He felt the room spinning around him. The air seemed cut off from his windpipe, his chest heavy as if it were being compressed.

Then she was on her knees in front of him, cupping his chin to face her. "I didn't do it."

"That man—was he a cop?"

"No." Her voice was emphatic. "Absolutely not."

He tore his eyes from her and returned to the newspaper. He had to read the article twice before it began to sink in, and even then, he wasn't sure he fully understood. Two people had been shot and killed shortly before he arrived in Lumberton—and shortly before he met Brenda. His mind raced through the timeline, and he fought to remember what she had looked like that first night, how she'd been dressed, how she had acted. There had been no blood. Of that he was sure. And he had seen her naked; there were no bruises, no signs of an altercation. No, he thought, wincing from his arm, he was in rough shape but she was untouched.

"Did *he* kill them?"

"I don't know. I think so."

"And now he wants to kill you."

"That's about it."

"Then we have to go to the police. We have to tell them what you know."

"I can't do that."

"You can't or you won't?"

A silence fell between them. He was acutely aware of the newspaper article, the picture, and the headline. And even more aware of her quiet reserve, and her eyes searching his.

"Brenda," he said, grasping her hands in his. "You are going to have to tell me everything. You don't have a choice."

She shook her head. "It's best that you don't know."

"He tried to kill me tonight. I'm in this, whether I want to be or not."

She looked away. He thought her lip trembled slightly, but she squeezed her eyes tightly and quickly composed herself.

He grasped her hands. "You're going to have to trust me."

Reluctantly, she looked back at him. She seemed to be weighing her words, and when she spoke, her voice was halting. "I was sent here. To Lumberton. I was to open a business—an Internet business—that I could work out of my house."

Chris nodded. "Go on."

"Nate—the guy who was murdered—worked at the bank. He was also to be one of my contacts."

"Your contacts?"

She swallowed. "His job was to—" she hesitated "—help me move money."

"Embezzlement?"

"No. It was my money. Money I earned."

"If it was your money, you wouldn't need help moving it."

He waited for her to respond. When she didn't, he said, "It was money laundering."

She appeared deep in thought. "I hadn't thought of it as that, but yes, I suppose you could say that."

He leaned back against the sofa, grimacing from the pain. His arm hurt a great deal for having only been grazed, and he didn't even want to think about pulling the duct tape off. She seemed to be waiting for a response from him, patiently watching his face, her hands still held within his.

Finally, he said, "I told you I work in Washington."

She nodded. "For a Congressman."

"That's right. That means my life is more transparent than most."

"I'm not sure I understand what you're getting at."

He leaned forward so his face was mere inches from hers. "It means my involvement in this could cost me my entire political career."

He could see his words soaking into her brain before she spoke. "I'm sorry I pulled you into this."

He ran a finger along her cheek and across her lips. "I'm not sorry we met. You awakened in me feelings— feelings that I thought were dead."

When she didn't respond, he continued, "Now we have to do what is right." His eyes wandered from her lips to meet her eyes once again. "And that means telling the police everything you know. They can protect you from that killer on the loose—and they can clear you of Nate's death."

He felt her stiffen beneath his touch. "I can't go to the cops."

"Why not?"

When she didn't respond, he asked, "Because you'll be charged with money laundering? Because you could face a prison sentence?"

She laughed, but it sounded more like a cackle. "That's the least of my worries. No; I can't go to them because the business I'm involved in—includes some very important people."

"Community leaders?"

"No. Much higher than that."

"Law enforcement? Crooked cops?"

She shook her head. "No. This reaches so high that any investigation could be squashed. And I could be framed for Nate's murder. And his wife's murder."

He remained silent for a long time. He studied Brenda's hands, her face, her lips, and her eyes. "The only ones higher than local law enforcement are the feds."

She nodded.

"Are you saying the FBI is involved?"

"Higher than that."

"Homeland Security? CIA? Defense?"

She shook her head at each question.

He stared into her eyes. "Is Washington involved?"

She hesitated. "Yes."

"Is it political?"

She hesitated again. "Yes."

"Brenda. I need you to think. You must be completely honest with me, do you understand?"

She nodded. "I won't lie to you."

"This money laundering, this Internet business, how high does it go?"

When she didn't respond, he asked, "I'm tired of playing twenty questions! Does it go to the highest level of our government?"

Her eyes did not waver from his. "It goes beyond the highest levels."

He leaned back again, but this time he felt no pain in his arm. His thoughts raced through the past twenty-four hours and then beyond to his political career—and his future.

After a moment, Brenda said softly, "Chris."

When he looked up, she continued, "I can't stop it. It's far bigger than me—or you."

"Then what do we do? Stay here the rest of our lives? Hide out forever?"

"You," she said, "*you* need to go back to Washington. You have a rental car; there's nothing holding you here. Get back home, and arrange for someone to tow your car back to DC. Get it fixed there, and put all of this behind you." When he began to protest, she placed her finger over his lips. "You are not involved in this."

"But I am involved," he said. He pointed to his arm. "I am involved."

When she didn't answer, he asked, "And what about you? What will you do?"

She sighed. "I need to destroy any evidence I have of the business. I have to shut down my part of it." She swallowed. "I have to get my money and disappear."

"And what of this?" Chris asked, pointing to the newspaper.

She fought back tears. "I can't bring Nate back."

"No, but you're implicated in his murder. That's going to follow you wherever you go. You can't just move someplace else and start a new life. They'll find you. Eventually, they'll find you."

She looked away from him. "We're wasting time." She glanced at her watch. "I have to get back to my house and get my backup. I have to get that evidence."

He started to rise.

"You stay here," she admonished. "Get some rest before heading back to DC."

"I'm going with you."

"No, you're not. You're in no shape to travel."

They were both standing.

"You just told me to get back to Washington."

"In a day or two. Rest. Get your strength back."

"Brenda, listen to me." He grabbed both her shoulders and squeezed them. "You can't go alone. You'd be no match for that man; he'd kill you. Let me go with you."

"I can take care of myself." Her voice softened. "Really, Chris. Stay out of this. It's for your own good."

He laughed. "I've been doing things for my own good my whole life. Let me help you. Please."

She hesitated, but he knew he could not allow her to leave alone. He might be injured and somewhat impaired by the alcohol she'd forced down him, but he was still larger and stronger than she, and at least as determined. The time seemed to stand still as they looked at one another.

"Okay," she said at last. "But we'll have to hurry."

21

Saturday, approaching midnight

Clouds had moved in by the time they reached Lumberton, the shifting gray masses obscuring the moon, plunging the earth below into darkness. As Brenda turned from the main road into a narrow alley, she cut off the headlights. A single light atop a pole shone down upon the alley, and she deftly moved past it, keeping the car in the shadows. With a three-quarter turn, she arranged the vehicle so it was facing outward, in preparation for a hasty exit. Then she shut off the engine.

Neither of them spoke. Chris felt as if they were frozen in their seats, his hands heavy on his thighs while hers grasped the steering wheel. They seemed to be absorbing the environment around them, the immediate silence replaced with the sound of dogs barking a few houses away and of occasional vehicles passing one street over.

He became acutely aware of the glass in the vehicle, of the wide windshield, the side windows, and the large back windowpane. He felt utterly exposed. Vulnerable. And now his heart was beginning to pound and echo in his head, the adrenaline beginning to rush through him, urging him into action.

Brenda wordlessly flipped the switch for the overhead light, ensuring it would not illuminate when they opened their doors. She reached for the door handle and then hesitated. When she turned to him, her face looked pale against the shifting shadows. Her voice was husky. Though it was barely above a whisper, it seemed to fill the car's interior. "Stay here."

"Like hell I am." His voice was clear; the firmness bespoke of a confidence he did not quite feel, but the mere sound of his own voice bolstered him.

She nodded. "I expected as much." She looked out the front window at the alley. "We'll have to move quickly."

With that, they opened their doors almost simultaneously, their closing sounding like the shutting of one door and not two. Then they were moving down the alley. A neighbor's kitchen window clad only in a scant topper cast a swath of light in front of them, and they jumped it as though it was a chasm. They turned at the corner and moved stealthily along back yard perimeters, allowing overgrown shrubbery to conceal their presence. A sudden yowl caused them to stop cold in their tracks, Chris' heart beating so loudly that he thought his chest might explode. Then a cat jumped the path in front of them and disappeared beneath some shrubs, its orange and white fur only a blur as it retreated. Then they were moving again, toward the back yard of Brenda's house.

They hesitated momentarily as they reached the edge of the shrubbery, their breath rising in small moist puffs. They both shivered in the cold night air, and Chris became aware once more of the new dress shirt he'd donned early that morning, one blood-stained sleeve now in tatters around his bandaged arm.

A street light near the corner of her house illuminated part of the yard. A swath of yellow crime scene tape seemed incandescent, the thin strips appearing more like a solid wall they should dare not cross. A stream of light angled across the steps leading to the back door. The door itself was encased in darkness, a black hole that could equally represent an inner sanctum or a bottomless pit.

Brenda took a deep breath and raced across the yard, taking the steps in a sprint before kneeling in front of the door. Chris saw a glint of metal as she raised a key to the door knob, but before she could turn the key in the lock, the door gave way with an unhurried protesting creak. He watched as she rushed inside, crouching against the street light that threatened to expose her.

The headlights from a lone car shone across the yard as it turned onto the side road. It traveled slowly, and Chris pressed his body into the shadows, watching as it moved past at a maddening crawl. The occupants seemed to be ogling the house and the crime scene tape, the driver's face wide and insipid as he stared. Chris' eyes roamed from the car to the house and the open door and back as it crept past. When it was finally out of sight, he realized he had been holding his breath. With a sudden burst of energy, he was leaving the obscurity of the shadows and sprinting across the yard, up the stairs and into the house.

It was dark inside, the interior cold and foreign. He hesitated as his eyes adjusted to the blackness that seemed to close in around him. Then thin streams of light made their way around the edges of a window blind, leaving a pockmarked glow across the kitchen. Gritting his teeth against the grating creak, he pushed the door shut behind him.

He spotted the back of Brenda's navy trench coat moving furtively through the next room, and he followed her as if she were a beacon of light guiding him. He took in packages of food on the kitchen counter, their labels too dark to read, and a welcoming teapot on the stove, the white ceramic illuminated by a swath of light. Despite the urgency of their situation, he wondered what it might have felt like to watch her cook, to sit at the intimate table in the next room on a lazy morning, sipping hot tea and reading the Sunday paper.

His heart began to slow and the rapid thumping in his head ceased as he made his way through the dining room to the living room. He caught a glimpse of her ankle-high leather boots just before they disappeared toward the top of the staircase.

He hesitated, listening as a car with a faulty muffler moved past the house, casting a glow through an uncloaked window above the door. The light moved around the room as though it were a spirit, illuminating the walls and corners.

In the fraction of a second, it had swathed an oversized photograph in its light, and his heart raced in sudden recognition. But when he stared at it again in the darkness, he realized it was only his imagination. It was nothing more than a beach at sunset, any one of thousands of beaches throughout the world.

The sound of Brenda's footsteps scurrying above him caused him to return to the present, and he felt a sudden surge. Pushing the living room and the photograph to the back of his mind, he mounted the stairs as silently as a cat, stopping only when he reached the top landing. He caught a glimpse of himself in a bathroom mirror, the image staring back at him with wide brown eyes, his hair tousled, his lips slightly parted. He felt at that moment as though he was living outside his own body, watching events unfold that had nothing to do with him, events of which he had no control.

He heard a sound akin to shuffling to his right and he moved down the short hallway, past the open banister and into a room at the front of the house. He stopped at the doorway, his mind absorbing the desk against the far wall, a bookshelf half full of books, and a floor littered with office supplies. His eyes came to rest on Brenda, furiously pulling items out of the closet and dumping them on the floor.

As he watched, she moved toward a waste basket beside the desk and turned it upside down, chucking the contents onto the hardwood.

"What are you doing?" he asked, his voice sounding strained in the small room.

"I need the bag," she said, pulling the white garbage bag out of the container. As he watched, she deposited several CD's into the bag, followed by papers, checkbook registers and deposit slips, and an external hard drive.

His attention moved back to the desk, where a mouse and a printer rested at opposite sides, a conspicuously empty space between them. "Your laptop?"

He could see the pain in her expression. "Gone."

He nodded silently.

She brushed past him, moving back down the hallway and stopping at another open door at the end of the hallway. He followed her, and when she moved aside, he took her place, his eyes absorbing the bed in the middle of the room, its pastel color somehow in contrast with her independent nature.

"Let's get out of here." Her voice jolted him, and he turned toward her. She stood on the top step, the bag in her arms, staring back at him.

He moved slowly toward her, motioning back toward her bedroom. "Don't you need anything else?" he asked. "Clothes—?"

"There's no time."

With that, she was racing down the stairs so catlike that her boots were barely audible on the hardwood steps.

He glanced once more at the open bedroom door, at the office door, and at his reflection in the mirror. He had his foot on the top step when another vehicle made its way down the quiet tree-lined street, the headlights casting a broad sweep over the staircase. He waited until it had passed before taking the steps two at a time in a mad dash to catch up with her.

He caught a glimpse of her as she hurried through the dining room into the kitchen, but as he followed he felt his own pace slowing.

"What is it?" she asked in a hoarse whisper.

"Your dog," he answered.

"I don't have a dog."

He pointed to the floor, where a trail of muddy paw prints meandered through the rooms.

"I don't have a dog," she repeated. "Come on. We're wasting time!"

Before he could move, the now-familiar sight of headlights moving beyond the windows heralded another passing car. But this time, the lights stopped in the middle of the kitchen, bathing the floor in a checkered glow between them. Then the lights abruptly disappeared, and a car door opened and shut only yards from where they stood.

22

Before Alec fully awakened, he could see his wife's face as clear as if she sat beside him still, looking at him with eyes the color of blueberries, the crescent shape always making her appear as if she were laughing inwardly over a private joke. He almost reached out to touch her long brown hair with the subtle streaks of reddish gold, to caress the locks between his fingers. But when she turned around, her hair was matted and soaked in blood, and then she lay dying, her heartbeat barely audible, a baby growing inside her.

His own gasp awakened him. For a moment, he expected to see Cherie sleeping beside him, but as his past collided with his future, he realized he had been dreaming about his wife and Peggy Lynn Landon at the same time.

As he opened his eyes, he became conscious of the fact that he had fallen asleep in the large brown recliner in the center of his living room. The television which had filled the room and his head with the sound of laughter and voices only a short time ago was now a multicolored screen announcing the station was off the air. He grappled for the remote; finally locating it beside the chair cushion, he reluctantly turned it off.

He sat up, pushing the footrest back into the recliner. He leaned forward for a long moment, his hands in his hair, his eyes closing once more as memories tumbled back to him.

The face he had seen with those eyes so full of mirth was Cherie's face at the last football game they ever attended. It was a high school game, the homecoming game, and a time when their son Sean had a golden life laid out before him. An athlete with recruiters already eyeing him and a full-ride athletic scholarship already secured at a choice university, he was the star quarterback and a rising town celebrity. Handsome and intelligent, he had a deep love of animals, a soft heart and a commitment to the community. So it was no surprise to see the town out in full force that night, cheering him on to certain victory.

He still remembered the aroma of popcorn, the pungent taste of mustard and relish as he bit into his hot dog, and his effort to swallow his food quickly so he could let loose with another wild cheer. He remembered the cup of hot chocolate held within Cherie's hands, the steam rising as she bent down to inhale the warmth…

The score had been close, the crowd worked into a fury as the final minute ticked down. With only seconds to spare, the team made a touchdown that put them over the top, sending spectators onto the field in a wild victory celebration.

He remembered remaining on the bleachers with Cherie, just soaking in the scene before them: returning Sean's wave from the center of the field before he was gleefully assaulted by fans and other players; of the coach being doused in Gatorade; of high school girls primping moments before parading past high school boys.

They caught up with Sean as he headed back toward the locker room, Cherie hugging him despite the sweat running off him, despite the grass stains that threatened to soil her thick plaid sweater and faded jeans. Then they were making their way to the parking lot, finding their car, and driving home as the clock ticked toward midnight, knowing their son would not be far behind in the aging Ford Mustang he'd purchased and planned to restore.

They made love, and if he'd known it would be their last time, he would have held her longer or kissed her more tenderly or not rolled over and gone to sleep afterward. He would have stayed up all night, telling her he loved her… But he didn't know. They had both gone to sleep when the call came, and he had been groggy when he answered, and the words on the other end of the line hadn't immediately made sense.

But as one of his fellow police officers described the accident, his stomach had tightened and his heart had seemed to hit the floor, and his chest had become constricted with lungs that could neither draw in fresh breath nor expel the old.

Sean was dead. Killed instantly less than two miles from home, when a drunk driver crossed the median and drove headlong into his car. The man had been driving a Hummer and was barely scratched; Sean never had a chance.

Alec tried to shake the memories as he rose from the recliner. Bits of pizza crust hardened on a plate, and he picked up the plate and carried it into the kitchen, dumping the food into an overflowing trash bin. Almost robotically, he returned to the living room and gathered a full ashtray and a handful of empty beer cans, which soon joined the other trash.

He glanced at his watch. It was after midnight. He had a long day ahead of him, and he needed sleep. But he fought the impulse to turn the television back on, to search for an all-night channel and try to drown out the memories that threatened to engulf him. He straightened the newspaper and his eyes came to rest on the photographs of Nate, Peggy Lynn, and Brenda Carnegie.

He thought of Peggy Lynn's last hours, and he searched Brenda's eyes in the photograph. Most murders were committed by someone who knew the victim. Motive, means, and opportunity. Brenda certainly had the motive; what was more compelling than jealousy? To have an affair with a married man, only to realize he was not prepared to leave his wife, and what's more, his wife was pregnant with their first child. It must have been an incredible blow to Brenda. He thought of the conversation overheard in the restaurant, of Brenda begging Nate not to tell his wife of their affair…

And when he remained unyielding, what did she do then? Did she already own the weapon that killed them, or did she buy it? He made a mental note to visit the pawn shop and local gun shops once the ballistics were known. She hadn't, in all likelihood, shown up at his house to reason with him, or to steel him away from Peggy Lynn. She'd come with a gun, of that he was sure. And she came to kill.

So she had the means.

And she had seized the opportunity.

He wondered if Nate and Peggy Lynn had both been home at the time Brenda arrived. He considered Peggy Lynn in her full winter coat and Nate minus his. He thought of the can of chili on the countertop, a Friday night meal more in line with a bachelor than a couple. He thought of Nate lying in a pool of blood in the kitchen floor, and of Peggy Lynn dragging his blood and hers down the hallway, grasping for the banister, her fingers dug into the hardwood floor… Had she begged for Brenda to spare her life? Had she begged for mercy for her unborn child?

He thought of the fear, the sheer terror, of knowing an infant child was inside her, of scrambling for the phone… And had she fallen face down in an attempt to shield her child from further assault?

He shook his head and turned off the lamp before heading down the hall toward the bedroom.

He felt his jaw stiffen and his lips tighten. He would find Brenda Carnegie if it was the last thing he ever did. He would find her and bring her to justice. And she would pay for killing two people, leaving an innocent child to grow up without ever knowing her parents. She would pay dearly.

He removed his clothes and slipped under the covers, the cold cotton sheets startling his skin. He turned off the light on the nightstand and rolled over.

No sooner had he closed his eyes than the telephone rang, the sound reverberating through the still room. Quickly, he grasped for the phone in the darkness.

"We got a call from Lumberton PD," the dispatcher said. "Someone's in the Carnegie house."

"I'm on my way," Alec said.

He was clothed and headed toward the door in less than five minutes, holstering his weapon and grabbing his keys from the sofa table, gladly leaving his house and his memories behind.

23

Edna McElroy was standing in Brenda's driveway when Alec arrived. She was speaking to a Lumberton uniformed police officer while her Jack Russell sniffed the bushes. Two police cars were parked on the street—one directly in front of the house and another along the side. As Alec parked behind the patrol car, it struck him that Edna and the officer were standing precisely where Brenda's Toyota Highlander had been parked. It was now conspicuously gone.

He lit a cigarette, introduced himself to the officer and greeted Edna. "Are you the one who called?" he asked.

She crossed her arms and spoke in her gravelly voice. "I am indeed."

He glanced at the house, where he could see two uniformed officers moving past the windows. The rooms on both levels were lit up like a party house.

"Lights were on in the house when we got here," the officer said.

Alec squinted at his name badge in the dim light cast by the street lamp. "So, Officer Manus, are they still sweeping the house?"

He nodded. "It's empty."

"I know she's in there," Edna said. "I got home just after midnight, like I always do. Took Jackie here on her walk. No sooner had I gotten out of the house than the lights upstairs went on. Just like they always do. She got up, made her way downstairs—"

"How do you know that? Could you see her through the windows?"

"Blinds were drawn. But I could tell she was moving through the house, on account of the way the lights were coming on. She went to the kitchen there, probably got herself something to eat, and went back upstairs. She was sitting in that front room there, working, just like always."

Alec crossed the street and stood on Edna's sidewalk. He could see the bedroom windows lit up. And if he stood in just the right spot, he could see the officers walking down the stairs through the window above the front door. Several downstairs lights were on as well, lighting up the living room and kitchen.

"When did you call the police?" he asked as he rejoined Edna and Officer Manus.

"As soon as the first light came on," she said. "I knew you were looking for her."

"And you didn't see her leave?"

She shook her head. "I was watching, too. Stood right there in my driveway, watching."

He pointed to Brenda's driveway. "When did she drive away?"

Edna glanced in the direction he pointed. "I don't follow you."

"Her car. It was here yesterday."

She looked again at the driveway as if she were seeing it for the first time. "Well, I'll be. I don't believe it was there when I came home. No, I don't reckon it was there when I left for work, either."

"What time did you leave?"

"Two thirty. I'm due at work at three o'clock, and I always arrive fifteen minutes early. Yesterday was no exception."

"And you're saying that at two thirty, her car was gone?"

"That's what I'm saying."

He looked again at the driveway and then at the house. One of the officers was exiting the back door. He scratched his head. "Help me out here, Ms. McElroy. Brenda returned some time yesterday after we left, and she drove away in her car. Then she came back here at midnight, turned on the lights, and started to work. How did she get here?"

"I didn't say that," Edna said. "I said she got up. She was sleeping and she woke up, just like she always does, and started her work day, just like she always does. Granted, her work day is the midnight shift—"

"So, where do you suppose her car is?"

"Young man," Edna said, her exasperation serving to emphasize her deep voice, "that is your job to figure out. Not mine. I am a concerned citizen who called you when I saw her home. Now you do your job, and stop asking me questions."

Alec returned her stare with unblinking eyes. Then with a tobacco cough, she gathered the little dog in her arms and stomped back across the street.

"She was more patient with you than she was with me," Officer Manus said.

Alec shook his head. "Too many unanswered questions." He turned back to the house. "I take it they searched the crawlspace?"

"Yep. We flipped a coin. Loser went in."

Alec made his way to the back door, where he mounted the stairs. He stopped to look at the damaged door lock. "You got somebody who can nail something over this door?" he asked. "Prevent anybody from crossing this tape?"

"We'll take care of it."

"Thanks," he said, before disappearing beneath the crime scene tape. He made his way through the kitchen and dining room and stopped in the living room. Nothing appeared any differently than it had a few hours earlier, except the rooms were illuminated with various lamps throughout the house. He passed one of the officers as he climbed the stairs. He went first to her bedroom, where he studied the neatly made bed. He kicked around for a moment, peering under the bed and looking in the closet, but the room was so bare that it offered very few hiding places.

He wandered into the bathroom in the hallway. He stopped at the tub, leaned in and wiped his finger along the tile. It was perfectly dry. He crouched and checked the bottom of the bathtub. It also was dry. He squeezed the towels hanging neatly on the rods. He found it hard to believe that she would return to this house, cross the crime scene tape, and return to her bedroom to sleep. Or that she would awaken at her usual time and not begin her day with a shower or bath—unless she took one before she went to bed, he reasoned. Still, the towels would not have dried out.

He returned to the hallway. He could hear the voices of the officers downstairs. He crossed to the front bedroom and glanced inside.

He felt his heart skip a beat as he surveyed the disarray in the middle of the floor. Cautiously, he stepped inside. He studied the table with the mouse at one side and the printer at the opposite edge. The laptop had been missing when he'd been there previously, he reminded himself, and nothing on the table looked any different than it had earlier.

But it was obvious someone had overturned the wastebasket, perhaps gone through its contents, and rifled through the closet, pulling out office supplies. He walked to the closet door and peered inside. What was she looking for? He wondered.

"Find anything?"

He turned to face Officer Manus. "It wasn't like this yesterday," he answered.

"What do you suppose—?"

"Money."

"How do you figure?"

"She's a strong suspect in the slaying of Nate and Peggy Lynn Landon. Passion killing. After she killed them, she realized she had to flee. But she didn't have transportation and she didn't have money."

Alec turned back to look at the closet shelves. Instead of clothing, they were filled with standard office supplies—paper, pens, computer CD's, envelopes.

"I suspect she had money hidden in the back of this closet," he said. "She waited until dark, returned here, got the keys to her car and her stash of money, and fled."

"And the lights?"

"It's obvious she turned them on as she was gathering her things. She probably figured on neighbors being asleep; by the time they noticed the lights on, she was gone."

"And the car?"

"I'm not so sure she got it before Ms. McElroy left for work. Otherwise, she would have gotten the money at the same time and left then."

"So what now?"

Alec started back through the house toward the stairs. "We secure the house. And notify the airports and train stations. Put out an APB on her car and license number. Get it on those electronic billboards on I-95. Make sure Virginia and South Carolina know about it, too. She could have already crossed the state line into South Carolina."

They made their way downstairs and exited the back door. Another patrol car arrived with a piece of plywood and as Alec drove off, they were hammering it into place at the back door. He glanced at his watch. In a few short hours, he would be picking up Dani and the day would start all over again. If he hurried home, he could get at least a few hours' sleep. He needed it.

24

Brenda and Chris drove south on I-95, turning onto Interstate 74 just fourteen miles from the state line. But instead of heading east toward Lake Waccamaw, Brenda turned the car westward.

"Where are we going?" Chris said.

She pulled the rental car into a service station parking lot and stopped. The station was closed, the windows clouded with grime behind black wrought iron bars. Signs announced they sold various types of chewing tobacco, boiled peanuts and fishing tackle. As Chris took in their surroundings, he became increasingly more apprehensive. Beyond the station were open fields filled with the remnants of craggy plants uprooted but not yet removed. Occasional lights blinked in the distance, appearing dim and bleak as they peeked through skeletal branches at the far edges of the fields.

"Nate's father owns a place out here." Her voice was hoarse with tension.

"Nate? The murdered guy?"

"Please don't refer to him like that," she said in a hushed voice.

"I'm not following your logic," Chris said. "Why would you want to go to a place owned by his father?"

She leaned against the driver's door. He didn't feel safe here, and he couldn't help but wonder how easy it would be for someone to sneak up behind her in the dead of night; with her head resting against the glass, she wouldn't know until they were upon them. He fought to understand his feelings, his instinct about this place, and why it generated so much apprehension growing inside him.

"It's an old hunting lodge. It was damaged by a hurricane some years back. It was too costly to rebuild, so they abandoned it."

"Then why—?"

"Nate stored information there. Things nobody else knew about. Things he didn't even think I knew about."

"Evidence?"

"I think," she spoke slowly, "if I can get my hands on that information, I can identify who killed him. And who is after us."

Chris felt a chill creep up his spine. He looked around them again—at the dimly lit service station with the iron bars across the windows, at the open fields, at the groves of trees scattered here and there, casting parts of the terrain into deep shadow. Interstate 74 was quiet, devoid of traffic, and though they weren't far from I-95, they seemed light-years away.

"This isn't the time," he said. "Wait until the sun is up. If it's abandoned, you won't be able to find anything in the dark, anyway."

She smiled wryly. "Nate kept electricity going there. And if we wait until daybreak, the hunters will be out and we might be spotted. It's best we go now."

They further debated the merits of going deep in the night versus the following day or at all, but in the end, Brenda won out. And in the end, she pulled out of the service station toward the west and into the darkness, away from Lumberton. And when they turned off the interstate onto narrow roads that curved through desolate swamps, Chris thought they had abandoned civilization altogether.

His life was filled with bright lights, with the population of a major metropolitan area, with cars filling the streets every hour of the day and night. And as they traveled deeper into the gloomy blackness of the swamps, he became increasingly more anxious. His heart quickened as the car barely missed overhanging branches from craggy trees that seemed bent on capturing them in their snares, past murky waters that rose almost to the road, filled with swamp plants and cypress trees, the cypress knees rising like an obstacle course in the brackish waters… Far-off howls and hooting owls reached his ears, noises with which he wasn't familiar, sounds that felt foreign and threatening.

They crossed small bridges over swampland and narrow streams filled with black water, until Brenda came to an abrupt stop.

"What is it?" Chris asked.

Without answering, she turned toward a grove of pine trees. Within the headlights' glow, he spotted an aging sign dangling by a single corner that announced *The Robeson Repose and Resort*, and in smaller letters underneath, *The Triple R Hunt Club*. As he watched, a gust of wind caught the sign, causing it to sway as if held by ghostly fingers. He thought Brenda seemed hesitant about venturing further, and they sat for a long moment, watching the sign sway and the thickening clouds blot out the moonlight.

Then she turned onto a dirt road that was almost overgrown with encroaching trees and swamp life, the car's tires barely seeking out the two ruts that comprised the roadbed, the vegetation between them dormant and dying, scraping against the car's undercarriage. The road twisted and turned, casting haunting beams of light across the swamp, occasionally catching an animal's yellow eyes before whipping around another turn. The bogs seemed to come alive around him, and as they ventured deeper and deeper into the darkness, every ounce of reason inside him begged him to turn around and go back.

At last, they crossed into a clearing that might once have been a parking lot. But now the thin pavement was broken, plants that lay dormant now in the cold of winter protruding from the cracks.

A building came into view. It was v-shaped, with the center of the "v" appearing two stories high with wings on either side only one story. The wings were separated from the main building by narrow, covered breezeways that allowed him to peek past to the swamp beyond. The center towered above the tree line against the night sky. Bats flew from the roof in droves, blackening the bits of moon that threatened to peak from the clouds, their wings almost audible. Chris became acutely aware of his breath fogging the car's windows, their breathing coarser than before. Brenda gripped the steering wheel with both hands, slowly driving past the sides of the building that extended beyond the center. They appeared to have once been motel rooms; they were one story with doors approximately twenty feet apart. But now, they were obviously abandoned, the light fixtures beside some of the doors filled with decaying bird's nests while others lay broken, the glass scattered across the ground. A sidewalk that wound its way in front of the building was heaving in places, as if unseen forces from below were trying to escape.

She pulled the car into the shadows near the center of the building. Wordlessly, she turned off the engine. She sat for a long time, and they listened to their breathing and the call of animals beyond the clearing. Then she removed the keys from the ignition and placed them in her left pocket.

As Chris watched, she reached inside the right pocket of her trench coat and pulled out a snub-nosed revolver.

"What's that?" he asked. For the first time since he awakened in the hotel room and searched for his wallet, he felt defenseless. He was the only witness who saw the evidence she'd taken from her home, who knew she had been involved in an illegal money scheme, who understood it reached past Lumberton and all the way to Washington and beyond. He had only her word that she had not killed Nate and Peggy Lynn, and as he stared at the revolver, he realized he could be staring at the murder weapon.

She smiled. "Smith and Wesson Centennial Airweight," she said. ".38 Special."

He tore his eyes away from the barrel and toward her face.

She tilted the revolver and checked the bullets in the rotating cylinder. "It's not that reliable for distance, but it's a good friend to have when you're close." She closed the cylinder and looked up, catching his eyes as they remained locked on her. "You're not afraid of me, are you?" She chuckled. "Come on; we're wasting time."

With that, she opened the door and slid the revolver into her pocket as she exited the car.

He hesitated. She had the only set of keys to the car, and he had just watched her return them to her left-hand pocket. Even if he had possession of them, he didn't know if he could leave her stranded there in the middle of nowhere—unless he was fleeing from her, running for his life.

She was approaching a doorway cast in shadows. She briefly turned and gestured to him to follow her. Slowly, reluctantly, he left the relative safety of the car and approached the building.

She juggled a set of keys, trying several before she managed to locate one that opened the door. Chris wanted to ask her how she happened to have a key when the owners of the property apparently didn't provide it to her, but he thought it wiser to remain silent. The less he questioned, the safer he might be.

Then they were inside. Brenda fumbled in the darkness, her arm brushing against him as she reached for the wall. With a constant, low buzz a single light flickered on, bathing the room in a dim light.

Chris found himself in a large room that had undoubtedly been an office when the hunting lodge had been in operation. Two desks were in the center of the room, piled high with aging computer printouts. Stacks of continuous feed computer paper littered the floor and almost every one of the half dozen chairs scattered throughout the room. Atop one desk was a single computer and across the room against the opposite wall was a television set.

Brenda crossed to the television and turned it on. As it came to life, the screen was blue and the picture blurry, like the sets Chris remembered from his youth after the stations went off the air for the night. Brenda smiled sheepishly. "Don't know why I thought I could get reception here," she said. She moved away toward a filing cabinet but kept the television on. Despite the fact that they could get no sound or picture, it cast a blue light through the room that helped to illuminate it.

"Tell me what you're looking for," Chris said. His voice sounded strained.

Brenda looked at him in surprise.

"I can help you find it," he said by way of explanation. "Then we can get out of here."

She hesitated only a moment before opening the top drawer of the filing cabinet. "Nate was into a lot of things," she said. "A lot of unsavory characters used to come here, after his folks closed their business."

Chris felt his breath grow shallower. "I can't picture you involved in that." He chose his words carefully, and hoped they didn't sound false in the still, dusty room.

"I wasn't involved in most of it," she said, her fingers coming to rest on a single file. "Just some of it." She pulled it out and looked through it. "This will help."

She rifled through the rest of the folders and then searched the other drawers. When she was done, she had several files, which she handed to Chris. Then she turned her attention to the computer.

He held the files within his hands, staring at them as though they held the secret to her past, the money scheme, and their own future. Somewhere in the back of his mind, he heard the whirr of the computer as she turned it on, and he sensed a chair being moved in front of the desk.

He had just begun to open the first file when they heard the sound of tires crunching on the broken ground outside the building. His eyes met Brenda's as she hesitated for a split second, her amber eyes wide, before she lunged for the light switch on the wall behind him.

25

The parking lot was shrouded in darkness, the thickening clouds effectively blocking the moonlight. Chris' impulse was to lock the door and remain inside until the coast was clear, but before he could stop her, Brenda stepped outside the building. He followed, realizing as he crossed the threshold that both the television set and computer screen were casting a blue glow that spread like tentacles through the doorway. Quickly, he reached behind him and pulled the door tight.

"Stay in the shadows," Brenda whispered hoarsely, motioning toward the edge of the building.

"You're not going out there!"

"Shhh," she admonished. "I'll be fine."

They watched as a sedan inched its way around the parking lot, the headlights shining across the decaying structure, illuminating the crumbling façade and clouded windows.

"They're lost," she whispered. "They've got to be lost."

"I'll check it out," Chris said.

"No," Brenda said, raising her arm to bar his way. "I'll go."

"Are you crazy?"

The car began to turn in their direction and she frantically motioned for him to hide. He moved backward, toward the edge of the tree line, as the car came to a stop.

He was standing in muck that threatened to submerge his polished Santoni shoes, but he remained perfectly still. He realized he had begun to hold his breath, but he became acutely aware of the vapor rising from Brenda's breathing a few yards in front of him, and he did not want to give himself away. The area surrounding the office door was cloaked in darkness, and he moved farther into the shadows, deeper into the murky blackness along the edge of the swamp.

Brenda stood at the edge of the building, her hands in her pockets. Chris wondered if she knew how to use the revolver she had so expertly brandished, and he wished he had control of it now. He realized she also had the key to the rental car, and if anything happened, he had no means with which to fight and no way to flee.

Brenda moved toward the stopped car. Then the driver's side window was rolled down. The clouds began to shift overhead, and Chris' heart quickened, but he remained in the shadows of overhanging evergreens and cypress. A sliver of moonlight shifted over the car, briefly revealing a petite young woman with light shoulder-length brown hair. She was very attractive, and Chris found himself staring at her before the moon was covered again in clouds. She was young—perhaps in her early twenties, and he wondered what a youthful, attractive woman would be doing at this abandoned lodge in the dead of night.

"Hello!" she called out.

Brenda's voice sounded incredulous as she stepped closer to the car. "Can I help you?" she asked.

It was a trick, Chris thought frantically, a trick to get her close enough to the car for someone to reach out and grab her. He thought of making his presence known, of moving toward the car with his hands in his pockets, perhaps making it appear as though he had his hand on a weapon, but before he could move, the young woman answered and Brenda stopped just beyond the car.

"I'm afraid I'm lost," the young woman's voice carried across the lot toward them. She had a Southern accent. "I was looking for the Triple R—"

"This is it," Brenda answered. "Or *was* it."

She moved toward the car, and Chris bit his lip to keep from calling out to her. She stopped abruptly and appeared to be looking into the vehicle curiously.

"There must be some mistake," the driver was saying. "You see, my parents stayed there on their anniversary and they just raved about how wonderful it was—"

"They didn't stay here," Brenda interrupted, her voice clipped and curt.

"So, do you have any vacancies tonight?"

Chris felt his jaw drop. For all of the young woman's beauty, she must have been missing a few cylinders. He peered around the crumbling structure. A blind person could see this place was uninhabitable.

"You'd be better off finding a hotel room in town," Brenda said. Chris thought he detected more than a bit of impatience.

"Are you sure?" the driver said. "I'm not from around here, and I'm *so* tired."

"Trust me," Brenda said brusquely, "you'd get more rest someplace else." She removed her left hand from her pocket and pointed toward the parking lot exit. Her right hand remained firmly in her other pocket, and Chris sensed she was keeping the revolver firmly in its grip. "Just follow this road until it ends. Turn right, and follow that road until it ends. Turn right again, and you'll see a sign—"

"Please," the driver pleaded. "Just let me get a few hours' sleep here tonight."

Chris could not see Brenda's face in the darkness, and he wondered if she were staring at the driver with the same astonishment he felt. "This place isn't for the faint of heart," she said after a pause. He thought her voice had taken on a conciliatory tone, and he wondered what she must have been thinking. Then she exhaled audibly. "Park over there."

Chris stepped farther into the shadows, one foot sinking into the mire. He hugged a tree as the car was pulled diagonally from him, hoping the headlights would not swath him in light and reveal his presence. Brenda was returning to the edge of the building and was intently watching the driver as she exited the car. The sound of the door slamming echoed in the silence of the night.

Chris watched as the driver approached Brenda, coming just a few yards from where he stood. She was several inches shorter than Brenda and very slender. Her hands were both visible, and he marveled at her trusting disposition. He wanted to step forward and warn her, to tell her to leave there immediately and never come back, but before he gathered his wits about him, Brenda said, "Better get your suitcase."

He knew he must have been staring at Brenda as if she had grown two heads. He couldn't imagine what she was thinking, as she watched the young woman return to the car and retrieve a gym bag from the trunk.

Then she was back, just inches from Brenda as they opened the door and moved inside.

Chris stood for a brief moment, watching the blue tendrils of light abruptly disappear as the door closed behind them. He tried to move but realized one foot had become stuck in the muck, and he grabbed the nearest tree and braced himself against it. As he wiggled his foot, he heard a sucking sound as he extricated himself. He must have had two inches of mud on his Italian dress shoe.

He moved back toward the parking lot, scraping his soles along a bed of pine needles. When he reached the crumbling asphalt, he wandered over to the young woman's car, glancing back at the building more than once. He glimpsed inside, but the front seat was bare except for a state map. The back seat was completely empty.

A brisk, cold wind moved through, causing the trees to bristle and weave and Chris shuddered involuntarily. He glanced at the license plate. It was from Arizona, and it didn't match the accent. He looked back at the building, now swathed in darkness. As another wind blew through, a blue light caught his eye.

He moved slowly in the direction of the building, toward the light. It emanated from the back. He hesitated at the edge of the building, pressing his back against the wall and peering around the corner.

It was coming from a window. Quietly, he moved around the corner, his feet finding their way hesitantly in the darkness. The light cast a dim glow through a window stained with dust and dirt, reaching toward the trees and the swamp like a person's dying breath. He moved toward it until he stood peering into the office at the two women.

Brenda was handing her a room key. He could hear the murmur of voices, but he was unable to decipher their words. When the young woman turned, he ducked quickly into the shadows. He could hear their footsteps across the floor just feet from where he stood. Then the door was opened and their voices became louder.

He heard the crunch of their shoes on the pavement, and he moved along the wall toward them. A branch cracked under his shoe, and he stopped, his heart beating so rapidly that his chest was beginning to heave.

They did not appear to have heard him. "You'd do well to lock your door," Brenda was saying, "and stay inside until morning. There's no phone in the room, and I'll be leaving shortly. There won't be anyone around if you need help."

Chris edged his way to the corner of the building. The young woman was walking toward the end of the building to the last room. His heart sank inside, and he suddenly felt very sorry for her. This was a horrible place for a person to be, especially a young woman all by herself.

Then Brenda was back at the door, locking it with feverish intensity. She caught a glimpse of Chris and hissed, "Do you have the files?"

He nodded.

He heard the faint sound of the room door closing, and Brenda turned to peer in the direction of the young woman's room.

"Let's get out of here," she whispered.

"The computer—"

"There's no time. Hurry, before she comes back."

He stepped into the hazy moonlight, his feet feeling like lead.

She was at the passenger door in a heartbeat. By the time Chris reached her, she had slithered across the console and was behind the wheel. He must have had a quizzical expression on his face because she said, "One door. One person."

He slipped in beside her.

He shut the door as she cranked up the engine. "Stay down," she said.

"You can't leave her here alone—"

"She's not our problem."

With that, they were moving quickly through the lot and back down the winding drive, the trees appearing lower and more ominous than they had just moments before, their naked branches reaching toward them in the darkness.

26

Joseph was back in his original hotel room, only one mile from the site of his earlier altercation. He wore a splint on his right wrist. He rose from his chair and crossed to the wet bar, where he poured some ice cubes into the plastic shopping bag he'd been given at the local pharmacy. Carefully arranging the bag over his wrist, he returned to the desk and the laptop. He hoped the ice reduced the pain and inflammation; the aspirin he'd taken earlier had not helped at all. He knew his wrist was sprained, but there was nothing more he could do about it now.

This would not have happened in his younger years; he knew that, just as he knew this career would soon come to an end. His instincts were not as lightning quick as he needed them to be; his physical strength had waned; and there were many more coming up through the ranks to take his place. This would be his last assignment, he determined. Then he would retire, not to Washington, but to New England, where he would open a knitting shop. Perhaps he would even give lessons.

The heavy drapes were not quite pulled tight, and he could peer outside and view the other hotel. It appeared quiet now, the police cars and fire trucks gone, the parking

lot still. Traffic in town had died, with only an occasional
vehicle touring the empty streets, and even the interstate
traffic was lighter than usual.

He found himself staring at the side door to the other
hotel, remembering his frantic activity as law enforcement
closed in and Christopher Sandige and Brenda Carnegie
escaped his grasp. He'd barely had time to retrieve his pistol
and silencer before returning to his room as hotel guests
streamed into the corridor in response to the pulled fire
alarm. He removed his bloody coat, folding it neatly over
his arm, quickly washed his face and hands, combed his
hair, and exited the building along with dozens of patrons,
his weapon secured in his knitting bag.

By the time the police had covered all exits to the hotel
and were securing the building, he was driving calmly away.
He turned onto Fayetteville Road, driving southbound as
a stream of police vehicles and fire trucks passed him in
the opposite direction. He continued a couple of miles
until he reached a corner pharmacy. By the time he
purchased bandages and the splint for his wrist, his head
was throbbing and his wrist was swelling so badly he was
forced to unbutton his shirt cuff. He chatted pleasantly for
a moment with the helpful woman behind the register before
leaving, purposefully shuffling his feet as if he were an
elderly gentleman.

A few minutes later, he was back at his hotel, passing
by the young lady at the front desk who always inquired
about his infant grandchild and the progress he was making
on the knitted booties.

Once he arrived in his room, he hadn't left it again. At
dinner time, he'd ordered room service, but the half-eaten
food now sat outside his door, waiting for the cleaning
staff to remove it. He'd downed two pots of coffee, and
now the last cup was half-cold, the powdered creamer
congealing along the top.

Though his wrist pained him, he continued to hunch over Brenda's laptop, as he had for the past several hours, trying various combinations to break through her password protection. He thought he knew all the tricks to bypass the standard operating system protection, but she had installed additional firewalls that were stubbornly blocking his every move.

He sighed heavily and leaned back in his chair. He could simply destroy the computer. It would be easy enough to remove the hard drive and incinerate it or throw it into the black waters of the nearby Lumber River. As he pondered this, his cell phone rang.

"Yes?" he answered.

"What do you know?" came the familiar male voice.

"I have a laptop. I can't get in."

"Can you connect it to the Internet?"

"Physically; through the cable."

"We can find it and infiltrate it."

He was silent as he connected the cable from the laptop to the broadband connection in the wall. "It's ready."

"Leave it on. I'll be in touch."

Joseph was preparing to click off the cell phone when the voice added, "We must know how severely the operation has been compromised; what their next moves are. We must know their complete intentions. Anything less is unacceptable."

"Sandige is intimately involved in the operation," Joseph spoke carefully. It was highly unusual for this much information to be shared over a phone line that could easily be compromised.

"He has orchestrated Congressman Jack Willo's campaign during his last two terms," the voice responded.

"Willo," Joseph repeated.

"That's right. He's on—"

"—I know; the committee overseeing Middle Eastern oil imports." His mind was racing.

"He just won a third term; Sandige served as his campaign strategist again."

Joseph was silent as this information sank in.

"There's more—he's considered one of the most powerful political architects in Washington."

"Then why haven't I heard of him?" Joseph felt his temples begin to pound.

"He stays in the background, shuns the limelight. But he puts people in strategic positions; he's a player."

"I understand," Joseph said, his voice barely above a whisper.

"He also worked for Senator Philipton."

Joseph sat on the edge of the bed. "That means," he said softly, "Sandige is here because of the oil."

"It appears that way."

Joseph's mind raced through the members on the congressional subcommittee, trying to remember the staffers who remained in the background but who courted powerful allies.

When the man spoke again, his voice was one of authority. "I have people working to find out every move he makes… what credit cards he uses, who he calls, where he goes. If he uses his credit cards for another hotel, a restaurant, gasoline… You'll know it while the card is being approved."

"Good."

"We're tracking down information on Willo and Philipton… details on the Middle Eastern oil agreements— exactly what their roles are."

"I see."

"Leave the computer on and plugged in. Our systems will find it. Our programmers will get into it. We must know how he knows Brenda Carnegie."

"I understand."

"Don't wait for us. If you are presented with the opportunity, eliminate them both."

"Understood."

Joseph hung up the phone slowly. He sat for a long time, staring at the wall. With a heavy sigh, he looked over his shoulder at the laptop. He had no doubt the programmers would remotely break through the firewalls and get to the data; they were the best in the world. He knew after he had eliminated Brenda and Chris, Washington would already be taking the necessary steps to protect the operation and to conceal their tracks. And he knew even after he'd retired from the business and was comfortably operating his little knitting shop, they would assassinate anyone else who had the audacity to attempt to interfere with the political machine they had created.

27

Sunday morning

Alec drove slowly north on Chestnut Street. The early morning service at the Trinity Episcopal Church would begin soon, and a steady stream of people were parking along the street and making their way toward the church. As he passed by, he returned Mary and Danny Pittman's waves before slowing even further as he approached the neat yellow house where his partner lived.

He was early, but he tapped his horn lightly to let her know he was there. A curtain parted in the house next door, and Dani Malleck's neighbor peered out. Her hair was tightly curled and even from this distance, he could tell she was dressed in her Sunday best. Alec waved, but she did not return his wave, preferring instead to glare at him for a long moment.

She remained at the window long after Dani exited the house and made her way to the car.

"What's the story with your neighbor?" Alec asked as she settled in.

Dani glanced at the window next door. "Oh, she's just curious," she said.

Alec nodded but he wasn't convinced. He pulled away from the curb and headed north toward the other side of town. "We got a call," he said.

"What's up?"

"Somebody read yesterday's paper and called the sheriff's office. Thinks he saw our suspect yesterday."

A few minutes later, they pulled into the parking lot of a rental car lot. A new truck was parked at the entrance to the office and as Alec pulled the unmarked patrol car alongside it, a face appeared at the double glass doors. Alec radioed their position as they exited the vehicle.

"Mornin'," the young man said as they approached.

"You Zach?" Alec asked as they entered the office. It was cold, as if the heat had been turned off.

"That's right," he said, motioning them toward the back. "It's warmer in my office."

They made their way down a hallway and stopped at an inner office.

"I understand you have some information for us," Alec said, "concerning a person we'd like to talk to."

Zach perched on the edge of the desk.

"Got a call 'bout this time yesterday," he said. "Brenda Carnegie wanted to know if I could rent a car to a friend of hers."

Alec glanced at his watch. "Are you normally open at that time?"

"Not for another couple hours. She called me at home."

Dani interjected. "So you know her?"

Zach nodded. "She's used our service department off and on. She's been a good customer. She's a nice person," he added. "Kind of makes me feel like a traitor just standin' here talkin' to you."

"Did you know her friend?"

"Never saw him before. He wasn't from around here."

"A man?" Alec was jotting notes in his notepad. "You get his name?"

"Yeah. Christopher Sandige."

"How do you spell that?"

As Zach complied, Alec printed it carefully. "Did you rent him a car?"

"Sure did. Got dressed and came on over. Opened the place up. We try to give good customer service. Matter of fact, I even picked them up at their hotel."

"Their hotel?"

"Yeah." Zach gave them the location. "Drove 'em over here."

"And you rented them a car."

"Well, yeah." His voice became faster and a little louder. "I didn't know they was wanted or nothin'. I just thought I was doin' a good deed."

Dani raised her hand. "We know. We're not saying you did anything wrong."

"Can you describe the man she was with?" Alec asked.

"Tall. Kind of lean. Wore expensive clothes."

"Hair?"

"Yeah, he had some."

Alec glanced at Dani. "Do you remember the color?"

"Oh, yeah. Brown. Had a little bit of gray right here." He pointed to his temple. "Not much though."

"So what age do you think he was?"

"I don't know, I'm not good at that stuff."

"Well, he had some gray so he probably wasn't a teenager, right?"

"Oh, no. He wasn't a teenager."

"You think he was about Brenda's age?"

Zach hesitated. "Maybe. No, I think he was older. Heck, you can figure out his age by looking at his date of birth." He walked around his desk to a filing cabinet, where he rifled through a few files before pulling out a paper-clipped batch of papers. He tossed them on the desk in front of Alec. "I rented him a car," he said. "We require i.d."

Alec could feel the adrenaline rush as he reached for the papers. He noted that Brenda's accomplice was from Washington, D.C.; Zach had made a copy of his driver's license so he also now had a picture to go by. He also had his social security number and his date of birth. "Bingo," he said to Dani.

He continued glancing through the paperwork. He also now had the make and model of the vehicle they were driving, the vehicle they probably had when they returned to Brenda's house and removed her car. And they had a license plate number.

"I need this," Alec said, holding it up.

"Just let me make a copy of 'em," Zach said. "If they don't return that car, I'm gonna need to show the paperwork to report it as missin'."

Reluctantly, Alec handed him the papers. "Where's your copier?"

As they made their way down the hall, Zach said over his shoulder, "By the way, I was checkin' the other cars yesterday, and two of 'em had been broken into."

"You report it?"

Zach stopped and stared at him as if he'd grown two heads. "I just did… To you."

"We don't have jurisdiction here for that," Alec said. "Best you call the Lumberton Police Department."

Zach shook his head and continued down the hall, where he started up the copier and loaded the papers in the feeder. "Darndest thing," he said. "Somebody went to all the trouble of breakin' into 'em and hot-wirin' 'em. I know they drove 'em, too, I compared the odometer readin's. But then they brought 'em back." He finished copying the papers and handed the originals to Alec. "Ain't that the darndest thing you ever did hear?"

28

Joseph was emerging from the shower when his phone rang. Wrapping a towel about him for warmth, he ventured into the bedroom and answered it.

"Credit card transaction was just submitted," the voice said.

"Where?"

"We're running it down now. It's part of a batch processing job from a chain of service stations."

"So they gassed up?"

"We'll know soon. Be ready."

Joseph clicked off the cell phone and returned to the bathroom, where he thoughtfully combed his hair. Bruises from his altercation the previous day were beginning to form, but there was nothing he could do about it now. He finished toweling off and quickly dressed. Then he rolled his shirt sleeve up and carefully placed the splint on his forearm. It had hurt during the night, the pain becoming more pronounced as the darkness set in. He'd discovered that most aches and pains were intensified in the wee hours of the morning, so he'd attempted to concentrate on other matters but his efforts had been in vain. Even a double dose of aspirin had done nothing to curb the pain, and now he worried it had been badly sprained.

He prepared his revolver, slipping it into one of his deep coat pockets. He slid the silencer into the other pocket. He draped the coat over his arm and grabbed his knitting on the way out the door. Until the next call came through, he would be downstairs, enjoying a full breakfast and completing another bootie.

29

Alec and Dani passed by the front desk at a Lumberton hotel.

"Morning, Ruby," Alec said to the young woman at the registration desk as he passed. "Any breakfast left?"

She nodded toward the dining area. "Plenty. Help yourself."

Alec stopped at the broad entrance, his trained eyes assessing the patrons in only a few seconds. This dining room was one of the nicer ones in town, offering a free, hot breakfast to hotel guests in a cozy atmosphere filled with nooks and various plants. It was also the perfect spot to take a break, fill out paperwork, and make a few phone calls. The food was free to law enforcement officers, but he always left a generous tip to ease his conscience.

He was relieved to find that today the dining area was quiet, absent of screaming kids who often touched every Danish and roll on the sideboard. There was a young couple on the far side of the room, each engrossed in their email on separate laptops. He spotted the crowns of a few silver heads on the other side of some plants, a constant, low murmur coming from the table. And alone in the corner sat an older gentleman with thinning salt and pepper hair, knitting something in pink. As he passed by, he gave him a cursory glance over his half-glasses, his eyes a startling blue, before returning to his task.

Dani filled a small plate with scrambled eggs and grabbed a plastic cup of orange juice on her way to a table. Alec took his time picking out the crispest bacon and brownest sausage, the most well-done eggs, and both a cherry and cheese Danish. He left the plate and utensils at the table and returned for a cup of hot coffee and apple juice.

As he returned to the table, the older gentleman was raising his coffee cup to his lips. His right wrist was encased in a splint not unlike those used with carpal tunnel syndrome. His eyes met his, and the man nodded in greeting. Alec returned the nod and sat down across from Dani.

They ate in silence for a moment. Dani was more engrossed in her food than usual and Alec thought she was less talkative. He watched her eat for a few moments and then said, "So, we got a good break, didn't we?"

Dani nodded.

"The computer techs tell me it won't take them much time to run down that credit card."

She nodded again.

The silence grew awkward and Alec felt as though each bite of food had more trouble making it down his throat than the previous one. He took a sip of coffee, but it did little to coat his throat.

"Listen, Dani, about last night... It didn't mean anything."

She stopped, her fork in midair. "Well, that's a nice thing to say."

"It wasn't the best choice of words," he said. Normally straight-forward, he felt tongue-tied, as if the right words eluded him. After another moment of silence, he said, "I was trying to comfort you, that's all. I don't want you to think that I was trying to muscle in on your husband—"

"We spend more time together than Martin and me," she interjected. She looked at his hand, still holding the cup of coffee. Though he was widowed, he continued to wear his wedding ring, and she seemed to pause when she saw it. Then she added, "We have to be careful."

Alec was aware of a growing silence in the dining room, and he realized the low murmur of voices he'd heard earlier had completely died. It was as if the other patrons were listening intently, though he knew that was unlikely. He took another sip of coffee and returned to his food.

He heard a rustle and four heads began moving at once, just beyond the plants. He recognized two of the women from his various errands around town. They all seemed to be glancing furtively in their direction.

They donned their coats and made their way around the plants toward the exit. One slipped a few bills to Ruby, who had entered the room and was visually inventorying the amount of food on the sideboard. "Thank you, Dear," the older woman said as Ruby accepted the tip.

Dani had stopped eating and was watching the women. When they turned back around, their eyes met.

"Danielle," one of the ladies said in greeting. Her eyes were veiled and she didn't smile.

"Good morning, Miss Nevin," Dani answered.

"We're off to church now," Miss Nevin announced. Her voice was thick with ice, her back ramrod straight. Each woman looked first at Dani and then at Alec before parading in single file through the lobby toward the front door. Alec could have sworn one of them was clucking.

A pall seemed to fall on them, though Alec was hard-pressed to understand it. He glanced several times at Dani, who was eating slowly but intently. He had opened his mouth to speak when his cell phone rang, and he answered it instead.

It was Kyle Emerson, the sheriff department's expert on computer technology. He was witty, quick, and loved a challenge.

"Got some activity on that credit card," Kyle said.

Alec removed his pen from his jacket pocket. "Shoot."

"Sandige checked into a hotel Friday night," he continued.

Alec wrote down the address as Kyle rattled it off. "Same one where Zach picked him up yesterday."

"Who's Zach?" Kyle asked.

"Never mind," Alec said. "That hotel is less than a mile from here."

Dani had stopped eating and was looking at Alec's notepad.

"Rented the car Saturday morning; time on the rental car receipt matches the time it was posted."

"Looks like we're going to be paying a visit to that hotel," Alec said. "He hasn't checked out yet?"

"If he has, the final charge hasn't gone through," Kyle answered. "But there's more… About two o'clock this morning, he filled up that rental car at a gas station, put it on his credit card."

"Where's the gas station?"

"Lake Waccamaw."

"Lake Waccamaw?"

Dani raised her eyebrows quizzically.

"Then we're going to Lake Waccamaw first," Alec said as he wrote down the service station address. He clicked off the phone and turned to Dani. "Sandige hasn't checked out of his hotel, but he filled up that rental car just a few hours ago—at Lake Waccamaw."

Dani rose and began clearing the table. "We can hit the hotel on the way out of town."

Alec shook his head. "I have a hunch we need to head straight for the lake. I don't want to waste the time at the hotel just yet." He tossed a few bills on the table and glanced at his watch.

"We'll go the back way," Dani said. "With any luck, we'll reach the lake in less than an hour."

30

Muted remnants of an early morning sunrise were streaming through the bedroom window when Chris opened his eyes. It was a startling contrast to the previous night, the abandoned hunting lodge, and the drive past desolate swamps. He rolled onto his side and placed his hand on the pillow where Brenda had lain. The covers were pulled back on her side of the bed, and he listened for the sound of running water or the clink of dishware. Hearing neither, he rolled back over, watched the slow rotation of a ceiling fan for a few moments, and then reluctantly crawled out of bed.

He took a quick shower, slipped on his clothes and made his way down the hallway to the kitchen. Sausage biscuits were lined up on a cookie sheet; they felt cool to the touch and the dough was hardening. The empty box was visible in the trash can, a thick layer of freezer frost still on one corner. A half-empty pot of coffee waited on the warmer, but there was no sign of Brenda.

He grabbed a biscuit and tried to chew it, but it tasted like pressed board and its toughness threatened to chip a tooth. He poured a cup of coffee and wandered around the small home, dipping the dough into the tepid liquid in an attempt to soften it. He had growing doubts that this lake home belonged to a friend of Brenda's. As he meandered from one room to the next, it occurred to him that it could very well belong to Brenda herself. He felt as if he were looking at the house through different eyes, and he stopped at each doorway and studied the contents within, trying to piece together the puzzle that somehow fit together into a tall, red-haired beauty.

There were two bedrooms in the compact, one-story structure. The one they had slept in had white-washed paneled walls, Spartan furniture painted a pale blue, and the bedcover pattern was reminiscent of lattice work with yellow and blue flowers peeking through. He opened the drawers to reveal women's clothing, the faint scent of lavender wafting upwards and tickling his nose. Taking a quick look at the sizes, he deduced they could easily belong to Brenda.

The second bedroom was more masculine with heavy oak furniture and a brown patterned comforter. The male clothing in these drawers belonged to someone shorter and smaller than himself. A variety of ship models on the dresser made the room appear almost juvenile.

There was one full bathroom between the rooms and a half-bath off the living and dining area. As he wandered around the living room, he studied a variety of photographs on the bookshelves—pictures of a young couple with two small girls, one blond and one copper-haired. He picked up one photograph. From the graininess of the picture itself and the clothing they wore, he imagined it was taken in the mid- to late-70's. He wondered if this little girl was Brenda; if the blond-haired girl was her sister. It still brought him no closer to determining whether he was indeed in Brenda Carnegie's home.

A sudden noise averted his attention, and he turned toward the dining room table. It was a round table situated in the corner of the combination living-dining room, enclosed on two sides by glass that allowed one to look out upon the lake. On top of the table was a laptop.

As he walked toward it, he realized an alert had sounded, heralding an automatic Internet update. He watched the screen for a moment. Then his eyes wandered to the external hard drive beside it.

He glanced around again. Having been through the house, he knew Brenda was not there. He stood at the windows and peered outside. The rental car was parked in the driveway only a few yards from the roadway. When he turned toward the back yard, a movement caught his eye. It was Brenda, sitting at the end of the pier under a small roof, sipping coffee and staring at the lake.

He watched her for a moment, her long hair catching on the breeze and swaying in cadence with the movement of the water and the plants along the bank. The pier jutted into the lake perhaps thirty feet from land, ending in the covered portion that housed a picnic table and benches. Beside it, also under the same roof, was a boat, the top encased in a gray cover, rocking in concert with the wind.

She sat on a bench, her feet resting on the rough-hewn railing. She appeared to be watching the sun as it rose higher, lifting her cheeks upward as if waiting for it to warm her face. But her heavy sweater spoke of a chill in the air, despite the sunshine.

He turned back to the table. Beside the laptop were the folders they had taken from the hunting lodge. He flipped through them. They contained printouts of bank transactions. There was also a printed spreadsheet with what appeared to be a schedule of internal bank audits, projected three months to one year in advance, depending upon the type of audit and account. He noted an audit was planned for the following week.

In the margin of one printout were two scribbled words, one directly below the other, that seemed to have no connection and no obvious meaning. A user name and password, he wondered?

He turned back to the laptop. He rotated it so he could watch the screen and still keep a sharp eye on Brenda. He'd been with her in the Lumberton house and knew without a doubt that she had not located or removed a laptop. This one, then, must not have been the one she'd been searching for. It had to have already been in the house before they got there. It was, however, the same external drive he'd watched her remove from her Lumberton home.

He pulled up a chair and sat in front of it, switching almost instantly to a list of files. He navigated to the external hard drive. It was full of files, but he didn't recognize any of the extensions. The names were intriguing, including one marked "Exit 22" and another named "Refineries." He double-clicked on the one named "Exit 22". It instantly requested a user name and password. He tried the words written in the printed file, but they were not accepted. He clicked out. He tried the second file, but when prompted for a user name and password, the words didn't work there, either. He attempted file after file, but was stymied at each effort.

A trash bag lay bundled on the top of the table. Remembering she'd taken more than the hard drive, he opened the bag and rifled through it. There were bank deposit slips from a local account and two off-shore accounts—one personal and one under a business named "Exit 22." He ripped a deposit slip out of each account booklet, folded it and slipped it into his pants pocket.

Brenda stirred outside and began to turn toward the house. He clicked back to the desktop and turned the laptop back to where it had been. He wrote the user name and password on a scrap of paper and tucked it into his pocket alongside the deposit slips before arranging the folders as he'd found them. Then he crossed to the back door and quietly let himself out.

The wind was crisp and he felt a chill as he crossed the back yard to the pier. As he walked across the boards, the sound of his footsteps must have alerted Brenda to his presence because she turned and smiled at him.

"How's your arm?" she asked.

"Good. Doesn't hurt at all," he answered. "You're good at mending bullet holes."

She flashed a conspiratorial smile. "I told you, you were just grazed… You didn't try to take off the duct tape?"

He shook his head. "Not even hot water budged it. And I don't intend to pull it off."

"Best you leave it in place for now."

He stood at the railing and stared at the current. Tall grasses swayed elegantly. A flock of geese passed overhead, and he shaded his eyes from the sun and watched them. When his eyes roamed back to the water near his feet, he was struck at how muddy his dress shoes were.

He stooped, removed both shoes and studied them. The expensive seams were packed with muck from the previous night's escapades. He bent to one knee, realizing too late that his new khaki pants would get soiled on the dirty deck. He raised his knee, brushed a bit of grime off the pants, and then carefully dipped one of his shoes into the swirling water. He used his fingers to loosen the mud and wondered if they would ever be the same; they'd been a special order and not easily replaced.

With his back to Brenda, he said in what he hoped was a casual voice, "Whose house is this?"

"Just a friend's."

"You don't trust me yet, do you?"

There was a long pause before she answered. "I don't trust easily."

"I know." He finished cleaning his shoes and sat beside her on the bench. He slipped his feet into the shoes and realized immediately that despite his careful efforts, they were now wet inside.

They sat for a time, just watching the sky turn from red to a tumultuous blue-gray. Brenda shivered, and Chris draped one arm around her, pulling her closer to his chest. He breathed in her floral-scented hair and ran his fingers over her thick cotton sweater.

"Brenda, I've been thinking."

She lifted her chin and looked at him with interest. "Do you do that often?"

"I'm serious," he said but he felt his heart grow lighter at the sound of her chuckle. "Run away with me."

She stopped and her smile appeared frozen. Then she laughed again. "Isn't that what I'm doing?" she said, waving her hand toward the lake house.

He placed his hands on her cheeks and looked deep into her eyes. "Come back with me, to Washington."

She didn't answer right away. She didn't push him away. She didn't even look away. He felt his heart beating faster and he felt emboldened.

"That isn't exactly running away for you, if we're going to your place."

"That's true," he said, realizing his voice had become a whisper.

"Besides, what would I do in Washington?"

"Whatever you want to do."

She reached for one of his hands, placing her small palm over it and holding it against her cheek. "You don't even know me."

"I know enough," he answered. "Enough to know I can't imagine waking up without you next to me. I can't imagine opening my front door and not finding you there. I can't imagine my life without you in it."

"Chris—"

"Come with me back to Washington. Whatever happened here—whatever you're running from, I can help you. I have friends—"

The sound of car doors closing caused them both to jump. Chris caught a flash of Brenda's wide, troubled eyes before he averted his attention toward the house. Through the glass corner of the home, he could see a dark sedan pulled across the short driveway, blocking in the rental car. Two people in dark blue suits were approaching the house. As one of them pulled back his suit jacket, the sun's muted rays bounced off a piece of metal.

Chris could feel Brenda's heart thumping rapidly against him, her breath coming in short, shallow bursts. The railing with the wide spaced pickets did nothing to shield them from the intruders, and he knew it was only a matter of time before they were spotted. But even as he watched them moving ever closer, he felt frozen in place like prey within a hunter's sights.

31

Alec had been driving the perimeter of Lake Waccamaw for only a few minutes before Dani spotted the rental car parked beneath the mature oak tree, its stripped branches reaching toward the roofline but doing nothing to shield its presence from the road. He straddled his unmarked car across the driveway, preventing the rental car's use in an escape attempt.

As they exited the vehicle, he was struck by the eerie silence. He'd grown up in nearby Laurinburg, and as a young boy, he'd visited Lake Waccamaw; in the summer months, a few of the homes were popular rental properties. He recalled the laughter and voices of scores of young children as they romped in the lake, rode their bicycles along the narrow roadway, and the calls up and down the road as mothers announced dinnertime. He remembered sitting at the end of the piers and eating shrimp boiled in beer alongside juicy watermelon, of watching for the ice cream truck with its distinctive bells that heralded its approach, and of the mosquito truck that wound its way around the lake at dusk, the neighborhood children running after it, oblivious to the heavy chemical fog it emitted.

Now all of those sites and sounds were gone. The tiny rental properties were intermingled now with larger, multi-storied structures; some of them appearing as though they were year-round primary residences. But the streets were empty. There were no children playing, no dogs barking, no boats skimming the surface of the lake. The heavy forestation that lined the narrow roadway was dormant now and lay brown and drab against the ground, the trees that normally draped the road now emaciated figures. He heard the twitter of a bird, but it sounded alone and lonely against the growing wind.

He surveyed the house as they approached it. Situated only a few feet from the road, it was a small structure. The roof was almost flat and made of metal, the green paint now faded so it would appear almost invisible when the nearby trees were thick with leaves. The front of the house consisted of two windows flanking a center door, and as they neared, he peered into the first window. Topped with a ruffled yellow curtain, it revealed a small but modern kitchen that was in contrast with the home's exterior. It was neat, the counters shining. And on the opposite side of the window was an automatic coffee maker, the light glowing red and the glass pot revealing diminishing coffee. A platter of biscuits sat beside it, and a presumably empty carton of frozen sausage and biscuits peeked out of the trash can nearby.

As he peered into the room, he realized a doorway faced him on the opposite wall, allowing a glimpse all the way through this end of the home to the pier and lake beyond.

Quietly, Alec and Dani made their way to the door, where Dani gently tried the door knob. It was locked.

Alec motioned toward the other window, and he stealthily made his way toward it while Dani remained at the door. It was more difficult to see inside the second window, as the curtains were almost drawn shut. But as a heater kicked on inside, they fluttered and he caught a glimpse of heavy oak bedroom furniture. The bed was made.

He moved toward the edge of the house. The cedar siding reached within five feet of the opposite corner where it gave way to a glass wall. In between the two corners was a small window with an internal crank that was partially open.

He returned to the front door. He stood on the right side of the door while Dani positioned herself on the left. Their eyes met briefly, and he nodded. She raised her hand and pounded on the door.

"Police!" she called out in a husky voice.

Alec heard the pounding echo through the house, and he listened intently for the sound of movement within. Hearing none, he signaled toward the opposite side of the house nearer the driveway.

While Dani remained at the front door, he moved to the corner and peered around it. The cedar siding here gave way to a glass wall about halfway down. He kept his back to the wall and made his way cautiously toward the glass. When he reached its edge, he peered inside.

Just inside the glass was a small round table upon which a laptop hummed along, a screen saver migrating around the screen. A chair had been pulled from the table, but it was empty. Beyond the table was a sofa and chairs, all facing the panoramic view of the lake. The back wall was made entirely of glass.

From this vantage point, he could see through the living area to another bedroom. This one appeared brighter, and a glimpse of the bed revealed covers that had been thrown back.

He heard a movement and turned back toward the front of the house, where Dani had appeared at the corner. He signaled toward the back of the house.

His eyes took in the entire room before he ventured past the edge of the cedar siding. He knew he would now be in full sight of the occupants, but now he also had an unobstructed view of any movement at this end of the house.

It was empty.

Empty, but it had been occupied, and from the red light on the coffee maker, the food on the counter and the laptop humming along, he knew they weren't far away.

Dani joined him at the back corner, her eyes searching the home's interior through the glass. "Looks like we just missed them."

Alec turned to face the water.

There might have been a scant twenty feet between the homes here, but their back yards were divided by wax myrtles that reached above his head. As they swayed in the breeze, they appeared as if they were coming alive, their long evergreen branches dancing rhythmically.

Along the back perimeter was the lake. The sun bounced off the waves as the wind increased. He listened to the sound of water lapping against a long wooden pier as his eyes skimmed it.

"I'm checking the boat house," he said.

"I'm going back around the house... I'll also call Lake Waccamaw Police, and let them know we're here."

"We'll want to—"

"—secure the rental car. I know."

He nodded before heading across the yard.

The water was shallow here, and as he moved along the wooden pier, he could see the bottom of the lake, the vegetation stubbornly holding onto the sandy bottom. About a third of the way, he noticed a clump of mud and he stopped and stared at it for a moment before glancing back at the yard. The mud was black and thick; the yard was sandy and brown. He stepped around it and continued.

He reached the end of the pier. He took in the picnic table. The bench furthest from the water was tucked neatly under the table, but the closest one was pulled out at a slight angle. On top of the table were two coffee mugs. He reached toward the one with a slight smudge of lipstick along its edge; it was cold. The other one was warm.

He stared at the lake. He could not see to the other side, but there were no boats here, no sound of motors, no sails peeking upward toward the sky.

He turned to the boat. It was perhaps twenty-one feet long. A gray cotton cover appeared to be a custom fit; it was snug against the hull and was perfectly dry. The boat itself was lowered into the water; he noted a cantilever boat lift. The boat was tied off, and as he inspected the ropes, they were dry. He stared for a moment at the gray cover and the way the wind barely budged it from its snug position.

He stepped back and almost slid into the picnic table. He caught his breath and looked at the floor beneath him. There were two pools of water just inches from the bench. The wood was old and worn, and the water was seeping into the fibers. They appeared to be about twelve inches in length; as he rested one shoe beside it, he realized they were roughly the same size.

He peered over the side of the pier; the water was clear, the sand rippled in response to the wind and waves. He looked back at the boat. He watched the wind rustle the cover, and then he reached for the gray cotton material.

32

On the opposite side of the speed boat, the cover was loosened, the material flapping against the side of the boat as the increasing wind caused it to roil and tumble within the rope constraints. Three feet down was a single Italian leather dress shoe, stuck in the mire and filling with sandy loam each time a wave approached the shore. Plant life stubbornly clung to the earth, moving in tandem with the current and threatening to bury the shoe.

A water line was barely perceptible along the side of the boat where the waves lapped against it. And in one corner, a greater watermark rolled off the side, a watermark the approximate size of two wet bodies that had scampered frantically into the boat.

Chris lay on the floor of the Bayliner, his feet pointed toward the stern. His dress slacks were soaked past his knees and clung to his skin in cold, wet folds. Both his socks were drenching the floor, and on one foot was the waterlogged match to the dress shoe lodged in the lakebed.

He lay on his side with one arm extended around Brenda's shivering body, her own clothes equally saturated, their breath intermingling in a visible vapor.

He breathed in the distinct odor of lake water and plastic seats, the perfume of the cotton boat cover absorbing the sun and water... The air was close and thick, the surface of the floor hard and cold, and despite his best efforts, he could not avoid trembling alongside Brenda.

He pushed his body closer to her, the minor movement feeling exaggerated in the close confines, and he soaked in her warmth and hoped his own body reciprocated. They were silent, listening to the lapping of the water and swaying in cadence with the current.

They lay for so long that Chris began to question whether their sudden panic had been out of proportion, and his mind raced through the possible identities of their unexpected guests.

He opened his mouth and was ready to whisper into Brenda's ear when he heard the sound of shoes on the pier. He knew she heard it also; at the sound, her body tensed. He felt his arm tighten around her, readying his own body to protect her from an attack.

He peered around him as much as he could without moving his body. With the boat cover on, it plunged them into semi-darkness. He squinted in an attempt to view his surroundings; a rope lay coiled not far from his hand, and he pictured its uses but could only think of it in terms of a noose. The rope reminded him that they were tethered to the dock, and any escape attempt by boat would be thwarted.

The sound of the footsteps were measured, as if the person were surveying his or her surroundings as they walked. It had to be a man, Chris reasoned; the sound was heavy, too heavy for a woman. He thought of the man in the hotel corridor, of their furious struggle, and of his wounded arm now wedged between his body and the floor, throbbing now that their lives might depend upon it.

He felt his breath slowing and then stopping as the footsteps advanced toward the boat. He pictured the man standing just a few feet away, and in his mind's eye he saw the picnic table where he had sat only a moment ago. He sucked in his breath as he remembered the coffee mugs. Brenda jerked slightly and squeezed his hand as if to warn him to be quiet, but he was already holding his breath again and struggling to determine the intruder's exact position.

The sound of footsteps stopped abruptly, and they lay there in each other's arms, rocking with the growing hostility of the wind. He pushed one foot against the edge of the boat in an effort to keep them from slipping, but as the boat continued to rock, he knew his efforts were futile. The cover rippled in the wind, the loose corner threatening to creep up the side and eventually retract to reveal their presence.

He turned his head, the movement excruciatingly slow, and tried to view his surroundings with more clarity. Their heads were close to seats and a console; there the boat cover graduated upward over a windshield before scooping back down toward an extended bow. He could barely make out a set of keys dangling in the ignition. On either side of their bodies, the boat widened toward the stern and as he glanced toward their feet, he realized there were two more seats along the back, separated by another console.

There was an outboard motor, but there was no way to determine if the boat would start right up or if there was sufficient fuel to allow their escape. He knew there had not been enough time to untie the boat, and inwardly he cursed their luck even as he continued to listen with bated breath.

He still could not hear anything more than the lapping of the waves and the low howling of the wind as it whipped across the water.

"Lake Waccamaw PD just arrived."

The sound of the police radio crackled to life only inches from Chris' head, and he jerked involuntarily. He could hear Brenda's heart beating rapidly and his own heart seemed to have leapt into his throat.

"Good."

The voice was calm and seemed to hang in mid-air just on the other side of the boat cover. As Chris peered upward, the material began to shift and he realized the intruder was unfastening the cover and would soon peel it back. He was caught between physically sheltering Brenda with his own body, and bursting toward the man in a preemptive strike.

"They have a problem with the search warrant," the radio cackled again. The voice was female, competent and strong.

The material stopped moving and he heard a heavy exhale.

"Better get back over here," the voice came again.

The man didn't answer. Chris got the sense that he was hovering just over them, one hand on the cover, thinking about his course of action. Then the cover was pulled taut, and with another strong exhale and a grunt as though the man were coming upright from a squatted position, he felt the weight of his body moving away from the boat. They listened, the sound of footsteps growing faint as they retreated across the pier toward land.

33

Joseph sat in the driver's seat of the dark blue Lexus, munching on a cheese Danish. A cherry Danish waited on a Styrofoam plate on the passenger seat beside him. With the engine turned off, the only sounds came from the wind as it whistled through the nearby trees and slapped against the car's windows, its urgency in contrast to his steady, rhythmic breathing. The car was backed into a gravel driveway so he faced the lake on the other side of a rural roadway. Only a few feet from the passenger side was a small, aging duplex. The surrounding trees swayed in the growing wind, their branches swooping down toward the roof of the vehicle, casting starfish shadows across the hood of the car.

What a lucky break, he thought as he monitored the activity at a gray cedar house about sixty yards away. To have been in the same hotel dining room as the two detectives who had been at Brenda's house, the male detective the same one whose picture was plastered across the front page of the local newspaper, the one he now knew headed the murder investigation and was now hot on Brenda Carnegie's trail… He couldn't have planned it better. And to be there to overhear their next destination was beyond luck. It was fate.

He'd waited until they left the hotel parking lot before venturing to his vehicle that waited at the edge of the hotel, just out of sight from the roadway. Rather than follow them and risk raising suspicion, he charted his course on the vehicle's navigation system, which took him first onto Interstate 95 and then onto I-74 heading eastbound toward the ocean.

He spotted their unmarked car leaving a service station just off the highway, hanging back as they crept along a tree-lined road that wound around a lake perhaps seven miles in diameter.

The lake was cast in a silvery blue glow as the sun attempted to peek through tumultuous clouds, the waves rising as the wind whirled across the open expanse of water. They'd driven along a stretch of road in which sleepy houses rested on only one side of the roadway, their front porches gazing lazily across the road to a lake dotted with patio furniture at the end of long piers that jutted outward to boat docks. He found it interesting when he spotted basketball hoops erected a few yards from shore, and tried to envision the game without the hard court needed for dribbling. Then his mind returned to the task at hand, and he returned to peering at each driveway as the car rolled past.

He saw the unmarked vehicle ahead of him as it reached a dead-end at one end of the lake, and he calmly pulled down another roadway and followed it as it gently swerved back toward the opposite side of the community. He carefully watched his rear-view mirror but the road behind him was empty. It was as if he'd come to a summer campground in the dead of winter.

He eventually made his way back toward the lake, where he continued driving the perimeter. He crossed into an area where the road curved away from the water; here there were houses on both sides, and he drove ever more slowly as he studied each residence for signs of life.

He spotted the sheriff's department vehicle again on the opposite side of the lake. It was pulled across a short driveway next to a one-story house, the angle effectively blocking a white Honda Accord. He felt the adrenaline begin to pump through him, but he calmed himself as he drove past. The two detectives were approaching the house.

He continued until he reached the duplex where he now sat, partly obscured by the shadows cast by the building. He watched as they peered into the front windows and cautiously made their way around the small structure, his eyes roaming across the terrain for signs of an escape while he calmly reviewed his options.

Brenda and Chris were nearby; he could feel it. He had an instinct for these things which hadn't been diminished by age. He'd seen yesterday's newspaper, courtesy of the hotel, and knew they planned to hide out until they could plan their next move. It was only natural. But his instructions had been clear: his superiors could not afford to have local law enforcement poking around their business, asking questions and determining motives. It was enough right now for them to believe Brenda committed the crimes in a passionate rage. But before they could discover otherwise, he had to eliminate both Brenda and her political operative, Christopher Sandige. And the time to do that could be only minutes away.

He wished he was not driving the Lexus. It would be too easy for a suspicious officer to run the license plates and discover they were stolen. But in his haste to reach Brenda and Chris before they were taken into custody, he hadn't had the time to hot-wire another vehicle. And, he consoled himself, if things went according to plan, this one would be back in New York before Monday morning, along with its original plates.

He calmly watched the lake house and the officers' movements. If they located Brenda and Chris and if they prepared to arrest them, he had no other option but to kill them all right here, at Lake Waccamaw.

His eyes rested on a propane tank beside the lake house. Ten years earlier on another job, he'd worked on a massive tank explosion; cutting the propane piping would cause a substantial leak, and as the combination of propane and vapor were released, it would simply ignite. He could help it, of course, with a match or something similar. With any luck, the tank was at least half-full, which could easily engulf the lake house, the cars beside it, and the people within fifty feet or more. The trick, he knew, was getting to the pipe and severing it without detection.

He waited patiently while one officer began walking toward the boat dock at the end of the pier. If they both ventured to the dock, he thought, he could get there, sever the pipe, return to his vehicle a safe distance away, and if it didn't ignite within a few short minutes, he could fire a shot to help it along. The bodies would be burned beyond all recognition. Mission accomplished.

He quietly, calmly opened his car door. He left it hanging open. He engaged the automatic trunk and slipped out of the car as it opened. By the time he was behind the vehicle, the trunk was open wide, revealing sets of tools— tools he'd used to crack open safes and doors, as well as those he employed for killing. He stared for a moment at a few sticks of dynamite, realizing that all he had to do was get them near enough to the propane to cause an explosion. His job had just become easier.

His hand was on the dynamite when a vehicle drove past him at a fast clip, stopping at the lake house. As he watched two Lake Waccamaw police officers exit the vehicle, he hesitated. Then he grabbed two sticks, slowly lowered the trunk just enough for it to gently click shut, and moved deeper into the shadows cast by the duplex.

He watched as the officer at the end of the pier returned to the shore. The officers conferred for a couple of minutes at the back corner of the lake house. He heard their radios crackle and come to life, but he was not close enough to make out their words. Two of them disappeared briefly toward the back of the house, beyond his range of vision. After a few brief minutes that seemed more like an eternity, they all returned to their vehicles.

His eyes roamed from the lake house to the Lexus, where the door still swung open. They would drive right past him, and they might mistake his vehicle for one used by their suspects. He slowly lowered the dynamite to the ground. Then as the cars backed out of the driveway and started down the street toward him, he walked to the sidewalk as if he were leaving his house and heading to his vehicle. He didn't avert his eyes as they drove past, but he looked at them with some degree of curiosity, even motioning in a half-wave as they passed by.

When they were out of sight around the next bend, he returned to the side of the house, where he gathered the dynamite. Then with a step that quickened as he drew closer to the lake house, he moved with a new purpose: if Brenda Carnegie and Christopher Sandige were hiding there, he would find them. And between his pistol and the dynamite, he would kill them.

34

It took every ounce of restraint for Chris not to throw back the boat cover and come out swinging. It went against his grain to conceal himself, and when he heard the radio, he knew without a doubt they were hiding from law enforcement. As this fact started to sink in, his temple began to pound and his heart raced.

When he finally moved away from Brenda, he was surprised to find that her right hand firmly grasped her pistol. She had been ready to shoot when the cover was peeled away.

"What were you thinking?" he hissed in the semi-gloom.

"This goes all the way to Washington and beyond," Brenda said, her eyes pleading. "They can't capture me."

"Whose side are you on?"

A flash of confusion raced across her face. "If you're asking me if I'm a spy," she said finally, "or if I'm involved in some sort of espionage, it's neither. I am doing nothing—absolutely nothing—against America."

He half-kneeled under the continued protection of the boat cover as they heard the sound of car engines starting. He tried to count the engines that turned over in a vain effort to determine how many vehicles had been there. He couldn't help but wonder how it was that one of them had been so close they could almost hear him breathe, only to be pulled away.

Brenda crawled on her belly to the rope that lay perfectly coiled near the front compartment. She dug around for a moment, her hands feeling their way in the absence of any real light. After a moment, she pulled out a four inch boat knife folded neatly into a hard plastic sheathing.

"Take it," she said, pushing it toward Chris. "You might need a weapon, and it's—"

"All you have?" he finished, looking pointedly at the gun. Without taking his eyes from hers, he took the knife from her and slid it into his pants pocket.

"We can't stay here forever," he said, feeling somewhat silly for stating the obvious. He realized despite the cold morning air that still skimmed across the boat cover, sweat was beginning to pop out across his forehead.

Brenda nodded. Her face reflected what he felt deep in his gut: that they had no way of knowing whether the coast was clear. Various scenarios raced through his mind: that they were alone now and safe; the officers were inside the house and would return shortly; or that additional reinforcements would begin to arrive. And as he played out each set of circumstances in the few seconds he could afford to digress, he began to think of the headlines in *The Washington Post* and how this predicament would not only impact his own political future but potentially that of every politician he'd helped to put into office.

"I have to check things out," he whispered finally.

"No—"

"They're not looking for me," he said firmly. "They're looking for you. If I'm spotted, I'll lead them away from you."

She searched his eyes, her own a mixture of confusion, fear and resignation. Then finally she nodded and swallowed.

He crawled to the corner of the boat farthest from the boat dock, which also happened to be in a position in which he felt he would least likely be detected from the house. He paused momentarily, listening for the sound of returning footsteps, of boat engines on the lake, or for any telltale signs of a nearby presence. Hearing none, he rolled onto all fours before climbing over the side, the boat cover reluctantly stretching over his body as his foot sought the water on the other side.

He knew in this moment he would be his most vulnerable. Unable to see for the heavy material that encased him, he knew his movements would alert anyone watching to his presence. The shape would be undeniably human, and by the time he extricated himself from the cover's grasp, he could come face to face with a loaded weapon, a set of handcuffs, and a whole lot of questions.

His foot found the water and he lowered himself gently, his other foot joining the first. It was then he chastised himself for forgetting to remove his one remaining shoe. The thought was immediately replaced by the resignation that it had been so thoroughly soaked getting into the boat, it was pointless to protect it now.

He lowered the rest of his body from the boat, feeling it rock harshly with the release of his weight. Then he pulled his head from under the cover and peered about.

The silence was eerie. It seemed as if the birds had stopped flying, the trees ceased to sway, and time stood perfectly still.

His legs were immersed in the cold water and though he did not need the boat for support, he remained close to it, bending to keep his head from rising above it. He crept to the bow, which faced the lake house.

His eyes moved purposefully over the winter grass, taking in the scores of bushes along the edges of the property. They wandered to the glass along the back of the house, where they searched for signs of life from within. Seeing nothing, he moved back to the stern and crossed behind it to the other side of the boat, where he could view the driveway.

The white rental car sat in the exact location they'd parked it only a few hours ago, in the protective darkness of night. The vehicle that had straddled the driveway had disappeared.

He loosened the boat cover. When he spoke, his voice was husky. "They're gone."

Brenda peeked over the edge. "Thank you."

He wanted to ask her why she was thanking him; why they were there, hiding in a boat at a lake he'd never heard of before last night; why they were running from the law… But instead, he threw the cover back, revealing the open stern, while he returned to the opposite side to find his shoe.

He had to kick around for a moment before he found it half-buried by shifting loam and sand. By the time he pulled it out and rinsed out the sediment, Brenda was standing on the end of the pier, looking thoughtfully at the boat.

"We can't stay here," she said, almost apologetically.

"I think that's a safe assessment," Chris answered. He moved back toward the pier, where he tossed the shoe onto the deck. Then he reached into the water, removed his other shoe, rinsed it out, and flung it onto the deck beside the first one.

He placed his hands on the dock ladder, the frigid steel biting his hands with an unexpected ferocity. Quickly, he began to scale the ladder as Brenda knelt down beside him.

She had just started to hold her hand out to assist him when a great blue heron cried out, it's trumpeting voice aggressive and hoarse as it floated on the wind just above their heads. Chris watched Brenda as she pulled back and tilted her head to admire the huge bird, the wind catching her hair.

He heard the sound of the shot in almost the same instant as he felt it whiz between them in the exact location where she'd knelt only a moment ago.

"Jesus!" he cried out, releasing his grip on the ladder and plunging into the water.

In a flurry of activity, Brenda threw herself back into the boat with a sudden fury, crossing the open stern as another shot rang out and echoed across the lake. Chris bounced out of the water almost the second his body struck it, flinging himself onto the deck in a fluid movement borne of a rapid surge of adrenaline. He half-crawled, half-propelled himself toward the rope that tied the boat to the dock as Brenda frantically tried to start the engine. As it sputtered and stalled and another bullet barely missed his bobbing and weaving body, he frenetically loosened the rope, his fingers feeling fat and uncoordinated and the rope stiff and unyielding.

His eyes darted toward the house as he threw the now-loosened rope into the boat and raced toward the bow, where it bobbled in the water with one remaining rope tethering it to the dock. The man from the hotel was walking calmly from the back door, his arm raised, his eyes measured as he crossed the small yard toward them. He was too far away for him to strike his target, but Chris knew it would be only seconds before he was close enough for his aim to be sure. Maniacally, he worked at the rope as the engine coughed, its slow groan in contrast with his rapidly beating heart.

As the last inch of rope was freed, he threw himself into the bow as another bullet whizzed past him and the engine sprung to life.

"Jesus!" he screamed again. "He's trying to kill me!"

Then he was throwing himself toward the steering wheel, pushing Brenda away as he thrust the boat into reverse. The boat's sudden movement knocked his breath from him, but his hands continued to grip the wheel with stubborn ferocity. Brenda pulled herself from the floor and raised her gun over the windshield. As he turned the boat from shore, he vaguely sensed her moving through the vessel, returning the man's fire as they sped away toward open water.

35

Chris cut the engine as the boat drifted from Lake Waccamaw into an adjoining canal. Once the angry noise of the motor had been silenced, it was replaced by the sounds of waterfowl hidden by thick cypress trees and water oaks. The water had been the color of iced tea, but now it turned brackish as it was almost overtaken with a plethora of plant life that lurked just below the surface of the water. As they moved farther inland, the swampy shores began to close in on them, the trees now so close together that their naked branches met overhead, effectively preventing the sunlight from reaching them. Marsh plants, now winter brown, seemed to spring to ghostly life as the wake from the small boat reached them.

Something bobbed a foot away, and Chris pointed. "An alligator," he said, his voice sounding more frightened than he would have liked.

Brenda laughed and reached out, pushing the obstacle. It bobbled and floated toward shore. "It's a log," she said.

"Are there alligators here?" he said, peering into the waters.

"Oh, about nine hundred of 'em," she said casually.

"*Nine hundred?*"

She laughed again. "Don't worry; they're hibernating."

"What the heck does that mean?"

"It means they won't hurt you."

As the weak sunlight disappeared, the air was replaced with a heavy veil that made it difficult to see more than a few yards ahead. It appeared more like the minutes after sunset than the hours of early to mid-morning.

Chris trembled from the cold air, realizing only now that he was drenched from head to toe. His clothes clung to him in sodden, frigid folds. His feet were encased only in waterlogged socks, his shoes left behind on the pier.

As if in response, Brenda retrieved two small blankets from the console. She wordlessly wrapped one about him, the odors of mold and damp rising to his nostrils as he tried to pull the dry material closer about him. She draped the second one around herself and sat on the cushioned side bench in the bow in front of the steering wheel.

She didn't direct his course, but as they continued their labyrinth journey, he realized he had no choice but to allow the current to propel them gently forward.

They were on the opposite side of the lake, away from the row of homes that overlooked the water. With each second that passed, they found themselves farther from the cozy lake home, the coffee warming on the burner, the warm bed... and the bullets whizzing past their heads.

Chris steered the boat toward the swampy perimeter, reaching for a tree trunk by which to stabilize and stop the vessel from continuing through the water.

Brenda did not stop him, but remained seated in the bow, watching him intently.

"Where does this take us?" he asked, nodding toward the ever-darkening waters.

"I don't know."

Chris clung tighter to the craggy trunk of the bald cypress. "What do you mean, you don't know?"

She shrugged. "I don't know. I've always turned around."

Chris peered behind them. "I don't think that's an option right now." When she didn't respond, he asked, "Any ideas?"

He followed her eyes as they studied his clothing.

"We need to get into dry clothes and get out of here," she said finally.

"And just how do you propose we do that?"

She looked in the direction from which they'd just come.

"Oh, no," Chris said. "We're not going back. The cops will see the boat is gone and they'll be looking for us. And if you don't think the man with the gun is trying to steal a boat right now—he might be riding around, just waiting for us to pop our heads up!"

"Relax," she said calmly. "We can go back a short distance and hide the boat in the swamp; there are plenty of places where no one could ever spot it."

"And what about us? How long do we stay hidden in the boat? I don't see a cabin in this thing."

"We don't stay in the boat," she said with a sly smile. "We walk through the swamp—"

"*Walk* through the swamp?" He knew his mouth was hanging open but he wasn't inclined to close it. "You didn't just see that alligator?" He looked at the water surrounding the boat. "And there's nine hundred of 'em out here?"

"I told you, it wasn't an alligator. It was a log. Alligators are cold-blooded creatures; they hibernate when it gets this cold. Trust me, they won't bother you."

"Yeah, right."

"Not far from here is a friend's house—"

"*Another* friend?"

She looked at him for a brief moment before continuing. "I know where the key is hidden. They won't be there. We can get cleaned up, grab dry clothes, and borrow their truck."

"How do you know so many people here? How do you know they won't be at home, and where their keys are hidden? How do you know these things?"

She glanced upward, but the trees blocked the sun. She said, "We're wasting time. You're just gonna have to trust me."

"Trusting you is what got us into this mess." Chris knew his tone was full of frustration, but he didn't avert his eyes. "And after all I've been through, I deserve some answers."

She let out a heavy, resigned sigh. Then she took a deep breath. "The house we just left belonged to my parents. We used to come here every summer. When they died, they left it to my sister, Emily."

"And Emily uses it only in the summer?"

She looked toward the lake and appeared to be listening. "Emily died about five years ago."

There was a moment of silence. Then Chris said, "I'm sorry."

She nodded. "The home's part of a trust for her son, Adam. He lives in California with his dad—they were divorced—and they don't come back here… The house is pretty much the way Emily left it, just before she died."

Chris grew silent.

"Anyway, we're wasting time," Brenda said, shuddering in the blanket. "Just a hundred yards back down this canal, we'll find a place where we can ditch the boat. We'll only have to walk about half a mile through the swamp to get to my friend's house." When Chris raised one eyebrow, she added, "My parents' friends. I grew up with their daughter. They live in Wilmington now and have the lake house here. They won't be there."

"Then how do you know a truck will be there?"

"It's a hunting lodge. But her dad hasn't been deer hunting in years; his health isn't too good these days... The old truck they used stays here year 'round."

Chris peered through the swamp, envisioning trying to walk through the black muck. A half mile on land was nothing, but as he studied the fallen trees, the years of undergrowth, and the thick green slime that coated the surface of the water, he involuntarily shuddered. It could take them forever to get through this stuff—and if they happened into the path of an alligator, they would have no real way of defending themselves. Well, he realized, Brenda had her gun.

He exhaled. "Let's get moving. We're wasting time."

36

Alec tossed his keys onto the desk. "Talk to me, Kate," he said to the crime scene technician. "I couldn't get a search warrant—lack of evidence—so tell me something that'll help me."

"Well," she said, pulling a chair toward Alec's desk, "I've got a file started for you." She plopped the file onto the desk as Dani joined them, perching on the edge and opening the manila folder.

"We got some good prints from the stair railing," Kate continued. "They belong to Brenda Jean Carnegie."

"Bingo," Alec said.

"And we found several footprints in the blood that appear to be from a woman with a size 7 or perhaps 7-and-a-half shoe." Kate leaned toward Alec and Dani. "But this individual—say it was Ms. Carnegie—walked through the blood after Peggy Lynn was shot. And the bullet's entry point shows that Carnegie could not have been the shooter."

Alec looked up from the photographs he'd been viewing of the crime scene. His brows furrowed. "Go on."

Kate rose from the desk. "Say this desk is the stairwell," she said, "and you're over here, looking down." She stepped back. "The victim is here, standing away from the stairs, toward the door." She retreated farther from the desk. "The shot came from here. From the direction of the kitchen, not from the stairwell."

"So she had an accomplice."

"Yes. But he's harder to identify."

"He?" Dani said.

Kate returned to the desk and rifled through the paperwork, retrieving a photograph of a shoeprint. "This was found outside the house near the deck. It's a man's overshoe—you know, one of those rubber jobbies that you slip over a normal shoe." She pointed to the emblem in the middle of the print. "These are very common, just not in North Carolina. They're generally used where there's slush."

"The northeast?"

Kate shrugged. "Perhaps. It's not enough protection to use in a lot of snow. They were popular some years back, when people dressed up more and didn't want to mess up their dress shoes."

"So," Alec mused, "what kind of a man would wear these today? An older man, perhaps, used to an older style of dressing?"

"He was smart. He didn't leave prints."

"What about the doors? Windows?"

"The front door had prints from two people, Peggy Lynn and Nate. Not many, so my guess is, they didn't use the front door too often. The back door had their prints, too. And two sets of additional prints."

Alec nodded for her to continue.

"Brenda Carnegie's prints were found both on the inside doorknob and the outside knob."

"The back door?"

"The one in the kitchen."

"And the other prints?"

"Nate's father, Jerry. One of his almost completely obscured one of Carnegie's. So it's my opinion that Brenda used the door first, and Nate's father used it after her."

"Do you think he could be the other person?"

"There's no evidence to support that," Kate said.

They were silent for a moment. Then Alec said, "Thanks, Kate. Good job."

"There's more."

He raised his eyebrow and waited for her to continue.

"Carnegie's fingerprints were upstairs, on a second bedroom. Only on the inside door knob."

"That would mean—"

"She walked into the room when the door was open," Dani interjected. "But she closed it once she was inside."

"Then she reopened it, walked down the stairs, stopped at the railing, witnessed her accomplice shooting Peggy Lynn, and left the house. The absence of the shooter's prints on the back door knob would lead me to suspect they left together."

Kate nodded. "It's plausible… And once they were outside, they split up. The shooter walked down the side of the house; we found some tire marks in the soft dirt beside the barn, where it looks like he might have parked a vehicle."

"Any identification on those?"

"We're still working on it. All we know right now is they were truck tires. And they were pretty bald. One of them had several nails in it. It's a wonder it wasn't flat. They wouldn't pass inspection."

"And the other prints led to the barn, and my guess is they belonged to Brenda Carnegie."

Kate nodded. "That's right. And she left by horseback."

"Were you able to follow the trail?"

Kate smiled. "With Jerry Landon. Turns out, Brenda's folks owned a farm about a mile away."

Alec peered at the crime scene photographs. "Past tense?"

"They died a few years back, willed the farm to Brenda Jean Carnegie."

"So the house on Elm Street—"

"I need a word with you two," came a booming voice at the other end of the office.

Alec turned to face the sheriff. "Now?"

"Now," he said before disappearing into his office.

37

The house was extraordinarily large for Lake Waccamaw standards: almost five stories. It was strategically built on a piece of land that jutted into the lake, its height providing a spectacular view of the water and the surrounding area. The front of the house faced the road; what would eventually become the front lawn was now a pockmarked booby trap of construction debris.

The entrance to the garage was on the side, and Joseph's Lexus was now parked inside, amidst ventilation ducts yet to be installed. There was no garage door yet, but it wouldn't matter; one would have to drive onto the property to see his vehicle. And that, he reasoned, was unlikely on a wintry Sunday morning.

He climbed each story until he reached the top level, where a broad, semi-circular balcony jutted out from the house, providing a roof for the floors below. A folding lawn chair was positioned beside one of the massive columns. He pulled it closer to the edge before seating himself.

He had in one hand a set of binoculars, another tool of his trade. He also carried a set of night vision goggles, but he wouldn't need those, although a storm was brewing. He also carried two biscuits and sausage.

As he munched on one of the hard biscuits, he peered through the binoculars, first performing a cursory review of the lake and the homes lined up around it. Not seeing anything out of the ordinary, he began studying it in more detail.

To his east, a Lake Waccamaw police officer was placing a boat in the water. He watched him curiously; once he was afloat, he followed him through the binoculars as he combed the lake, no doubt searching for the same target as he. But the lake was choppy and the storm kicking up high, cold winds; there were no boaters or skiers on the lake today, and there was no sign of Brenda and Chris.

To his west, two Lake Waccamaw police officers were securing the lake house where he had been only a short time ago.

He should have hit his target. He looked at his right wrist and the splint that held it immobile. It shouldn't have made a difference in his marksmanship. He'd been farther away from them than he would have liked, and perhaps he should have continued his approach until he was sure of his shot. But ten years ago, he would have made it. They both would be dead, their bodies dumped in the lake or the surrounding swamp, to be found long after he was out of the state—if they were found at all.

It was substandard work. The whole operation was shoddy. It was his last job, and he didn't want to finish like the once-great singers who continued croaking out their tunes long after they should have stopped. He wanted to go out at the top of his game. But the top of his game was five years ago, maybe ten, only he hadn't recognized it then.

As he watched the police scour the lake and the house, he pondered this turn of events. Things were usually very methodical, as they had been when he arrived at Nate Landon's house. He was given an assignment, provided floor plans, and someone on the inside gave information that allowed him to gain access—in Nate's case, through a back door habitually left unlocked. That part had gone well. Even with the unexpected appearance of Nate's wife, he normally would have been done and back on the road before anyone knew anything was amiss.

But this assignment included two hits. And if it hadn't been for the nosy, dog-walking neighbor, he might have accomplished the second one. Maybe he should have taken her out, too, he thought. And taken the little Jack Russell terrier home with him.

But he hadn't, so here he sat, surrounded on both sides by police officers that were leaving no stone unturned. And he knew he must bide his time—for now.

He dialed a number on his cell phone and waited for the familiar voice to answer.

"Can you monitor police communications at Lake Waccamaw?" he asked.

There was a slight pause. "Yes. It will take us a few minutes."

"They're searching for them."

"They can't be taken into custody."

"They won't be."

He clicked off the phone and sat in the lawn chair, huddled against the brisk wind. The sky was gloomy, the clouds roiling now with an angry vengeance. He wished he were sitting beside a warm fireplace, knitting. Soon, he told himself. Soon.

38

The ground just ahead of Chris appeared solid, the soil formed into an earthen mound that rose slightly above the surrounding mud. Yet when he stepped upon it, it sank lower than the ground around him, sinking him ankle deep into muck.

It had been that way for excruciating minutes that had turned into an hour-long battle against the terrain. They had ditched the boat some distance behind them, but he worried that it had not been adequately concealed. In warmer months when the trees were in full foliage and the undergrowth forming a more solid barrier, it might have been easier to hide a motor boat. But with the trees naked and the brush brown and wilted, the white vessel seemed to shine like a beacon in the swampy forest.

Brenda had made it sound so simple—a cabin in the woods only half a mile from where they'd begun their trek. But now all of the trees looked exactly alike. And when he peered behind him, his tracks were instantly covered with mud and brackish water and a film of green slime. He had begun to worry that they were traveling in circles.

In addition, they were both shaking from the cold air that hung oppressively from the tree branches. When he

tried to examine the sky amid the Byzantine network of
tree branches, he saw only glimpses of roiling dark clouds.
If there was any semblance of sunlight at Lake Waccamaw,
it was not finding its way through those trees.

Brenda stumbled beside him, and he instinctively
grabbed her arm and kept her from falling. The green wool
blanket she'd tried to keep above her waist was now
streaked with thick, black mud; the many missteps she'd
taken had shaken it loose too many times to count. He
knew he looked every bit as bad; glancing down at his
clothing, he realized he was covered in mud at various
stages of hardening. The only silver lining in this trek were
the cold waters and chilly air that kept them from being
eaten alive by mosquitoes or water-borne parasites.

His eyes darted about, looking in the shallow swamp
for alligators, but thankfully he had seen none and he hoped
it remained that way. Each time his bare foot stubbed
something heavy and he was forced to step over it, he
immediately envisioned it as a hibernating gator. Then once
he passed over it, he sought to calm his pounding heart by
convincing himself that it had been only a fallen log.

Brenda weaved through the thickly wooded swamp,
stopping frequently and peering overhead as if to get her
bearings, but she continued to travel in a labyrinth of north,
east, south, and west, until at last she stopped.

"There it is," she breathed. He wondered if the relief
in her voice belied her waning confidence in her ability to
find it.

It was still a short distance away, but with the goal in
sight, they tried to redouble their efforts. Chris' toes were
raw and the soles of his feet felt blistered from the uneven
and unforgiving terrain. He noticed Brenda had slowed
dramatically as well. He alternated between keeping his
own steps steady and assisting Brenda, reluctantly slowing
to an agonizingly time-consuming pace. Then finally they

reached a swath of deeper water that stood between the woods and the cabin.

As they felt their way into the creek, the cold water rushed above their knees, causing them both to gasp. With each step, Chris felt as though he were being stung a thousand times by the freezing water. By the time he was midway across, it had risen to his waist. He knew it was worse for Brenda, who was submerged almost to her chest. Each time they raised a foot, it was as if they were dragging ten pounds of mud along with it.

Halfway across, he realized with a rising sense of panic that if they stood still, they would most likely sink as though the mud were quicksand. He grabbed Brenda's arm and urged her onward, their only hope to keep going, to fight against the cold waters, to trudge steadily onward, their eyes riveted on the faint blue outline of the cabin.

When they reached the shore and solid ground, Brenda sank to her knees. Her legs were streaked with mud and they were trembling fiercely. He stopped beside her and rested the palms of his hands on his knees, almost doubling over to maintain stability. Though he knew they could remain there for a time in an attempt to recover, the wind was picking up, and once he steadied himself, he reached down and hauled her to her feet.

She stood shakily, and he realized both of her ankle-high boots were missing, no doubt sucked into the muck left behind them. The thick layer of mud that streaked across her legs appeared to dry and cake almost as quickly as the air hit them, and as they moved shakily toward the safety of the cabin, it fell off in chunks, leaving a steady trail behind them.

They made their way onto a screened back porch. The floor was a solid slab of concrete only a few inches from the ground, and Chris wondered how easily it could flood when the waters rose. It was filled with black wrought iron furniture. Along one side was a set of storage benches that he envisioned held cushions for the patio furniture. And against the back of the house was a refrigerator, humming away.

They were overcome with thirst, Brenda's parched and chapped lips mirroring how his own felt, and he crossed quickly to the other side of the patio and opened the refrigerator door. Inside was a hefty stock of beer.

He closed the door quickly, the blast of cold too much against his wet clothing. Alcohol was the last thing they needed in their condition.

Brenda pulled a chair into the center of the concrete slab.

"What are you doing?" he asked.

"There's a spare key up here," she said, her voice raspy and uneven. As Chris watched, she stepped on the seat and felt along the top of the exposed beams.

She let out a shriek as a black snake fell from the beam onto the floor below, landing with a thud.

Chris jumped for her, grabbing her around her waist and whisking her toward the opposite side of the patio before turning back toward the snake. He instinctively looked for a makeshift weapon to kill it, but he quickly realized as it remained motionless that it was already dead, its four-foot-long white belly exposed and decomposing.

When he turned back to Brenda, she opened her hand so he could see a dull, tarnished key. She forced a nervous smile before crossing to the back door and wiggling it into the rusty keyhole.

A moment later, the door was open. The space inside was more frigid than the outside air and smelled about as stale as a freezer turned off for months.

Chris watched as Brenda went directly to a thermostat near the door and flipped on the furnace, as though she'd done it a hundred times before. The distinct odor of burning oil accompanied the first blast of hot air, but as it began to take the chill out of the cabin, the stench slowly dissipated.

They stood in the middle of the room, which appeared to be a combination living and dining area. Their expressions mirrored their physical exhaustion. Her copper hair was now streaked with thick strands of mud of varying degrees of hardening, the gentle waves now pulled straight from the additional weight. Her fair skin was streaked with grime, and her hands looked almost like huge lumps of coal from the thickening muck. He couldn't remember what color her clothes had been; both the blanket she'd worn about her shoulders and every inch of clothing looked as if she'd taken a mud bath. And at this moment, he thought he'd never seen a woman more beautiful.

Reluctantly, he surveyed his own appearance. His brand new khaki dress slacks from which he'd removed the price tag only yesterday looked aged and decrepit. The ironed crease was long gone, replaced with mud so thick he could no longer see the material. His shirt was worse; the button had popped off one cuff, leaving it hanging forlornly, while the other sleeve lay in tatters around duct tape that had begun to peel. The shirt tail hung in grimy folds around his waist, clinging in some places and pulled away in others. His bare feet made him appear as if he were a young boy wearing his father's black overshoes, except for the muddy cracks beginning to appear between his toes.

She crossed to him and laid her head against his chest. When he touched her hair, it was cold and he involuntarily shivered. She peered into his eyes, the light amber color appearing almost startling against the smudges of grime. When she spoke, the hardened mud gently crackled on her face.

"There's a butcher's shower behind that door," she said, leading him to a three-paneled door with white paint as thick as biscuits. It creaked when she pushed it open, revealing a large open shower with two shower nozzles mounted on adjoining tiled walls.

She continued leading him into the shower, stopping only to reach inside and turn on the water. She tested it several times while they stood just beyond the water, shivering from the cold. When they finally stepped inside, the water was warm and soothing as it streaked down their clothes.

Chris started to remove his shirt, but she stopped him. "It's better to leave it on until most of the mud has washed off," she said with a shy smile.

"But won't it—?"

She shook her head, her hair so thick with mud that it appeared like blackened plaster hanging from her scalp. He gently leaned her head back so the water flushed the mud from her. They stood for a long time, allowing the steamy water to soothe their aches, the mud swirling at their feet before rushing down the oversized drain.

"Where are we?" he whispered.

"It's a hunter's cabin," she said.

"There seem to be a lot of hunters in these parts."

She smiled tiredly. "There's a lot to hunt."

He didn't respond, and she continued, "They butcher the deer right outside, and then come in here to wash the blood off."

She tilted her head further backward and allowed the water to pour over her scalp and shoulders, washing the mud from her in thick rivulets. She pulled Chris toward her, playfully pushing him under one of the shower heads, and he closed his eyes as he felt the water massaging his aching muscles.

She turned him away from her and leaned her head against his back. Then her fingers were on his shoulders, kneading them gently. He moaned quietly, almost imperceptibly. If he could just freeze this moment in time—the feel of the hot water running over the length of his body, her hands on his shoulders, easing away the tiredness…

And then he was turning to face her and running his hands through her hair, revealing more of the copper color and gentle waves as the hardened mud softened and turned to a thick liquid and then to tea-colored water as it washed away from her. Then her skin was peeking through, and when he pulled her toward him, he realized his feet no longer hurt and he no longer cared about the deep scratches that still bled; his muscles no longer ached and his shoulders no longer felt heavy; and the world outside no longer mattered.

39

Sheriff Czarnecki was in his late 50s but his shaved head and dark brows made him appear at least ten years younger. He was a commanding figure with broad shoulders and imposing biceps that bespoke of his propensity for bench-pressing. He'd inherited a troubled department and he'd performed wonders with it, and he didn't like murders in his back yard—especially murders relating to high profile, leading citizens.

"Have a seat," he said as he stood behind his desk.

Alec and Dani took their seats on the other side of the desk. He couldn't help but feel awkward as he looked upward at The Czar, as they were prone to call him. And when he didn't take his seat but remained standing, Alec was tempted to stand up again.

"So what have you got?"

Alec filled him in on the details Kate and Kyle had provided to them, as well as the appearance of another suspect, Christopher Sandige, and their ability to trace them to Lake Waccamaw.

"We believe Brenda hired this guy Christopher Sandige to kill Nate and Peggy Lynn Landon. They split up after the murder but reunited later, at a hotel in Lumberton.

They've now fled the hotel—we got the rental car records—and they headed to the lake. Lake Waccamaw Police are keeping an eye on the rental car for us, while we gather enough evidence for a search warrant. I want that car; it might have blood in it, maybe even the murder weapon…"

"Any idea where Carnegie and Sandige are now?"

"We believe they're still at Lake Waccamaw. We're following up on a few more leads here, then heading back out there to get that search warrant. With the Lake Waccamaw Police keeping an eye on the lake house and rental car, I doubt they'll get away."

Sheriff Czarnecki nodded.

Alec stood.

"Not so fast," the sheriff said.

He slowly returned to his seat.

"Dani requested a reassignment."

"She did?" Alec turned to her. "You did?"

Dani avoided his eyes, but looked briefly at the sheriff before becoming acutely interested in her hands.

"I know it's difficult for a man and a woman to spend so much time together—" Sheriff Czarnecki began.

"Is this about me giving you a hug at the hospital?" Alec said, his mouth agape. He turned back to the sheriff. "Okay, maybe it was inappropriate. But it wasn't sexual. She was crying because of the baby—Peggy Lynn's baby—and I was trying to console her. That's all. It didn't mean anything else."

"I know it didn't mean more," Dani said. "It just *looked* like more."

"What's that suppose to mean?" The heavyset woman with stark white hair flashed before him, and he relived that moment with Dani in his arms as he'd wiped away her tears, the large woman's nostrils flaring in anger.

Dani shook her head and didn't answer.

"What, because one woman sees me trying to console my partner, you want to be reassigned?"

"It wasn't just her," Dani said. She looked to Sheriff Czarnecki but he didn't jump to her aid. "The women at the restaurant this morning… They overheard us, and now they think we're having an affair."

"So, they're wrong. We all know they're wrong!"

"My neighbor next door—"

"The nosy lady who stares at me every time I pick you up in the cruiser?"

Dani bit her lip. After a moment, she said, "I know there's nothing between us. And the czar—sheriff—knows. But this is a small town, and gossip can take on a life of its own…"

"It can do that anywhere. It's no reason to quit on me."

Her jaw jutted forward. "I'm not quitting. But in case you haven't noticed, I am a woman. And you are a single man. And I'd just feel a whole lot more comfortable if I was with somebody that the townspeople knew couldn't possibly be a love interest."

"But—we work so well together."

"I know."

"You think the way I think. You—"

"—finish your sentences. I know."

Alec exhaled sharply. He felt his nails digging into his palms.

"Well, if I didn't know better, I'd say you two were having a bit of a spat," Sheriff Czarnecki said calmly.

When Alec looked up, the sheriff's neutral expression served to calm him. He thought he detected something in his eyes—compassion, perhaps—that caused him to relax his grip and lean back in his chair.

"In any event," the sheriff continued, "I can't take you off this case right now."

"But—" Dani interjected.

"Don't beg, Dani. There's no begging in police work… Fact is, my phone is ringing off the hook. Everybody wants this case solved and solved fast. And they want the perps to hang."

Dani fell silent.

"I can't guarantee the hangin', but I can certainly give you what you need to solve this crime and make some arrests. When this is over, we'll talk about reassigning you, Dani."

An awkward silence ensued. Alec was caught between the desire to return to his case and the longing to just go home and brood.

"So, what do you need, Alec?" Sheriff Czarnecki asked smoothly.

Alec thought for a moment. "Search warrants. I need physical evidence to tie Christopher Sandige to the murders. I think there's blood in that rental car, and I want it impounded. I also want in that lake house. I want access to Brenda's house on Elm Street and her farm—the barn as well as the house. We've already requested an APB on the interstate signs for Brenda Carnegie. We've tied her to the scene; I want her in custody. And something tells me, when we find her, we'll also find her accomplice, Sandige, who I believe actually did the shooting."

40

Chris hovered between a half-awakened state and the beckoning warmth of a too-soft mattress. He lay on his side, his nostrils inhaling the sweet fragrance of freshly shampooed hair, sleepily burying his face in the now-dry curls.

Barely opening his eyes, he pulled a blanket closer to them, covering Brenda's naked shoulder. She murmured and moved, and he found himself not wanting to let her go, to hold onto this one moment for the rest of his life.

When he fully opened his eyes, she had turned onto her back. "What time is it?" she asked drowsily.

"Who cares?" he whispered.

A sudden noise similar to the furnace reached them, and she raised her head and glanced at the doorway. "The dryer," she said.

Chris pictured their clothing tumbling in the aged but functional dryer, now pristine and warm, the swamp cleansed from them. And as they lay in the warmth of the small bed, he wanted nothing more than have their ordeal fade to the relevance of a bad dream.

But as his sleepy state gave way to wakefulness, the reality of their situation began to sink deeper into his consciousness. And when Brenda groaned and sat up, he didn't attempt to stop her. When she rose with an exhausted sigh and left the room, he hesitated only a moment before joining her.

The cabin was much smaller than the lake house. The center was a combination dining and living area with a kitchenette tucked into one corner. A bathroom with the butcher's shower and a toilet was located on one side of the house, and within inches of the toilet seat were a washer and dryer that appeared to be at least twenty years old. Off the center room were three additional doors: one opened to a minuscule closet while the other two revealed small but functional bedrooms. Each was equipped with a single bed whose width was somewhere between a twin and a double bed, the springs noisy and sagging. Beside each bed was a single table of pressed board, and a child's dresser stood in one, its size enough to dwarf the tiny room. None of the furniture matched.

The refrigerator was stocked with bottled water and condiments of suspicious age. It had obviously been cleaned just before the previous inhabitants had left it. The electricity had not been disconnected but had remained on, as if the structure were waiting for its owners to reappear at any moment, and as the furnace continued to warm the rooms, it was beginning to feel somewhat cozy.

Brenda was examining the contents of the kitchen cabinets. She turned to him as he approached.

"You have your choice of instant grits or instant oatmeal," she said.

"Oatmeal," he answered.

"Just like a Yankee," she said.

He sat at a small round table with an Early American pedestal and dark pressed wood, and watched her boil water on a stove top that was so small, the four burners almost met.

"So what do we do now?" he asked.

"I've been thinking about that."

"I was sure you were."

She stared out a small window onto thick woods before turning around to face him. "Here's the plan."

"It sounds so sinister," he joked.

She didn't smile. "You need to get back to Washington. And you need to forget all of this ever happened."

He felt his smile freeze on his lips and then gradually sink into a frown. "I can't—"

"Listen to me," she said, crossing to the table as he rose to confront her. "It's easy to get your car towed back to D.C., you know that. You can rent a car and be back there within a few hours."

He opened his mouth to object, but she placed a finger over his lips. "The man who is after us is after me, not you. He won't pursue you; he doesn't care who you are or what you do… The cops are after me, too. Not you."

"But what will you do?"

She smiled and cocked her head.

"Don't get smart with me," he admonished. "I deserve a serious answer."

She paused for a long moment. "Yes, you do."

The teapot began to whistle and she hesitated for a moment before returning to the kitchenette, switching off the burner, and pouring the steaming water into two bowls of instant food. She stirred them for a moment before carrying them to the table. "It's not much," she said, "but it's something in our bellies."

Chris waited until she sank into a chair before joining her. But though his stomach was crying out for nourishment, he could do barely more than swish the lumpy oatmeal around.

"This business I told you about," she said, enunciating each word as though she'd thought each one out carefully, "it's brought me a lot of money."

He stopped stirring and looked at her. "Oh?"

She avoided his eyes. "Enough to live on for the rest of my life."

He didn't answer but continued watching her.

"I have off-shore accounts," she continued. "All I have to do is get out of the country."

He thought of the bank deposit slips he'd stuffed into his pocket that morning, and wondered what shape they would be in after a trip through the swamp and the wash-and-dry cycles. "Is that all?" he said. He realized his voice sounded edgy with sarcasm, but she hadn't seemed to have noticed.

"My parents owned a farm in Robeson County, not far from Lumberton. It's been in the family for generations… They died, and they left it to me." She looked at him as she slipped a spoonful of instant grits into her mouth. After a moment, she said, "You asked what I'm planning to do… Well, I'm going back to the farm, packing some bags, taking some cash I've squirreled away, and I'm leaving for the islands. And from there… maybe Argentina. Brazil. Chile. Any number of countries who don't automatically extradite when the United States comes calling."

He set his spoon down. "If you didn't kill those people, why won't you stay here and clear yourself? I'm a witness to the man who tried to kill us—"

"To stay here means to tell everything I know," she said abruptly. "And that's worse than a double-murder charge."

"Then I'll go with you."

She laughed, but it seemed forced. "And throw everything you have away? Don't do that to yourself."

He tried to argue, but she wouldn't hear him. "I don't know much about your life in Washington," she said, "but

I can imagine you have a nice career there, a bright future. Don't throw it all away on me. I'm not worth it."

They sat in silence for a long time. The oatmeal had cooled off quickly and tasted like paste.

"I'm going with you," Chris said at last.

She stood and gathered her bowl and spoon. She returned to the tiny kitchen sink, where she carefully washed and dried them and placed them in the cupboard. "We're going to clean up the mess we made—" she nodded toward the tiled floor with their trail of mud "—and then we're heading back toward Lumberton, to my parents' house. From there, we'll part ways."

Chris felt his heart sink. He wanted to shout at her, to kiss her, to pull her to him, to tell her how stubborn she was—but he remained seated. It didn't matter what she planned, he told himself. He was stronger and smarter. He would take her back to Washington with him. Once there, he would call on his powerful friends to help them. But for now, he would let her think she was calling the shots. For now.

"So," he said, hoping his voice sounded flippant, "do we walk back to Lumberton?"

She poured the pot of coffee into a huge Thermos and nodded toward the kitchen window. "There's a truck parked just outside… And if memory serves me, the keys are kept in the ignition."

Chris rose and joined her at the window. A few yards from the cabin was a battered and rusty pickup, the windshield coated in bird droppings and the tires sitting low to the ground. "You're not serious?" he murmured.

She secured the top on the Thermos and turned away. "Unless you'd rather go back the same way we got here," she smirked.

He heard her moving toward the opposite end of the cabin, but he remained at the window, staring at the weather-beaten old truck and wishing he was back home in his spacious house, eating croissants with red currant jelly, and reading the morning newspaper with Brenda by his side.

41

The drive back to Lake Waccamaw felt ten times longer than the one Alec and Dani had taken only hours before. The silence was oppressive, hanging over them like a thick veil.

When they first left the sheriff's office, Alec had been fuming. But as they drew closer to the lake, his anger had turned to sadness. Only one year ago, he was living the perfect dream—a stunning wife, happy marriage, a smart and successful son, and a job he enjoyed. He could never have envisioned the twists and turns his life would take, could never have imagined starting over in mid-life, a widower and childless.

Perhaps Dani would feel more comfortable working with a happily married man, Alec thought, but what she didn't realize is he wanted to be that man.

He turned onto Old Lake Road. Within a brief time, he spotted the lake, now a deep shade of blue-gray, as if it were reflecting the tumultuous sky above it. The current was strong as the winds increased, heralding a colder than normal winter day.

He turned just yards from the lake and began the drive to the lake house. As they rounded the bend, his heart felt as though it skipped a beat.

In front of the lake house were three Lake Waccamaw Police Department vehicles.

"What the—?" he began as he pulled alongside one of them.

One of the officers spotted them immediately and made his way to them. As Alec stepped out of his car, the officer held out his hand and introduced himself.

He was a young man with sandy hair and wideset eyes, and as he spoke Alec got the distinct impression he had moved to the area from the midwest. His speech was quick and to the point, unlike the more relaxed speech patterns of the natives. His name was Jack MacClurie.

"The officer who was here earlier left the house when he got your call; he met with the magistrate and got the search warrant. In the few minutes he was gone, we got reports of shots fired," he was saying as they approached the back of the house. "Gun shots can echo across the lake so it's hard to figure out just what direction they're coming from. But with fugitives possibly hiding out here, we converged on this house."

The back door was open. Alec paused just as he stepped onto the back deck; something was gnawing at him, and he turned around. "The boat—"

"Gone. As you can see," Jack answered. "Our PD just got our first patrol boat," he said with more than a hint of pride. "The Chief is checking out the lake now… There're no outlets. None. We'll find 'em shortly."

Alec nodded and stepped inside. Two more officers were inside the house.

Jack handed over the search warrant to Alec. "With the gunshots and the missing boat, we had reason to come in anyway."

Alec watched Dani as she wandered down the hallway toward the bedroom. Jack nodded his head in her direction. "No signs of any crimes having happened here, but it looks like someone slept here last night, used the shower, and made breakfast… And the trash can in the kitchen had a couple of bloody towels in it. We're getting those processed for DNA now."

Alec stopped in the center of the living area and turned to look at the pier and boat house. It was an odd feeling, knowing he'd been there only hours earlier when the boat had been there, too. And wondering how close he might have come…

"We got another report, too," Jack was saying.

"Oh?"

"Yeah. Right after the shots were fired, a resident spotted a man running from this place to a dark sedan, parked a couple of houses down."

Alec's mind jerked back to the moment he left the lake house. As if in slow motion, he saw the man walking toward the car, waving as he drove past. "Which house?"

"You can see it from here," Jack said, walking toward the glass wall at the corner of the house. "That duplex right over there."

Alec peered through the trees. In the summer months, he had no doubt both houses would be shrouded in privacy from the thick bushes and trees that surrounded most homes. But now, in the bleakest of months, all that separated the two was a road and spaghetti-like branches of gnarled and aging red chokeberry bushes and the sparser winter foliage of wax myrtles. He stared at the side of the duplex, at the ancient oak tree that bowed toward its roofline, and at the empty spot where the sedan had been parked.

"The neighbor called in a license plate," Jack said, handing a piece of paper to Alec.

"New York," Alec mused, turning the paper over in his hand as if it could answer all his questions. "That common, for folks to come here from New York?"

Jack shook his head. "We know everybody who comes here," he said. "The full-time residents, who has keys hidden, the places that are rented out… We have the phone numbers of every owner in town. The owner of that place lives in Ohio, rents out the duplex every summer to the same two families. It's vacant now. We checked it out, and nobody's been inside."

Dani joined them and Alec handed her the license plate number.

"No sense in running it," Jack said. "We already did. Belongs to a white Mazda Tribute."

"That's an SUV."

"Yep. Plates reported stolen about a week ago."

Alec nodded. Somewhere in the back of his mind, he felt Jack move away from the window. He didn't remember when Dani left, but when he glanced around him, they were both gone. In the kitchen area to his right, he overheard the other two officers debating football teams. He longed to have a partner he felt that closeness with, someone he could have a beer with after work, somebody who could come over on a Sunday afternoon and watch a game with him, somebody who could just shoot the breeze with him on a Friday night… He liked Dani and he thought she was capable, even if she was a bit too preoccupied with what people thought, and he wondered if he would be destined to work alone simply because his most likely partner was female. It wasn't right, he thought, that a few false rumors or assumptions could derail a good working relationship.

A whirring sound caught his attention and he turned toward his left, where a small round table was nestled into the corner. On top was a laptop, the screen erect and the hard drive buzzing.

He looked around the room but there was no one else around. He stepped toward the table and wiggled the mouse. The screen sprang to life, displaying an automatic virus scan.

His palm remained poised on the mouse, his eyes locked on the screen.

A man and a woman, he thought, his heart quickening. Walking into a spare bedroom, closing the door... witnessing a double homicide. A house with one room ransacked... one room. A table with a mouse on one side, a printer on the other. A laptop in a lake house, turned on and running.

"My God," he whispered.

He turned as Jack and Dani reentered the house from the back door. "My God."

"What is it?" Dani said, her eyes raking over the table, the computer, and back to Alec's face.

"I've been wrong all along," he said, realizing his voice sounded dazed. "They weren't having an affair. They were working together!"

42

It was late in the afternoon by the time Alec and Dani returned to Lumberton. In keeping with the season, what little sun there had been throughout the day was waning. As they approached Brenda's house, their unmarked car's headlights cast a set of sinister tentacles across the wood siding before Alec shut them off.

There had been no sign of the missing boat at the lake house, though the Lake Waccamaw Police had patrolled the lake for hours, searching boat docks and a few tributaries that petered off after a few hundred yards. The staff at the Lake Waccamaw State Park had joined in the search, and word had spread rapidly through the small, close-knit community. Now every citizen was on the lookout for the two suspects, and roadblocks had been set up on every road out of the area. There would be no escape for the fugitives, if they were still in the vicinity.

And now, under the direction of the Lumberton Police Department, a locksmith was just finishing his work at Brenda's house, turning over a new set of keys to the officer. They were handed over to Dani as they approached the house, and after they crossed the threshold, Alec was vaguely aware of the crime scene tape going back into place in front of the doorway.

The stairway was directly inside, and he hesitated only briefly. He could see the living area; through contiguous doors into the dining room and kitchen, he could also view the length of the downstairs area. Everything was as neat as a pin except for the dog prints that muddied the floors. And except for one magazine slightly askew, even the pile of reading materials on the coffee table was precisely stacked. It was as if this were used as a model home.

He climbed the stairs two at a time, and went directly into the bathroom. He opened the medicine cabinet and peered within. There were the usual items one would expect to see: a toothbrush, toothpaste, dental floss… and on one shelf, there were cosmetics: foundation, lipstick, mascara. Alec removed the bottle of foundation and handed it to Dani.

"Can you tell if this has been used lately?" he asked.

She looked at him curiously before removing the cap. "This foundation is water-based, which means it will separate if it's left for any length of time," she said. "I used to use this brand." She held it under the light fixture. "It's been sitting a day, maybe two. But it isn't as if it's been unused for weeks."

Alec nodded. "That's what I thought."

He rifled through the rest of the cabinet. He located a round blister pack of birth control pills. The dial pointed at Saturday. "This mean her last pill was Friday?" he asked.

Dani took the pack and turned it over. "Looks like it. She took a pill and turned the dial so it would be ready for Saturday's dose."

He moved past Dani and entered the bedroom. The bed was made, the spread pulled tight. No one had even sat on it.

He opened each drawer in her dresser, revealing perfectly neat stacks of undergarments, blouses and sweaters, jeans and casual slacks. The drawers were not filled to capacity, but they weren't nearly empty, either.

Under Dani's watchful gaze, he strolled to the closet, where a set of luggage was lined up neatly under hanging clothes. He rummaged through the clothes. Only two hangers hung empty between the clothing.

He turned back to Dani.

"If you were having an affair with a man and you wanted to convince him to run away with you, would you pack your bags?"

Dani shrugged. "It depends on how confident I was, and when I expected to leave."

"What if you were planning a murder? Would you have the confidence to carry it out and simply return to your own home, go back to your usual business?"

Dani shook her head slowly. "No way I'd stay in the same town. Especially a small one."

Alec nodded. "But she didn't pack any clothes. She didn't take her makeup…"

"She even left her birth control pills."

"She didn't plan to murder them."

"You think maybe she went over to talk to them, and things got out of control?"

He mulled this for a moment. "Out of control, when she had an accomplice with her? What was going through her head—that she would witness their killings and then just return to business as usual?"

"It would take a pretty tough woman to do that. A woman without a conscience."

"But if she wanted Nate dead because she couldn't bear the thought that he wouldn't leave his wife for her, she had a heart, right?"

"One that was capable of being broken…"

Her eyes were narrowing, and before Alec spoke, he knew she understood where he was heading.

"This way," he said, moving past her. He marched to the second bedroom, where they both stopped to survey the assortment of office supplies haphazardly spread across the floor. He meandered around them, using the toe of his shoe to move items out of the way so he could see underneath. Then he turned around to face the desk. He studied the computer mouse at one side and the printer opposite it.

"The first time we went through this house, do you remember seeing a laptop?"

Dani shook her head slowly. "No; there wasn't one."

"I didn't think so."

"So Brenda left her clothes, her makeup, and her pills, and she took only the computer? It doesn't make sense."

Alec turned back to the heap of supplies. "And sometime after we left, we got a call that Brenda was here. And when we arrived, only this room was touched."

"Do you think…?"

"I think it was someone else in the house. Someone looking for something. Someone who knew the answer wasn't going to be found inside a closet full of dresses. The answer was here, in her work." Alec caught a flash in the corner of his eye. "What was that?"

Dani glanced out the window. "Car driving past?"

Alec brushed past her as he made his way into the hallway. He stared into the living room at the base of the stairs. The light was on.

He raised his finger to his lips while his other hand rested firmly on his pistol. He knew without looking that Dani was readying her own weapon as she followed him quietly down the stairs.

They paused every few steps while he peered into the room, the contents becoming clearer and more visible as he descended. It was exactly as they'd left it, except for a lamp on the end table. It was on.

He kept his back to the wall as he moved from one room to the next, through the dining room, through the kitchen, into the hallway at the back of the house. He kicked the door to the bathroom open, his pistol ready, but it was empty.

Dani was moving through the house behind him.

There was nowhere to hide. The home was sparsely furnished, the floor plan open and simple. No one was there.

Alec crossed to the lamp and followed the cord. "Well, I'll be," he murmured.

As Dani joined him, he held up the timer. As he allowed it to drop back toward the floor, he rushed upstairs. He tried to remember Edna McElroy's explanation of Brenda's work hours: the bedroom light coming on after midnight, the lights upstairs, the downstairs light, making coffee… the lights in her office burning until the wee hours of the morning.

It was all there: the timer on the nightstand that came on automatically at 12:15; the hallway set for 12:20; the second bedroom for 12:30. Lights downstairs that went on and off at all hours of the day and night, some remaining on for only fifteen minutes at a time while others, like the office light, turned off at dawn.

He stood in her bedroom, staring at the lamp on the nightstand, envisioning the complex illusion of life in the house… of a car in the driveway and then missing, of basic items left untouched but office papers thrown about. He turned to face the only artwork in the room: a photograph in a simple black frame, depicting two figures riding camels, their trail stark and alone across the vast desert sands, and yet just beyond them rose a modern city of glass high-rise buildings and neon signs amidst palm trees. Something about the photograph bothered him, but he couldn't quite put his finger on it.

When Dani joined him, his face felt chilled to the bone, though the air in the house was warm. "The answer lies in their work together," he stated flatly.

"But they didn't work together," Dani said, her words coming slowly. "Nate worked at a bank—"

Before she could finish, Alec was moving downstairs toward the front door. "Who do we know that works at the bank?"

"I know the President," Dani said as she hurried down the stairs behind him.

"Get him on the phone," Alec said as he reached the front door. "I want access to everything Nate was working on—especially if it involved Brenda Carnegie."

43

Chris stood at the door of the cabin. What he'd originally thought was the back door turned out to be the only door. He heard movement behind him and knew it was only a matter of a few short minutes before they would be on their way back to Lumberton.

He stared at the snake, but he looked at it blindly, not really seeing the white belly turned up toward the ceiling. His mind was set on the red-haired enigma he was falling hopelessly in love with. His heart told him to abandon everything he knew just to remain with her, while his brain begged him to turn her in. Who would she have to know, he wondered, to have knowledge of a hidden key in the rafters, to be familiar with this tiny hunter's cabin, and how to reach it on foot through a Byzantine swamp?

He pieced together the few facts he knew about her and her family. She said they'd owned a farm, yet she didn't seem like a farm girl to him; quite the contrary. And just one hour from their main home, they had a secondary home, albeit small, on the lake. That meant they'd been financially successful, at least enough to own two properties. And lakefront homes couldn't come cheap.

She seemed very intelligent, well-educated, and yet…

How could she have gone from a well-heeled upbringing to running from the law like a common fugitive, with two murders hanging over her head?

He thought of the pistol she'd displayed at the abandoned lodge, the same one she'd been so quick to use when they fled the lake house. Where would she have learned to shoot, he wondered, and why? Had she always been a tomboy? Perhaps she learned to hunt with her dad? Maybe that's why she knew so much about hunting lodges, how she could make her way around the most rural part of the county… Or could there be more, much more than he knew or could even imagine?

As much as he wanted to know more about her, to be able to connect all of the dots, all of his efforts boiled down to miserably scant information. And none of it brought him any closer to knowing details about her illegal activities, and why they were fleeing the authorities as well as a man who wanted to kill them.

The reality of his situation was bearing down on him and bearing down hard. He didn't live in this world of concealed weapons, of hunting lodges at every turn, of butcher's showers and swampland. He knew the inner workings of national politics, of getting people elected and placed into critical positions, of political damage control and inflicting damage on those who didn't share his agenda. But his damage wasn't physical; it was on paper, a strategic email, an anonymous source. And while he couldn't say his decisions were rooted in some naïve notion encircling the good of his country, it had never resulted in vigilante justice.

He was in deep enough to understand the events of this weekend could never make it back to Washington. It would destroy not only his own career but those of a half-dozen well-placed senators and congressmen, merely by association. And if they toppled, it could devastate their plans to control the oil arriving on American shores.

It was time to consider his future, to do whatever was necessary for self-preservation.

"You ready?" Brenda's voice was tinged with anxiety.

Whatever was necessary. "Almost," he said.

She slid a pair of boots to the floor. "Think these'll fit?"

He studied them momentarily. They were a full size smaller than he normally wore, but his options were scant: barefoot or boots.

A few minutes later, his fingers moved mechanically to open the door. When he stepped onto the screened porch, he was cognizant of the heavy boots that were so small that every step pained him. Brenda's boots were worse; male boots into which her small feet disappeared.

Their clothes were washed and dried, courtesy of a clothes washer and dryer the likes of which he hadn't seen since he was a child. His new slacks were now about two inches shorter than when they'd gone into the dryer and the waist and crotch were decidedly tighter. The tattered shirt sleeve was unraveling and it barely concealed his wounded arm; and now he knew just from the corner of the duct tape that fell away from his skin that he hadn't been merely grazed, as Brenda had said. He pushed the thought to the back of his mind for now, and tried to push off the inevitability of assessing the wound for himself.

They made their way to the rusting pickup in what vaguely constituted a yard.

"This tire is almost flat," he muttered as much to himself as to Brenda.

"It'll get us where we're going."

As Brenda opened the battered driver's side door, it creaked in the silence of the night, stopping only partway open as the door hit a wrecked section of the front panel.

Brenda slid inside and Chris closed the door behind her before making his way to the other side. The passenger side was even worse, and he found himself slipping sideways into the vehicle and slamming the door shut several times before it actually latched.

But when Brenda turned the key, it roared to life immediately. They sat in the cab, blowing their breath on their hands while the truck slowly warmed.

When they finally began to move, it lurched forward over uneven ground. They made their way around the now-darkened cabin to the opposite side from the swamp. They were bounced and jostled as she navigated the pockmarked excuse for a road, once bottoming out on a steep embankment. Chris was curious how she could plot a course across the terrain, as she kept the headlights off and the moon provided only scant light.

After a few minutes, they reached a paved road. Brenda stopped the truck at the tree line and watched the roadway. It seemed stark and desolate, the only sign of life from frogs that sounded as large as dogs.

After a moment, she edged forward but slammed on the brakes. As Chris grabbed the dashboard to keep from crashing into it, he caught sight of a set of headlights moving slowly toward them. Brenda backed the truck between the trees, the shadows blending the rusted vehicle with the pines and cedars, and Chris felt them both holding their breath, hoping the thickening clouds would continue to obstruct the moonlight.

The sports car drove slowly past them, the taillights disappearing around a bend.

"They'll be back this way soon," Brenda said, her voice sounding loud and unnatural in the silence of the cab. "That road dead-ends shortly."

"So we wait until they go back the other way?"

"No. We leave now."

Chris felt his heart leap into his throat as she thrust the truck forward, the heavy vehicle bounding along the uneven ground like an inflatable standup punching bag.

She headed in the same direction as the car, but when he tried to protest, she silenced him. "There's an old road near here," she said hoarsely.

She leaned forward, as if searching the side of the road for the opening. As they rounded the bend, he could see the car performing a three-point turnaround, its headlights reflecting on the heavily wooded swampland. In another minute, they would be turned around and heading straight for them.

"There it is!" she said as she careened onto an asphalt road whose surface was divided by deepening cracks with brown foliage peeking through.

The pavement ended only a few yards from the road, turning into two lines of sandy soil barely large enough for their tires. She pulled alongside another tree line and stopped the vehicle, her eyes riveted on the rear-view mirror.

Chris turned and looked behind them, searching what little bit of the main road he could see through the branches that wove their way from one trunk to another. After a long moment, the car moved past, going even more slowly than before.

It felt like an eternity that they sat there, their breath fogging the windows, the sound of the motor running seeming to intensify in the still night.

Then she moved forward, steering the truck back onto the makeshift roadway and moving away from Lake Waccamaw.

"Where are we?" Chris asked as he stared into the pitch blackness around him.

"When I was a child, we called this Coffee Ground Road."

"Why?"

"I have no idea. We just did."

She kept the lights off, and for the life of him, he couldn't figure out how she managed to stay on the road. Or, for all he knew, they'd left it some time ago and were bound for another desolate swamp somewhere in rural North Carolina.

44

Alec and Dani drove down Elm Street and turned right onto Roberts Avenue. The bank was ten minutes away at most, and the bank president was already in route.

The sky was black, the clouds obscuring the moonlight, which only made the signs at business establishments seem brighter and somehow more flamboyant. They crossed over Fayetteville Road and past a row of pharmacies, fast food restaurants, and *The Robesonian* newspaper buzzing like a beehive. They were coming up on the rental car business when Alec began to slow.

"What is it?" Dani asked, following the direction of his gaze.

"Is that Zach?" he asked. But he knew the answer. In front of the glass showroom, parked under a brightly lit parking lot light, was the white pickup truck. And sitting in the front seat was Zach, a rifle held across his chest. The truck was running, the exhaust sending a cloud of condensation against the glass building, fogging the windows.

Alec pulled into the lot and parked beside the truck.

Zach rolled down his window.

Alec turned off the car and opened his door while Dani exited and made her way around the vehicle.

He leaned on the open door. "What're you doing, Zach?"

He pointed the barrel of the rifle toward the parked cars. "I told you, somebody's been messin' with these cars."

Alec shut the door and came to stand beside the truck. "I called Lumberton Police about that."

"Yeah."

"Did you speak to them?" Dani asked.

"Yeah. They took a report."

"So… what're you doing out here, Zach?"

He pointed the rifle barrel again. "You see Lumberton Police out here, patrollin' my lot?"

Alec and Dani glanced around, but the point had been made.

"You planning on sitting out here all night?"

"If that's what it takes."

"Why?" Dani asked.

Zach stared straight ahead and chewed on the inside of his lip. "My dad started this business," he said finally.

"Does he know you're out here?" Dani asked.

"He's in the hospital."

"Was he hurt when the cars were taken?" Alec asked.

"Warn't nothin' like that. Gall bladder attack."

"So, you're taking over until he gets back?"

"Yep."

Alec nodded. "Why don't you show me which cars were taken?"

Zach's eyes widened, and Alec thought he detected a sense of relief as the young man opened the truck door and slid out.

"You can leave the rifle here," Alec said.

Zach hesitated for a brief moment before sliding it onto the front seat. "I reckon, since you two're armed," he muttered.

Alec and Dani followed him across the lot to a Ford Taurus.

"This one here was took," Zach said. He pulled a set of keys from a large key ring and fumbled through them. "See that window broke back there?" he motioned with his head toward the rear window. A small vent had been busted open, the glass cleaned neatly away from the edges.

After Zach unlocked the doors, Alec opened the rear door and peered inside. Broken glass was scattered across the back seat.

"I figure he unlocked the back door after breakin' that glass," Zach said.

"You'd figure right," Dani said, moving around the vehicle.

"Then he hot-wired the car. Drove it less than twenty miles. Then parked it right back in the same spot."

"Why would anybody do that?" Alec said as he examined the dash.

"You tell me," Zach answered. "Anybody use this car to rob a bank or somethin', and you heard it from me first that it was stole."

"You said there was more than one?"

"Yup."

Zach closed the door and locked it before turning toward another area of the lot where an aging white minivan sat. Alec could see before they'd reached it that the passenger side vent was broken.

"Same thing?" Alec asked. He bent down to the pavement and peered at the tires. They weren't brand new, but they weren't bald.

"Almost exact same thing. Broke the window. Hot-wired it. Drove it a few miles, then brought it back. Now I got to get them windows fixed, and get them wires fixed, and where's that money gonna come from?"

"So two vehicles were broken into on the same night," Alec mused.

"Ain't just two. There's one more."

"Another car?"

"Truck."

Zach led them to an old truck that looked as if it had spent a lifetime on a farm. The bottom of one door was rusted out, and in one spot, Alec could see through to the inside.

"You planning on selling this?" Alec asked.

"It ain't much," Zach said, bristling a little, "But you know what, you ain't got to have it in the greatest shape if'n you're using it for huntin'. You can keep it at a farm, and as long as it stays on private property, it ain't even got to pass inspection."

Alec bent to the pavement. The tire was bald.

"Now, this truck's sellin' for next to nothin'," Zach said. "I got some spare tires in the garage over thar, and I can slap them tires on here and it'll be good for another hundred thousand miles."

Alec was making his way around the truck, peering at each tire as Zach followed him. He reached the front passenger side, which was swathed in shadows.

"Can you back this truck up for me?"

"I can back it up," Zach said, flipping through his key ring. "Or you can back it up. You can even take it for a spin."

"Just back it up, put it under that light," Alec said, motioning toward a parking lot lamp post.

Zach hopped in. "I gotta fiddle around with these wires," he said sheepishly, "on account of the hot wirin'. But I'll get that fixed for you, when we open up Monday mornin'."

After a moment, the truck sputtered to life and Zach backed it out of the space.

Alec watched the tires rotate slowly as the truck continued to creep backward.

"Whoa!" he called out.

Zach stopped the truck immediately.

As Alec made his way to the vehicle, Zach slipped the truck into park and opened the door. "What?" he called out.

Alec squatted beside the truck. "What's this?"

Zach peered over his shoulder. "Oh, that's nothin'. Just, when you got a farm truck, there's nails just about ever'whar. I told you, I'll throw in a set of tires—"

Dani was beside Alec, staring at the tire.

"Zach," Alec said, rising. "I'm afraid we're going to have to take this truck."

"I'll give you a good deal—"

"That's not what I mean." He was aware of Dani moving away from the truck, speaking quietly to Dispatch. "There's a possibility this truck was used during the commission of a crime."

Zach raised both hands. "I just now told you, if'n one of these was used in the robbin' of a bank—"

"I know. We're not accusing you of anything."

Dani rejoined them. "Kate's on her way."

A short time later, the front of the dealership was lit up with police spotlights as the crime scene technicians processed the three vehicles.

"Bank president's waiting on us," Dani said as she hung up her cell phone. "He knows we might be awhile."

Alec finished smoking a cigarette and lit another. "Man, am I hungry."

"We got us a vendin' machine," Zach volunteered. He seemed genuinely happy that law enforcement had descended upon his father's dealership and his report had been taken seriously. "I can open it up, and give all of y'all somethin' to eat."

"Thanks, Zach," Alec said, "but if you'll just show me where it is, I'll buy a candy bar from you."

Zach led the way into the dealership. The phone began to ring as they crossed the showroom. "It's back there," he said, pointing down the hall. "Hello?" he answered as Alec disappeared.

A moment later, Alec was back with a couple of candy bars and a bag of chips. Zach was chuckling.

"Can you believe it?" he laughed. "Sheriff's Department just called me, asked me to tow a truck to y'all's lot. We got the contract for that stuff... they didn't even know it was my truck!"

"Isn't that something?" Alec said. He passed through the showroom and met Dani on the front sidewalk. "Candy bar?" he asked.

"Thanks," she said. "Listen, Alec, I'm sorry—"

"I know."

They stood in silence as they watched Zach open the large garage doors and back out a tow truck. On top of the flat bed was a sand-colored Toyota Highlander.

"What the—?"

Alec was beside the tow truck instantly. Zach was opening the door and preparing to get out.

"I just gotta unload this car," Zach said. "Only take me a minute."

"Where'd you get this?"

"Why, it's—" Zach stopped. "It's Brenda Carnegie's."

"Where—?"

"When she rented that car the other day, she told me her car wouldn't start and she asked me to bring it in. I did; I towed it right in. We got good customer service here."

"We know you do," Dani said.

"She keeps a spare key under the hood; I told her not to, those things fall off, but she ain't listened to me."

"Okay…"

"So I get her car here and I start it up—and it roared right up. Nothin's wrong with it."

"Why didn't you start it up before you towed it?"

Zach looked at his shoes sheepishly. "Well, thing is, if'n I went to her house and started it up, I can't really charge her nothin'. In good faith, you know. But if'n I towed it here and it wouldn't start up, well, then…"

"Yeah." Alec walked around the vehicle. "So when did you pick it up?"

"Oh, Saturday sometime. Maybe around noon. I don't rightly remember." He reached inside the tow truck and the bed began to lower. "I had it on the truck here, ready to drive back to her house first thing in the mornin'. I didn't know I'd need the tow truck."

"Yeah." Alec watched as he removed the car from the truck and parked it alongside the showroom. He met Zach as he headed back toward the tow truck. "Leave her car here, Zach. We'll be back for it."

"Okay if I park it inside the garage? She's real particular—she don't want it stolen or nothin'."

Alec looked at him for a moment. "No, I don't reckon she does."

45

Alec could see the bank lobby from the desk where he sat. It looked stark and sterile, the floors shiny and spotless, the counter vacant. Enough lights were on to illuminate every desk, every teller window, and every counter, but they looked to him like the lights used in a museum to shed light on paintings. And that's what he felt like, he realized, like he was sitting in a museum after closing time. The rooms felt larger, the walls thick and cold, and the vault on the other side of the lobby formidable.

Nate Landon's desk was clear and neat, the surface as shiny and smooth as the lobby floor. On one side of the L-shaped desk was a black telephone with two dozen buttons, a pencil and paperclip caddy, and a photograph of Nate and Peggy Lynn, holding each other against the backdrop of a stunning waterfall, a single flower in Peggy Lynn's long brown hair. Hawaii, he thought, as he looked at the photograph.

He turned his attention back to the computer in front of him, the information he sought accessible by an Intranet connection from Nate's desk.

Only a short time ago, Randy Williamson, the bank president, had met them at the bank. Alec politely delivered a court subpoena authorizing the review of all deposit accounts and account documents associated with Brenda Carnegie, Nate Landon and Peggy Lynn Landon. The subpoena had been signed just moments before they left for the bank, heading off any objections involving privacy issues.

Once Randy had reviewed the document, he'd led them down the hall to Nate's office. Dani had gone to school with his daughter as well as Nate and Peggy Lynn, and they had a brief, bittersweet conversation that brought memories of good times but also of the untimely deaths.

Now Randy stood behind Alec, reaching past his shoulder to enter passwords and select options that led to Brenda Carnegie's bank accounts.

It was, as Caroline Rauch Taft had reported: Nate had opened a bank account for Brenda with a stunning deposit of two million dollars.

Almost immediately, a check was written to a local real estate agency; from the amount, he assumed it was payment in full for the house on Elm Street. Directly following that expenditure was another deposit for an additional two million dollars, and then a series of deposits, each for $9,000 but totaling three million, were electronically transferred to an account in the Cayman Islands.

As he scrutinized the transactions, he mentally grouped them into two categories: the mundane activities everyone engaged in—grocery shopping, pharmacy, retail expenditures—and a spectacular trail of deposits and transfers that depicted tens of millions of dollars.

"Take a look at this," he said, shifting away from the screen so Dani could see the transactions.

Her eyes grew wide. "Where would you get this kind of money?" she breathed.

Randy studied the screen over Dani's shoulder. "She opened the account under a corporate name," he said matter-of-factly. "That means we'd have photocopies of the corporate documents. The computer techs scan the images, and they're available right on your screen."

"Can you do that for me?" Alec said. "Bring it up?"

"Sure."

Alec moved out of the way while Randy's fingers flew over the keyboard. He barely looked at the screen as he worked through the options, as if they were indelibly etched on his brain.

"There," he said.

"Exit 22," Alec pondered. "What kind of a corporate name is that?"

"Funeral parlor?" Dani quipped.

Their eyes met over the monitor. "No," they both said simultaneously.

Randy reached across the keyboard and hit a button. The documents began printing on the laser printer at the end of the desk. "It's a foreign corporation," he said.

"What does that mean?"

"The business was incorporated out of state—the Cayman Islands. North Carolina recognizes out of state corporations doing business here, but they're listed as foreign corporations." He handed the newly printed documents to Alec. "Here are the scanned corporation papers; they were required for her to open the account."

"That's interesting," Alec said as he read through the documents. Under the business certification information was a single line entitled "Description." Beside that were two words: "Oil Refinery."

"An oil refinery in North Carolina?" Alec mused.

"It's not unheard of," Dani said. "In fact, there was a company in the Cape Fear region that was re-refining used oil. But their name wasn't 'Exit 22'."

"Is there really this much money in oil refining?"

The three stared at each other for a long moment. Alec removed a cigarette and absent-mindedly placed it in his mouth. When he removed his lighter from his pocket, Randy cleared his throat. Alec returned the lighter, but kept the cigarette between his lips.

"I don't know about you two," Alec said, "but I'm picturing a Gulf Coast kind of oil refinery. The kind you can't miss. Just how was Brenda Carnegie refining oil out of a small house in a Lumberton neighborhood?"

Dani shook her head. "And how was she able to earn this kind of money?"

Alec hadn't noticed that Randy had returned to the computer and was studying the bank transactions again, until he spoke. His words were measured and in the type of hoarse whisper that comes with tension. "What I want to know," he said, "is how all of these transfers were done by one bank employee—Nate Landon."

Alec peered over his shoulder at the list of transactions. "What does it mean?"

Randy shook his head. "It takes two people to wire money overseas to prevent fraudulent transfers… Most people think the Cayman Islands' main source of revenue is tourism. It isn't. It's banking."

"And Nate was transferring all this money to a bank in the Cayman Islands?"

Randy nodded. "There may be nothing wrong with that… but there have been Congressional hearings about shell corporations opened in the Cayman Islands specifically. Because they are not within United States' jurisdiction, corporations there don't owe taxes and don't have to adhere to U.S. tax and corporate law… or criminal law, for that matter."

"And Brenda's account?"

"The account he was transferring to was under the same corporate name—'Exit 22.' Had it been under her personal name, an internal audit would have picked it up within three months. But it wouldn't have been flagged going from one corporate account to another... Some of these banks even have offices set up within the United States so it's not immediately apparent that the money is going overseas."

"Then the advantage of moving money to the Cayman Islands—"

"—means it can be used in drug trafficking and other illegal activities," Dani interjected.

"Well, yes," Randy said. "But because of that, banks must follow pretty stringent procedures. And after 9/11, things have tightened up a lot more... You know, following the money of suspected terrorists, broadening the scope to look for those engaged in terrorist activities or related to weapons of mass destruction."

"So how was Nate able to circumvent those procedures?"

Randy shook his head as he scrolled through the transactions. "We have dual controls and separation of duties to prevent just such a thing from happening. He would have to know how it worked and what the triggers were. Plus, we have a risk scoring," he continued. "It's a complex mathematical algorithm we use, to determine the likelihood of an account used in illegal activities."

"And that's it, just the number assigned to somebody?"

"Well, there are many factors that go into it. As I said, it's pretty complex. One of the factors is whether the bank knows the person and what type of business they're engaged in. Bill Gates, for example, could buy and sell half the United States and it wouldn't set off any alarms... he's just known to earn that kind of money."

"So, Nate might have vouched for Brenda somehow?"

"Very possibly."

"But, wait a minute," Dani interjected. "In this day and age, customers can hop on the Internet—like we just did—and transfer money without ever having to fill out a piece of paper or go through a bank employee. I do it all the time."

"Yes," Randy said, "but you're not wiring money across the border. To minimize the risk associated with possible illegal transactions, they require not one, but two, bank employees for wiring money. And according to these records, Nate handled all of that. And somehow, he was managing to do it without triggering the internal controls."

"And what was in it for Nate?" Dani asked.

Randy moved through the screens until he pulled up a list of Nate's personal bank accounts. "There are several accounts here for him," he said, scrolling through them. "Checking, savings, certificate of deposit… they are all joint accounts. Oh, but here's one in Nate's name alone."

As Alec and Dani watched, he pulled up the transaction records. "Nine thousand dollar deposits," he mused, "Hundreds of them. From an off-shore account."

"And I'd just bet," Alec said, "that every time money was transferred, a deposit was made to Nate's account."

Randy nodded slowly.

"And the reason it was transferred from another bank is, it would raise fewer flags than money moving from a customer's account to an employee's account within the same bank?"

"Another set of controls," Randy said, nodding. "It would have triggered a third party to investigate possible suspicious activity."

Alec sat on the edge of the desk, his eyes moving from Randy's face to the computer screen and back. "So, Brenda Carnegie comes to town and Nate Landon opens her bank accounts. And every time she wires money to an off-shore account, he personally conducts the transaction. And it would appear that for his efforts, he was being paid handsomely."

"But, wouldn't that have triggered a flag?"

Randy shrugged. "Here in the States, yes. Overseas… who knows? It all depends on the country. In fact, once the money went into the Cayman Islands account, who's to know if it went into a Swiss account from there? It could disappear through an international web."

They were silent, each contemplating the scenario Randy painted.

"You mentioned 'triggers'," Alec said. "What are those?"

"The computer should pick up any suspicious activity and automatically flag it," Randy answered. "Such as one employee making the transfer and not two, as required… Plus, we have routine audits."

"These audits, are they on a schedule?"

"Internal ones occur every six months; external ones once a year."

"Is it possible," Dani said, "that Nate was getting nervous? That he might have known an audit was approaching, and he wanted out?"

"We keep the schedule completely secret, just to prevent an employee from knowing how much time they have before they could be caught… There's also no way for them to know which accounts were scheduled."

"And you're sure—absolutely positive—that there's no way for anyone to get that schedule?"

"I wouldn't say it's impossible," Randy said thoughtfully. "But highly unlikely."

"What if he did get it?" Dani asked. "And he got scared?"

"Maybe scared enough to meet with Brenda about it… And maybe they met in a restaurant and argued over it?" Alec added. "And Nate said he was feeling guilty, that he was going to tell Peggy Lynn, and Brenda begged him not to?"

"And maybe…"

"Just maybe, he couldn't get out. Maybe he was so deep into money laundering that the only way out was—"

"Death."

Alec nodded. "Then my next question is, who is Brenda Carnegie working for?"

46

Never in his life had Chris traveled through a moonless night like this, where everything around him was in such total blackness that it left him disoriented.

The thick, tumbling black clouds he'd seen from the cabin had moved in, completely covering any semblance of light, concealing the moon and every star in the night sky. Added to that was Brenda's insistence that they drive with the headlights off. Even the dashboard was in complete and utter darkness.

The truck bounced around on rough ground, reducing Chris to holding onto the door handle to keep from flying across the seat, though he was securely buckled in. How she managed to avoid the trees that must surely surround them, he'd never know. He just knew with every moment that passed, his arm hurt worse, and by the time they arrived at a paved road he felt bruised and battered.

When they stopped at the edge of the pavement, he peered at Brenda. She looked every bit as disheveled as he felt, her long hair wild and unfettered, her eyes wide as though she'd traveled miles without daring to blink.

She sighed and leaned back against the seat.

"I'm amazed you didn't crash into a tree," he said, his own voice sounding husky and tense.

"It's not the trees I was worried about," she said. "It was the deer."

He visualized for an instant how a buck could have come crashing through the windshield. It was best he hadn't known about that hazard until now. "Where are we?"

"Just outside of Lumberton. From here, we take back roads to my folks' farm."

"Back roads—"

"They're paved." She turned on the headlights but before he could question her action, she volunteered, "From here on, we'll raise less suspicion if the lights are on."

Chris nodded silently as she pulled onto the road. For several minutes, he heard the sound of mud and sod dropping off the tires, and he wondered if he might ever have an occasion to see the terrain they'd driven through in the daylight. It was an odd feeling, not knowing where he had been—or where he was going.

Despite himself, he had to admit his respect for Brenda's survival instincts was growing. He could only hope his own would be as good.

They drove at a higher speed now, past vacant farmland with spotty lights of scattered homes that appeared like beacons in the darkness. His only glimpse of his immediate surroundings was through the narrow beam the headlights cast as they sped along the outskirts of town, sometimes catching animals' eyes in their glare, sometimes trees that threatened to encroach into the roadway, and sometimes long rows of vacant fields.

A service station's bright lights beckoned through the darkness, and he caught Brenda glancing repeatedly between the dashboard and the station.

"What is it?" he asked.

"I don't know if we have enough gas to make it all the way," she said. "I hate to stop, but I'd hate it worse if we ran out of gas out here."

"We don't have any other option. Stop."

She slowed as they neared the service station, pulling the rusty truck beside the pumps and cutting off the engine. It was perfectly quiet. A neon sign indicated the station was open 24 hours a day, but there was no one in sight.

They both exited the vehicle and met at the pump. Chris got the gasoline started, and they stood beside the truck and tried to keep warm.

"Get back in the truck," he said. "There's no sense in both of us freezing."

"But—"

"I'll finish pumping, and I'll go inside and pay. I won't be long. In and out."

She nodded and reluctantly returned to the truck.

When the pump cut off, he replaced the nozzle and put the cap back on the gas tank. As he neared the building, he heard the truck start up behind him. He didn't turn around, but he was oddly resigned to a sinking feeling that she might not be there after he'd paid for the gas.

An older woman sat behind the counter, the only sounds coming from the constant hum of the refrigeration units and an electric space heater at her feet.

He pulled his wallet from his pants pocket and started to count the exact amount when he abruptly stopped. He didn't know when he might need cash, he reasoned. His life had taken too many unexpected turns already. Instead, he handed her a credit card.

Two minutes later, he was exiting the station. Brenda was still there. She'd pulled the truck alongside the building and was waiting for him. As he appeared, she reached across the seat and opened his door for him.

Then they were leaving the station and the bright lights behind, moving deeper into darkness.

At last the truck began to slow and then they were turning onto a narrow graveled drive between towering rows of oak trees. The drive went straight back until a serpentine pond came into view; then Brenda turned along the embankment on what appeared to be little more than a path. It angled around the pond to the other side and crossed behind a stand of evergreens that swayed in the wind.

The road took a hairpin turn and then became straight again. As they neared their destination, Brenda slowed the truck and Chris got a clear view of the farmhouse.

It was a two-story structure, much larger than he had anticipated, with four columns that each appeared to be almost two feet in diameter and nearly thirty feet tall. The siding was clapboard and was in dire need of painting, and as they neared, he spotted one of the plantation-style shutters swinging away from the window it had once sought to shelter as the wind quickened and grew in ferocity. The other shutters were fastened tight, their dark color against the once-white siding appearing like soulless eyes noting their arrival.

Overgrown Leyland cypress bowed in the wind over flanking flower beds; as the headlights moved over them, he noticed the disintegrating brown bedding fading into the soil and the gloomy stalks of flowers he envisioned once vibrant and tall, now wizened and brown, drooping back to the soil from whence they'd emerged.

As Brenda slowed to turn, Chris noted a massive front door that once must have appeared in splendor but which now looked aged and worn. It was flanked by wide, tall windows, one on either side. As the lights struck them, he noted their wavy appearance, as if they were centuries old.

The second floor was almost a mirror image of the first; a set of glass double-doors were set diametrically above the front door, opening onto a broad balcony. On either side of those doors were windows set directly above the others.

Brenda turned, following a narrow path around the house. The home was as long as it was wide, boasting three oversized windows on the side on each level. At the back of the house was a one-story structure that jutted out from the main house.

She navigated the truck in a circle behind the house, concealing it near some evergreens and pointing toward the road on which they'd just arrived. As she turned the vehicle 360 degrees, he spotted a massive red barn with a functioning pole light at one corner, illuminating the wide entrance. Farther down, the pond curled around the house and the barn, leading his eyes to two smaller structures that appeared in need of repair.

She breathed a sigh of relief as she turned off the ignition. "We're here," she said, almost shyly.

"I wish I knew where 'here' was," Chris responded.

The truck doors creaked and groaned when they opened them, and the sound of the doors slamming shut reverberated through the night air. Brenda was obviously more familiar with the terrain, but he stumbled in the darkness, stubbing his toes on tree roots or rocks as they neared the back entrance.

The back of the house looked like a scaled-down version of the front, the center back door not nearly as massive and grand as the front door. On one side was a tall window and on the other was the additional one-story room. Above the sloping roofline was a second-story window, which was only the first in a string of three that appeared as though they were watching them.

He heard the sound of an owl in the darkness, its cry sounding inquisitive and sinister.

She unlocked the back door and opened it easily. She motioned for him to follow her, and when he moved past her, she turned and closed it. He heard the sound of deadbolts and chains and then the room sprang to life under a dim, yellow lamp.

He found himself in a hallway at least twelve feet wide, staring straight through the house to the front door. The walls had dark paneling along the bottom, interrupted by a chair rail that ran the length of the hall. Above that was burgundy wallpaper with the faint outline of lattice work in cream. Photographs lined the walls, and as Chris stared through the dim light at one of them, he noticed the glass was slightly bubbled and the sepia photograph was of a woman in period clothing.

As he turned back to face Brenda, she offered a faint smile. "This is where I grew up," she said.

He noticed the light emanated from a Tiffany-style lamp on a stand beside the door, its base nestled onto a white crocheted doily. As Brenda moved down the hall, she turned on a light switch; he noted the outlet box was mounted on the outside of the wall and not within, and as his eyes moved upwards, he found himself staring at a tube containing the electrical wires, affixed to the wall and covered in generations of paint, disappearing as it reached the ceiling high overhead.

On his left was the entrance to the additional room; the three-paneled door was open to reveal a kitchen that would have appeared right at home in the 1940's, the porcelain sink oversized, the walls covered not in built-in cabinets but in freestanding cupboards. He wanted to venture into the room but Brenda was moving farther down the hallway, a backwards glance conveying her message for him to follow her.

He was struck by the highly polished wood floor broken only by thick Oriental rugs, as though someone still lived in the home. There were two massive doors on either side of the hallway, each with an arched glass window above them; through one door, he spotted an enormous dining room table and matching cabinet; through the other, he saw a neat bedroom with a three-quarter mahogany bed, the white bedspread appearing as if it had been made only that morning.

As he followed Brenda toward the front of the house, the hallway opened through opposing open arched doorways. On one side was a baby grand piano, the black lacquer highly polished and surrounded by old-fashioned settees. On the other side, behind a curving staircase, were two more modern sofas that faced each other. In the center and to the side was an immense wood fireplace.

Brenda walked into the room and plopped down on one of the sofas, patting the cushion beside her as though this was their home and they'd been gone only for a routine but exhausting workday.

As Chris joined her, he realized he knew less about this enigmatic woman than he had even imagined.

She turned on a lamp on the end table, swathing the large room in a gentle yellow light. The questions began to form on his lips, but when she laid her head tenderly against his shoulder, he leaned back against the soft sofa. And as her measured breathing reached his ears, they lulled him into a soothing sleep.

47

The sun had long since disappeared beyond the horizon and still Joseph sat in the lawn chair, hunkered against the chill. The rain had not come, although distant thunder had reached his ears. He thought that was interesting, as thunder generally occurred in warmer weather, and he wondered if there were competing weather fronts at work there. He moved his chair farther into the confines of the structure, but the partially constructed home provided no real protection from the increasing wind and the night air.

And yet he knew the time was near. He could sense it, the same way a pianist feels the fluidity of the music building to a crescendo. The same way a mother knows when birth is near; he could sense when death was not far away.

When his cell phone rang, it sounded loud and rude in the quiet of the lake.

"Yes?"

"Christopher Sandige just used his credit card."

"Where?"

"Service station in Robeson County."

"Where's that?"

"Just outside of Lumberton." He rattled off the address while Joseph wrote it down.

"Where are you?"

"About an hour from Lumberton."

There was a moment of silence. Then, "Don't let them slip through this time." The voice had a hard edge to it.

"They won't."

Joseph clicked off the cell phone and then logged onto the Internet through his phone. He navigated to a mapping service and entered the address of the service station. Within seconds, he was looking at an aerial view of the station and vicinity.

So they had evaded the police. He felt a tinge of respect, not unlike a warrior might feel for the opposing side if they were worthy enough to warrant it.

Where does she go from here? He wondered. He looked at Interstate 74 leading away from Lake Waccamaw, and how it crossed I-95. The Interstate should have been the fastest route; within a few minutes, she could have been in South Carolina and headed farther south toward Florida. Or she could have picked up Interstate 20 in South Carolina and headed west… But she was going back, back to Lumberton, back to the area where Nate and Peggy Lynn were killed, back to the town where her picture was flashed across the front page.

And he had no choice except to follow her.

48

Alec stood quietly in the corridor, studying the tiny body in the incubator. Her yellow cap had been replaced with a white one, and under the clear polythene blanket, he could see her petite diaper and white socks. She lay on her stomach with her diminutive fist by her head, but she could not have sucked her thumb even if she'd been so inclined; the tubes in her nostrils, taped across her little face, and the needles in a hand the size of a doll's were stark reminders of her ordeal.

As he watched, a movement caught his eye and he turned to see a nurse gently rocking another infant to sleep. This one was larger and no needles or tubes intruded upon her; she sucked on a pacifier while the nurse tucked a cozy cotton blanket around her. The nurse seemed to have sensed Alec's presence because she looked up and smiled demurely, her eyes hidden by long lashes. Then she glanced across the nursery at the incubator, as if in response to his silent questions. After a moment, she rose very slowly so as not to awaken the sleeping infant in her arms; she returned the child to her bassinet, lovingly wrapping the small body in the warm blanket.

She wandered to the incubator, where she stood for a moment watching Peggy Lynn's baby. She gave Alec a thumbs-up signal and smiled reassuringly, as if to communicate that everything was alright. As she leaned toward her, her shoulder-length honey blond hair caught the lights from the overhead fixtures.

His cell phone rang, jerking him back to reality. He turned away from the window and answered it.

"You about done?" Dani asked.

"I'll be right down," he answered.

Dani had stood in the same spot only a few minutes earlier, alone in her thoughts as she'd watched the baby breathing. But when she left, Alec hadn't been quite ready; he didn't know what held him there, but the pull was undeniable.

He clicked his phone off and turned toward the elevator when he found himself face to face with the nurse.

"You're the detective working the case," she said. Her voice was soft, and Alec wondered if her timbre was cultivated for working with infants.

"Yes."

She looked through the window. "The baby is doing fine," she said. "There's so much that can be done for preemies these days."

"I'm glad," Alec said. "It's a miracle she survived."

"A few more hours, and…" her voice faded off, the unspoken words hanging in the air.

"What will happen to her?"

"I'm told that Nate's father, Jerry, will petition the court to adopt her. I'm sure it will go through… Jerry is a good man."

"Yes. So I hear."

Her eyes were blue-green, the color of an ocean that changes shade as the waves sweep across the surface. He found himself drawn to them, to her shy smile, and to her soft voice.

His cell phone rang again, and he inwardly cursed it as he grappled for it. But it wasn't Dani calling to rush him along, as he'd suspected; it was the Sheriff's Office.

He excused himself as he moved toward a private corner.

"I bypassed those passwords," Kyle Emerson said. The sound of pride in the computer technician's voice was unmistakable. "You know, on the laptop you seized from Lake Waccamaw."

"Great," Alec said. "Anything of interest?"

"You'd better come down here," he answered. "There's a lot you'll be interested in."

Alec and Dani flanked Kyle as he scrolled through the file list. "I'm not sure what you were looking for," he was saying, "but there's none of the usual stuff you might expect—word processing documents, spreadsheets, etcetera…"

Kyle's fingers could move faster over the keyboard than Alec could think; he suspected with his brains and ability, he would rack up some experience at the sheriff's department and then move into a lucrative position in the private sector. Alec just hoped it wasn't any time soon.

"You see this list of files here?" he was saying. "These are places the user has visited on the Internet. Interesting stuff."

He clicked through one of the files. The Internet Explorer opened and a moment later, a web site requested a user name and password.

Kyle entered the information and waited for the next screen to appear.

"How did you know—?"

"It's too easy," he said, his face erupting into a Cheshire grin. "There is nothing out there that can't be cracked. *Nothing.*"

A list appeared on the screen and Alec leaned in closer to read it. "What am I looking at?" he asked.

"Transactions."

"I know, but—"

"It's oil."

"Oil?"

"Oil. Take a look at this." He moved the cursor to a specific transaction and clicked through. "Oil is shipped from Canada to America, only it's recorded as coming from the Middle East—"

"Why?"

"Well, this program doesn't answer the 'why's' but if I had to speculate, I'd say because Middle Eastern oil prices are set by OPEC, and Canada isn't a member—yet. But that's sheer speculation."

"But would it be financially advantageous to come from the Middle East, versus Canada?"

"Financially advantageous for those involved in shipping the oil, but not those buying it… certainly not for the consumer."

Alec nodded. "I understand. Does the program say what happens next?"

"This program records its arrival on our shores. From there—"

"From there, it should be transferred to a refinery," Dani spoke up. "My uncle works at one on the Gulf Coast. I took a tour of it last summer. Fascinating, if you like that kind of stuff. Anyway, the crude oil is unusable in its present form, so it's shipped to a refinery, where it's processed into all sorts of products—most notably, gasoline, but also diesel fuel, petroleum gas, heating oil, kerosene…"

"Right," Kyle said. "And it's also used in the development of plastic products, even detergents and solvents. It's also part of polyester and nylon clothing."

"So is this the business Brenda Carnegie was engaged in?" Alec asked. "Oil?"

"This is where it gets good," Kyle said. "Pull up a chair. You'll want to see this."

Alec and Dani seated themselves in chairs on either side of Kyle. Their eyes were riveted on the screen as though they were looking at a hologram that would come into focus at any minute.

"The oil comes through these various ports, into the United States. But instead of being shipped to one of the major refineries, it's sent to a tiny company employing one person."

"Brenda Carnegie."

"Yep. All that oil is shipped to a post office box, one of those with a street address, like it's going to an office."

"But that's physically impossible."

"Tell me about it," Kyle said with a touch of sarcasm. "Then it's processed right here in beautiful downtown Lumberton... turned from crude oil into products used in vehicles, plastics, and clothing."

Alec leaned back in his chair. "But—where? There are no refineries in Lumberton. And if there were, they'd have to employ hundreds of people, wouldn't they?"

"Unless," Kyle said with a twinkle in his eyes, "This company named 'Exit 22' doesn't really exist."

"Like a shell company?" Alec said, his voice growing quieter.

"Exactly."

"Refineries, by law, have to be located away from residential areas," Dani interjected. "It's too combustible. There are also a lot of waste products. Refineries are incredibly complex operations..."

"So if you had a shell company, it means they aren't really doing the work, but they're getting paid for it," Alec mused. "Then who does the work? And why stick a middleman into the mix?"

Kyle brought up a separate screen. "Every time the oil is transferred, it raises the price. And in a lot of cases, it doesn't go straight from the oil company to the retailer. There are wholesalers and distributors involved. The thing is, if one company is doing the bulk of the work, they're capped at how much they can charge."

"But if it goes through multiple companies, through multiple processes, each time it raises the price."

"Exactly."

"Then, if you showed—on paper, anyway—that it was going to a particular company and somehow being processed, it gets bumped up to a higher price."

"And it keeps getting bumped up."

"Then before you know it, we're paying astronomical prices at the gas pump," Dani said.

"And for anything else that uses petroleum products."

"But," Alec said thoughtfully, "how could you remain competitive? I mean, if your product has to go through extra steps to be processed, while your competitor can do it in a more streamlined fashion, why wouldn't everybody just buy from your competitor?"

Kyle shrugged. "Haven't you noticed it almost doesn't matter where you fill up your car? You're going to pay the same price, within pennies."

"Are you saying—?"

"I'm saying it's kind of curious, don't you think? But then again, to pull something like this off, you'd have to get the cooperation of people in pretty high places—"

"Government officials?"

He shrugged again. "I'm not making any accusations. I'm just saying it's right curious."

Alec settled back in his chair. The wall clock ticked off the minutes, the sound growing louder in the quieted room.

Finally, he spoke. "So, what we have so far is this: Brenda Carnegie was operating a shell company, a company that looks like it was refining oil when the oil never even got near Lumberton."

"That's right."

"She was making an astronomical amount of money," Dani said. "We saw that from the bank records."

"It was so much money, that a typical bank employee might be tempted to point it out, wouldn't you think? But if she had an inside accomplice, somebody to handle the transactions who knew what was going on…"

They grew silent again. Kyle clicked through various screens while they pondered.

"He wouldn't have to know much, just that she was transferring large sums of money in and out of her account," Alec said. "He might not have even known where the money was coming from; he might have assumed drugs or any number of other things. But he had to have known that he was engaged in money laundering. And maybe he started asking questions—"

"Or he wanted out," Dani finished. "And that was not an option."

"So as his conscience got the best of him, he told Brenda he wanted to go clean. Tell his wife. Get out. And that's when Brenda begged him not to. She had to have known they—whoever 'they' are—would not permit him to just leave the business. That he'd be risking his life."

"So this guy, this Christopher Sandige, shows up to kill him. What's Brenda's role in the murder?"

Alec stroked his chin thoughtfully. When he spoke, his own words astonished him. "She set him up," he said slowly. "She was there, in the house. The hit on Nate looked professional—one shot in the eye. Dead instantly. Peggy Lynn—maybe she wasn't supposed to be there. Maybe she was collateral damage."

"It makes sense," Dani said, her voice soft. "Brenda would have to turn on Nate. If she didn't, she risked the entire operation. She risked all the money she'd made, she risked prison time... You're right, Alec. There can be no other explanation. Brenda facilitated the murders."

49

Sunday evening

The hotel room was chilly and dark when Joseph stepped inside. He quietly closed the door behind him and flipped on the hall light. Out of habit, he glanced inside the bathroom, peering behind the door and into the tub, before moving into the bedroom, where his eyes swept the room.

The bed was made now and the curtains were pulled apart, but everything else was just as he'd left it this morning. He crossed to the thermostat and turned on the heat. Then he closed the heavy drapes and turned on additional lights.

He turned his attention to the laptop. Where he had left it connected to the Internet, it was now displaying what was known as the "blue screen of death" which strikes fear in the heart of every computer user. But to Joseph, it meant his associates had located it through the Internet, had copied what they needed—which might have been the entire disk—and then destroyed the data on it.

He unplugged it and popped open the battery compartment and removed the battery. He retrieved his screwdrivers from his luggage, returning to the computer, where he pried away the section with the serial number. Then he flipped the laptop upside down and removed the bottom of the case. He disconnected the hard drive and pulled it from the machine. He held the thin piece of equipment in his hand for a brief moment, turning it over and studying it. Then he set it on the desk and pried it open, revealing a disk that didn't appear much larger than a typical CD or DVD. He removed it and tossed it onto the desk.

He pulled an empty gym bag from the closet floor and unceremoniously dumped the computer and parts into it. He had seen enough swampland around Lumberton to know exactly where he could unload it. The plastic piece with the serial number and the hard drive would be disposed of separately.

He zipped up the gym bag and placed it at the door to his room. Then he pulled a briefcase from the closet floor, took it to the desk and opened it.

He rifled through it, revealing a manila folder he'd been handed only forty-eight hours earlier, which contained information on his two targets. Everything had been in there—the floor plan of Nate's house and Brenda's house, their daily activities... the exact location of Nate's farm.

He pulled out his cell phone and connected to the Internet, where he navigated to Google Earth.

Sometimes he wondered what he ever did without the Internet. He still received files with photographs, and he occasionally received film footage. But now, as a matter of course, he studied the house and surrounding property through the aerial images that were made possible through Google Earth's satellite technology.

Once only available to the military, it was now at the tip of his fingers. And as technology advanced, it was rare not to find an exact location where he could point the satellite simply by scrolling through the Internet images.

He entered the address for the service station where Alec had recently purchased gasoline. He switched to the aerial view, displaying the station in real time. There were a couple of vehicles at the station now; one was parked behind it, which he presumed belonged to a station employee. Another was at the pumps. He watched a person filling up their vehicle's tank before crossing to the station's store.

Then he zoomed out and surveyed the surrounding land. The station appeared to be adjacent to acres upon acres of farmland.

Next, he entered Nate's address. The house was instantly displayed. It was familiar to him, etched into his brain through his preparatory work when he originally received his assignment. It was dark now, barely visible except for the night vision scope used by the satellite. As he zoomed out, he noted the brightly lit house next door that belonged to Nate's father. There was a steady stream of people arriving and departing. The funeral, he realized, would most likely take place within the next day or two.

He charted a course from the service station to Nate's house. It was as he suspected: it was almost a straight shot from one to the other.

But why would Brenda return there?

He removed another manila folder from his briefcase. When he opened it, he found himself staring into Brenda's eyes. It had been a surveillance photograph, but she had turned and looked directly at the camera just as the picture had been taken. He had no doubt that she had never known her picture was being taken; the clandestine photographers were the best in the world. Their equipment was almost impossible to detect.

Under the photograph were her vital statistics—date and place of birth, height, weight, and physical characteristics. And then there was her history—where she'd grown up, where she'd attended school, a list of friends both past and present and sometimes a forecasted future. Every home she'd ever lived in was there, every person she'd ever spoken to. If she chewed gum in the third grade, he thought it was noted there.

When he received a case, he focused on the present. It was best not to know that much about his targets, he reasoned, especially if they had spouses or children or pets. He normally did not need to know who they sat next to in their sixth grade classroom, which churches they'd attended, or what their extracurricular activities had been ten or twenty years earlier.

But then there were the times like these, when success depended upon his ability to put himself into the target's mind, to feel what they were feeling, to think what they were thinking, to know what they knew… and to predict their next move. Like the time he followed a target halfway around the world, only to lose him in Africa. He had pulled out his file then, too, dissecting his entire life, studying his hobbies, until he'd found a tiny piece of information that put Joseph on the path to success: thirty years earlier, when his target had attended high school, he had journeyed to Africa with his father on a safari. On a hunch, Joseph traced the man to the wilds of Zambia.

He'd caught up with him just as he was getting ready to shoot a zebra at a reserve guaranteed to net a kill. He'd spotted a reserve employee in the brush, the zebra in his sights, preparing to fire simultaneously with their client; the client would undoubtedly miss, but the reserve employee would not, and the client would not be the wiser.

So as Joseph's target prepared to fire, Joseph aimed his rifle upon him. And when the shots rang out, there were three of them, not two: the zebra collapsed to the ground in a gushing pool of blood, the client's shot presumably went astray, and the client lay dead in the Zambian dirt.

As the safari employees scrambled to the aid of their client, Joseph had ducked into the tall underbrush. He had traveled on foot for a time before transferring to a waiting vehicle, and eventually he made his way across the borders and to a waiting plane, where he was whisked back to the States.

It would be that way again, he thought as he studied Brenda's file. He had never experienced an unsuccessful assignment, and he would not have one now. Especially when it was his last one.

He flipped through the pages, noting she'd been born in Lumberton at Robeson County Memorial Hospital, and had attended county schools. *County schools.*

He searched through the records until he located information on her parents: her father had been a successful farmer, highly regarded, and her mother had been a homemaker. And they'd lived on their farm until their deaths.

He located a rural route number for their farm and switched back to his cell phone's Internet connection. Using Google Earth, he located the tract of land and the large house set far from the road. Zooming out, he studied the surrounding area.

Eureka, he thought. Their farm was adjacent to the Landon property.

He felt his pulse quickening as he zoomed back in. He wanted to rush right over there, driving pell-mell down the road, but he knew success would depend upon careful planning. He studied the house from every angle, memorizing the front porch and balcony and the location of the doors. As he peered at each side, he realized light was filtering from the house in one location only, the dim light stretching across the lawn and into the nearby trees. Someone was home.

His breath grew shallow.

He reached for his other cell phone and dialed a number. "Yes?"

"Blueprints."

"What's the address?"

Joseph read off the address.

"It's an old home," the gravelly voice said. "I don't know if we'd have the blueprints… Give me five minutes."

Joseph clicked off the cell phone and returned to the satellite image.

There were several barns on the property, he noted. One appeared to be fit for livestock, another looked to be a smokehouse, while others were tobacco barns in varying stages of decay. He memorized each of them, the footpaths to them, the locations of their doors and openings, and their proximity to the house.

His cell phone beeped and he scrolled to an incoming attachment. The blueprints were there.

The house had been built in the late 1860's, he noted. Plumbing, electricity and heating had been added in the mid 1950's. Major renovations had taken place in the 1970's, including upgraded plumbing, heating, and even central air conditioning.

As he scrolled through the plans, he memorized the location of each room. He compared the upstairs bedrooms with the location of the light filtering from the window on the satellite view. That would be her bedroom, he deduced.

He studied the house further, looking for the easiest point of entry.

The original home had been built with a basement. No, he realized, not a basement but a coal cellar. There was a chute outside the house where the coal was presumably delivered. And inside, the cellar was accessible only by a narrow spiral staircase leading to a short door into the main house.

He had just located his point of entry.

50

Chris awakened to the comforting scent of wood burning in the fireplace, the logs radiating warmth throughout the large room. In a state between sleep and wakefulness, it vaguely registered that Brenda was no longer beside him, but he found himself too sleepy to care. He dozed off and on for some time before he gradually became alert enough to look for her.

As he wandered through the downstairs, he was struck by the normality of the home. As they'd approached it earlier, it seemed like a crumbling relic of the past, the unkempt landscape providing the impression that it was deserted and no longer maintained. But as they'd walked through that door, he encountered quite the opposite: an immaculate home, obviously very old but well-maintained, with aromas he recalled from his grandparents' house— lemon furniture polish, a strange mix of floral fragrances, and that unique odor that comes from old wood and aging stuffed furniture.

He wandered throughout the downstairs, pausing in the kitchen to admire a wood-burning stove side-by-side with a more modern one; an icebox across the room from a large two-door refrigerator, and a tiny room off the kitchen that contained a deep freezer, washer and dryer. It was a paradox, this mix of old and new, a paradox not unlike Brenda Carnegie herself.

Having meandered through the rooms and still unable to locate her, he began an ascent up the curving staircase with banisters so wide his hand could barely wrap around the handrail. When he reached the second floor, he found himself in a hallway as wide as the one downstairs. On each side were two doors under arched windows. As he wandered through each one, he found each contained a bedroom with massive armoires in lieu of closets. One of the bedrooms housed a half-dozen rifles, some of which appeared to be very old—perhaps dating back to the Civil War. Between the pair of bedrooms was a bathroom containing a free-standing bathtub with clawed feet, a toilet and a pedestal sink. It looked newer than the rest of the house, and he wondered if they might have added the kitchen and bathrooms at the same time.

He found Brenda in the bathroom on the opposite side, asleep in a bathtub filled with bubbles. He stood in the doorway and studied her face in repose. It was relaxed but a few telltale lines bespoke of her tiredness. Her hair had been pulled away from her neck, but as she'd fallen asleep, she'd sunk a little deeper into the tub and now part of it was hidden by bubbles. One hand was grasping the side of the tub; a well-manicured hand, he noted. One that spoke of gentility.

He leaned against the doorframe and it creaked unexpectedly. Brenda was awake in an instant, sitting up with both hands ready to catapult her out of the tub, her eyes open and flashing. It was so unexpected that he was at a loss for words; he suddenly felt like a voyeur.

But when she realized it was him, her face softened and she leaned back into the water.

"How long have you been standing there?" she asked tiredly.

"Only a minute," he lied.

She nodded and closed her eyes.

"I like the house," he said hesitantly.

"I grew up here."

"It feels like an old house. Not that that's a bad thing."

She smiled sleepily. "It's been in the family for generations. It was built right after the Civil War ended; it's been passed down my father's side of the family ever since."

He thought of the small house in town and the sparse accommodations. "Do you live here?" he asked softly.

She opened her eyes and looked at him for a long time before answering. "Yes. I do."

"I thought so."

She didn't respond but continued looking at him, as if to gauge his reaction.

"Live alone?"

"Yes."

He looked beyond the bathroom into the adjoining bedroom. Logs blazed in the large fireplace, casting a warmth over the room. The furniture appeared to be heavy mahogany, the dark wood softened by pastel bedcovers.

"How did you come from all this—" he waved his hand "—to running from the law?"

She leaned her neck against the back of the tub and for a long moment, he thought he would not receive an answer. He had turned and was preparing to leave when she began to speak. Her voice was soft but relaxed, her eyes closed. He stopped and listened.

"Things didn't happen overnight," she said. "They happened a little bit at a time. Sometimes, I didn't even know my life was moving in any direction at all."

"What do you mean?"

She kept her eyes closed and moved her hand lazily through the bubbles. "I was recruited in college. I was young, probably more naïve than I recognized at the time…"

Funny, he thought. Of all the words to describe her, naïve would not have been among them.

"I went to work in Boston, working as a programmer. My specialty is finance." She paused. "So for a time, I handled the programs for payroll, accounts payable, receivables…"

"What line of work was the company in?"

"Oil."

"Drilling?"

"Refining."

He nodded.

"Do you know how powerful oil lobbyists are?" she asked.

He felt his body stiffen as if ice had been applied to his back, though the warmth of the fireplace still radiated throughout the rooms. "You worked for oil lobbyists?"

She smiled and briefly opened her eyes. "No. But things have been changing with the oil industry… There's been less oversight, fewer questions, not as many regulations…"

"Oh?"

"It's been very favorable to the oil industry. Especially to bottom-line profits."

He remained silent.

"Ever wonder what happens to crude oil when it reaches our shores?"

"Not really."

She opened her eyes and fixed her gaze on him. "Maybe you should. You can make a lot of money."

"I still don't understand," he said softly, "what that has to do with our present situation."

"Every time oil is refined, it increases the cost. I handled the accounting for all the processes it went through… And somewhere along the line, way above my head, someone else was watching the numbers. And this guy wondered what would happen if a couple of additional processes were added?"

"What kind of processes?"

She shrugged. "Converting it to other uses… What if one company handled two processes? How would that differ from two companies handling them separately?"

His voice was barely above a whisper. "And what did you determine?"

"The profits could skyrocket, just by moving the oil from one place to another, putting it through a different process in each location…"

He remained silent and she looked at him for a long time before continuing.

"But if both processes were done by the same company, it was much more efficient—and less costly. So a shell company was formed. And I was put in charge of the accounting, monitoring the revenue, paying out dividends…"

"Are you saying that this company you work for has one refinery handling two processes, but you created a separate entity to make it look like it was more involved?"

"That's about the gist of it. But I didn't create the company."

"Who did?"

Her expression hardened. "It's such a labyrinth of people, a conglomeration of American citizens and politicians… and even some high ranking people in the Middle East."

"And you handled it all."

"I handled the accounting."

"So why are you here in Lumberton and not still in Boston?"

She shrugged. "I could have been anywhere. But a shell company needs to have at least some semblance of legitimacy, you know?"

"So the company is registered here."

She nodded.

"So, what's in it for you?"

"Skimming."

"Skimming?"

"I transfer money earned in the U.S. to an off-shore bank account. The money is then disbursed to groups of people, but it isn't taxed. As it filters down—or up—to the principals, it's out of the jurisdiction of the IRS."

"So it's pure profit."

She nodded. "And it's lucrative."

"I'll bet it is."

She turned on the hot water faucet with her toes. After a moment, she turned it off.

"And you got a piece of the action?"

"A small piece. A minute piece, really. But enough to last me the rest of my life."

They were silent for a moment.

"Then why," he asked, "the extra home in town? If you could work anywhere, why not here?"

"Internet connection."

"What?"

"It's an old house and it's way out here in the country. I didn't have a good Internet connection."

"That's all?"

"That's all."

"So, you went to work every day at another house, and I guess people around here thought you lived there?"

"I suppose they did."

"That's why you needed the backup, why we had to go back there…"

"That's right."

"But the hard drive—it was left at the lake—"

"It doesn't matter."

He remained silent, and after a moment, she continued. "I shut down the operation. And I took all of the money in the off-shore accounts and wired them to a personal account."

"You did what?"

"You heard me."

"But—why?"

"You see what's happening here. Two people have died because one of them was about to blow the whistle on the whole operation. I didn't kill them. But the people at the top are ready to frame me for the murders… If I live through this."

His throat was dry. "So that's why we're here. You're preparing to flee the country."

"And there will be plenty of money waiting for me when I get there."

"And where is that?" he asked.

Before she could answer, they were plunged into darkness, the lights suddenly extinguished, the furnace and appliances instantly quieted. "The wind," she said. "Happens a lot out here. A tree falls on the power lines… They'll get it fixed. They always do."

51

Southeastern Regional Medical Center was located just off Elm Street, only a few blocks from Brenda Carnegie's home. Joseph pulled into the parking deck, circling the floors until he reached the top level. He backed the Lexus into a corner spot and removed the New York plates. North Carolina only required one plate on the back of the vehicle, so the lack of a front plate would not arouse suspicion.

He carried the plates with him to a trash can located by the elevator, where he buried them under a pile of soda cans, empty cigarette cartons, and various wrappings from fast food.

Then he took the elevator to the ground floor. The parking deck elevator was separated from the hospital, and he found himself at the front of the building only steps from the door. As he began to walk toward it, a movement caught his eye and he turned to face a security guard.

"Good evening," Joseph said.

"Evenin'," the guard answered.

"Looks like we're going to get a storm."

Joseph reached the door to the main lobby and casually entered it. The lobby was expansive; at the center back wall was a large information desk with a prominent sign requiring visitors to register. A line was formed in front of the desk.

He walked past it through the doors leading into the main hospital. He moved easily through the corridors like a doctor accustomed to navigating the large facility. Eventually, he reached an elevator.

It was very quiet as he waited for the elevator to arrive. The hospital was hushed. There might have been a hustle and bustle near the emergency room, but in this section of the hospital, it almost felt as if he were the only person in it.

The elevator arrived and he stepped inside and pushed the button. The door closed and he heard the smooth whir of the machinery as it whisked him upward toward the nursery.

52

The winds had become ferocious. As Brenda lit candles in the corner bedroom, Chris opened the window. The storm pelted his arm as he reached for the shutter slamming against the house, pulling it taut against the window and fastening it. With his shirt now drenched, he closed the window. As he locked it, the room became quieter, the thick walls and shutters serving as an effective barrier against the rain.

As he turned to face Brenda, a low rumble began. He waited for the lightning but saw none. "I've never heard thunder this time of year," he remarked.

She shrugged as she pulled a heavy sweatshirt over her head that reached almost to her knees. Below it was a pair of jeans she'd donned only a moment before. "We can have thunder here any month of the year," she said. "Warm fronts move in, and…"

"Ice on Friday and thunder on Sunday. Interesting."

The lights flickered, came on briefly, and then the house grew dark again.

"It happens out here in the country," she said. "You learn to make do."

Chris took one of the candles from the dresser and carried it to a corner bistro table with two chairs. "Come and talk to me," he said, gesturing.

She complied, bringing a second candle. They placed them on the center of the table and settled in. She reached toward the bed; pulling a coverlet from it, she draped it over her legs.

"I have a proposal for you," Chris said. His voice sounded hoarse and tense to him in the semi-darkness of the room.

She looked at him over the flicker of the candles. "Oh?"

"I've been giving all of this a great deal of thought," he began. "You know that I am a political strategist?"

"You mentioned that."

"Part of my job is to get people out of—well, let's just call it 'situations'."

He waited for her response but she only continued to look at him, her eyes veiled. She leaned back, farther into the shadows.

"The thing is I believe I can get you out of this situation."

"I'm listening."

"Hear me out; I know that some of this might be difficult to hear." He took a deep breath. "No matter what happened, we can alter the facts simply by putting a different spin on them." He peered through the darkness, trying to see her eyes. "Nate's dead. We can pin everything on him."

Her eyes widened and she sucked in her breath, but she didn't say anything.

After a short hesitation, he continued, "It was all Nate's idea, this business you two were in. You were a victim, pulled into it against your will, taken so deep so quickly that you were in over your head before you knew it. Ever since, you've been trying to find a way out, but your life had been threatened."

"And what about witnesses?"

"They'd have to fall into three categories," he said, his political survival instinct kicking in, "they're in it with you—in which case they won't dare come forward, or they'd simply be bringing unwanted attention—and maybe the law—upon themselves."

"Go on."

"Or it's their word against yours, and they have no concrete evidence."

"And the third?"

"The third consists of people who have evidence. In which case, if I know who they are, they can be compelled to forget it, lose it, or change it."

Another low rumble of thunder began. Chris listened to it for a moment. It sounded far away.

"And what about Nate's murder? And Peggy Lynn's? How do I explain those?"

"They weren't after Nate. They were after you. Nate was setting you up, maybe—"

"Maybe," she interrupted, "I was there."

"Where?"

"At Nate's house."

Chris swallowed. He wished he had a tall glass of water right now. "He set you up," he continued, his voice thick. "He asked you to come to his house. You were the one who was to be killed. But things went wrong, and Nate and Peggy Lynn were killed. And you fled."

"And why didn't I go to the police?" she asked quietly. Her voice sounded like silk.

"You were running for your life, hiding from the man who wants to kill you."

"Why couldn't I have called?"

He waved his hand toward the candles. "Do you have a phone here? Does it work?"

He caught a glimpse of her teeth as she smiled fleetingly. "No; when the power goes out, I lose my phone service."

"I haven't seen you with a cell phone."

"Don't carry one. They have GPS. They can be traced…But the storm just began. Where was I Friday night? All day Saturday? Why didn't I come forward then?"

He thought for a moment. The rain pounded against the shutters as the wind rattled them. "Wait a minute," he said. "You don't have to tell them anything… You work for me, for the feds. It's a matter of national security."

"Pretty far-fetched, don't you think?"

"I've heard worse. Or better, depending on how you look at it."

"Or your relationship to the dead."

"I suppose."

"Assuming this little scheme of yours works and it keeps me from being charged with Nate's and Peggy Lynn's murders… What about the guy following me? The guy who wants to kill me? I don't think a little spin action is going to change his mind."

"You'd have to trust me," Chris said. "Tell me who he is, what you know about him. My friends in Washington will do the rest."

"I don't know who he is."

"You said you'd met him once."

"I lied."

The room grew quiet as if they were in a tomb in the midst of a swirling storm.

"Okay," he said slowly, "so you lied. What *do* you know about him?"

She leaned even farther back in her chair, the back resting against the wall. The candles flickered just beyond her reach, casting her in complete shadow. "Nate was going to go public with his knowledge of my cyberbusiness. Guilty conscience. Though he'd never displayed any reluctance to accepting the money."

He waited for her to continue.

"I couldn't allow that to happen. It compromised everything I'd earned, everything I'd worked for… And it wasn't like I made up this business all by myself. It would have been like a set of dominoes, a house of cards. One weak link and everything topples."

"And Nate was the weak link."

"Yes."

"So, did you arrange Nate's murder?" His voice sounded foreign to him, and he had the sense he was outside of himself, watching events unfold from afar.

"No. Yes; I mean… " She sighed. "I passed along the information."

"That Nate was going public."

"Yes."

He waited for her to continue. When she didn't, he asked, "And then what happened? How did you go from passing along the information to sitting in a restaurant while Nate and Peggy Lynn were being murdered?"

"Not 'murdered'," she said. "Assassinated, maybe. Eliminated, certainly. But not murdered."

"Call it what you will. How did you go from Point A to Point B?"

She sighed heavily. A long moment of silence passed. Chris had begun to think he'd gone too far and the conversation had ended when she continued. "I was told they would take care of him," she said.

"And that was it?" His voice was soft. "That's all they said? Then the next thing you knew, they were dead?"

"I supplied… information."

"What kind of information?"

"Habits… Things like, Nate never locked his back door. Like Peggy Lynn was supposed to be out of town, attending a work conference that weekend. So he was supposed to be alone."

"I see."

She sat forward, her face now cast in a flickering glow from the candles. "And Nate wasn't supposed to leave work until 5:30. He shouldn't have been home until close to 6 o'clock. Nate was early, and the assassin was early."

"How do you—?"

"How do I know? Because I was there."

He sucked in his breath. Forget the water; he needed hard liquor.

"I didn't know what they would do to him," she said. "But I knew he was soon going to be out of the picture. And I also knew he kept a list of bank passwords on his personal computer at home… So I went over there when it got dark, and I let myself in through his back door—"

"—that he always kept unlocked—"

"—and I went upstairs, to a spare bedroom, intending to copy the files from his hard drive to a flash card."

"And did you?"

"I was copying the files when he came home. He was at least a half an hour early. And then the assassin came. Just my luck," she laughed wryly, "both of them were early."

"And Peggy Lynn?"

"She was never supposed to be there. I don't know why she came home, but she did."

"And where were you?"

"Hiding in the spare bedroom. I thought I was dead, too. I was preparing to open the bedroom window and crawl outside, scamper down a tree or something." Her voice sounded incredulous. "But he killed them, and he left. Just like that."

"And then—what did you do?"

292   p.m.terrell

"I waited until I knew he was gone, and then I finished copying the hard drive, walked downstairs, and let myself out."

"Why didn't anybody spot your car? Nate—or the assassin?"

"I wasn't in a car." She waved her hand as though pointing outside the window. "I have three horses. I rode one of them over to Nate's house and put her in the barn. I'd expected to be gone before Nate got home... But when I finally did leave, I rode my horse over here. The Landon farm adjoins this one. Always has."

Chris listened to the wind whipping around the corner of the building. "If you were here Friday night, why didn't you stay here? What brought you to the restaurant, where we met?"

"I figured if the assassin knew all about Nate, he'd have to know all about me, too. So he'd have to know I lived right next door."

"So you thought the assassin would follow you here."

"Yes."

"Then... why are we here now?"

She leaned toward the table and drew an imaginary circle with her forefinger. "I figured he would work outward... He'd come here first. When he didn't find me here, he'd look for me on Elm Street..."

"And when he didn't find you there, he'd—"

"Go to Lake Waccamaw. So, you see, I've been thinking like him all along... I knew when we saw my house on Elm Street that he'd been there... And we both know he was at Lake Waccamaw. He's still there; I'm sure of it. He thinks we couldn't have gotten far with just that boat and no outlet from the lake. He's probably scouring the neighborhood right now, searching for us.

"So, we're safe tonight," she said. "And we'll leave here before dawn. By the time he realizes we're not at the lake, we'll be hundreds of miles away."

53

It wasn't a full moon, but enough to see the trees bending and twisting in the growing wind, their branches raging against the tumultuous clouds. There were flashes of lightning in the distance and the low rumble of thunder. Judging from the clouds and the direction of the wind, Joseph knew the storm would soon be full upon him.

He sat in a white Ford pickup with a West Virginia license plate, watching the Carnegie house from a dirt road that wound its way around the property. His Lexus was packed and ready to go, parked at a discount store's crowded parking lot right off Interstate 95 at Exit 22. The truck he'd stolen from a nearby motel; if things went according to plan, it would be returned to an adjacent lot before the owners awakened the next morning. It seemed that half the population of Robeson County owned white pickup trucks, a fact he considered while casing the parking lots. It was important to blend in.

The rain had arrived in advance of the main storm, drenching the roads and causing some flash flooding in low-lying areas. Fate was with him once again, he thought as he stared outside the window at the water forming gullies in the old tobacco fields. After stealing the truck, he'd made his way to the Lumber River, which was roiling and tumbling in the approaching storm's onslaught. He dropped the laptop in bit by bit, watching as it disappeared downstream. On his way to the Carnegie farm, he tossed the hard drive off a bridge into a swamp. He watched as the swirling water whisked it under the road and toward a low-lying area filled with cypress and slime. With any luck, it would be washed into the thick vegetation and would soon be covered in muck.

He wore a black overcoat and a hat with a plastic cover. Both were drenched, the water running off in rivulets onto the seat and floorboard. He wore rubber overshoes, but now he reached into a bag and pulled out another pair, folding it neatly into his coat pocket. He would wear one through the rising waters to the Carnegie house; once inside, he would slide them off so the mud would not pose a slipping hazard. He would then don the other pair, which would prevent his own shoes from leaving an imprint in the blood.

He slipped on a new pair of surgical gloves. The temperature was warming and his hands were sure to sweat. But his movements had been carefully planned out; he would not be inside for more than ten minutes. He hoped to be out in five.

He watched as Chris opened the window and leaned out to pull the shutters close to the pane. When he secured it, the dim flicker of light that had remained was snuffed out.

It didn't matter. Joseph knew exactly where they were.

His Smith & Wesson Model 351PD Revolver was in the inside pocket of his trench coat. Seven bullets were ready. He had more in his pants pockets, but he wouldn't need them. One shot each, perhaps two, and he would be gone and on his way back to Washington, destined for retirement and a new career with his knitting shop.

He opened the truck door. The light remained unlit, as he knew it would. He closed the door behind him; in the howling wind, it would not be heard.

It was a quarter of a mile to the main house. He walked briskly, deliberately. He knew he was making tracks in the mud, but it wouldn't matter. The storm would erase most of them. Any that were found would be evidence of a common overshoe, one he never used in his other life.

There was no need to remain in the shadows. The house was isolated, a good mile from the nearest home—Nate Landon's house. The older Landon home was on the other side of that, too far away to see the Carnegie house, even if it were engulfed in light. He didn't fear being spotted by Chris and Brenda, either; the wooden shutters now securely blocked every window.

He reached the house. He located the coal chute easily; it was exactly where it had been shown on the blueprints. The coal chute door was made of cast iron, the pattern an intricate fleur-de-lis that bespoke of a bygone era. It took him longer than he would have liked to open it; it was obvious it had remained unused for some time. When at last it screwed off, he was left with a round hole the approximate size of a New York manhole.

He slipped inside, his feet touching the floor before his head had disappeared from the side yard. He slid the door back in place but did not rotate it completely. He would be exiting in a few short minutes.

Hunched over, his back almost scraping the ceiling, he used a pen flashlight to peer through the pitch black interior. The light picked up a blackened floor and walls that still held thick remnants of coal dust. Cobwebs and spider webs crisscrossed the room and as he shone his light, fat hairy spiders scurried into nearby crevices.

Besides the iron door he had just used, there was a wooden door about four feet high on the opposite side of the room. He made his way to it, brushing the webs out of his way. When he reached the other side, he studied it carefully.

His flashlight revealed a simple door with no frame on the cellar side. It was at the top of a rickety iron spiral staircase. He could shine his light around the edges, revealing a glimpse at an old-fashioned metal gate latch. It was approximately one inch wide and if memory served him well, it would lift straight up and the door should open.

He returned the light to his pocket. In the darkness, he removed his overshoes and slipped on the new pair. He removed his coat and his hat and laid them at the entrance. His gun was in place.

He was ready.

54

Brenda leaned forward. "My parents' car is still in the garage. I never got rid of it. It's a Cadillac sedan, something that won't raise suspicion on the Interstate."

"Then we leave now," Chris said. "I know we're both exhausted, but we don't have time to waste. You get us out of Robeson County and onto the Interstate. We'll trade back and forth while the other one sleeps." He looked at his watch. "It's already after two o'clock... If we leave now, we can be in Washington by the tail end of morning rush hour."

Brenda slid to the floor and reached under the bed, pulling out two suitcases. "I'd like to pack a few things," she said. "Not much; just..." She looked around and sighed wearily.

Chris squeezed her shoulder. "I know it's hard to leave. But we'll start a new life together. Anything you could possibly want, we'll get for you."

Tears began to well up in her eyes as she looked at him. Then she squared her shoulders and looked away. "I'll just pack a few clothes then," she said. "Just enough to get me through the next few days."

He nodded and watched as she slid the luggage onto the bed.

"What about your things?" she asked.

"We can't risk going back to the hotel," he said thoughtfully. "When we get to Washington, I'll arrange to have my car towed back there. I'll call the hotel and tell them I forgot to check out or something… The only thing I really need is my briefcase. I'll get them to ship that back to me." He thought of the suitcase full of new clothes, clothes he'd intended to wear on his Florida vacation. He would just have to arrange another trip, he thought, and this time he'd have a beautiful woman with him. Perhaps they would travel to Europe or Hawaii or some exotic locale. And he'd buy all new clothes for that trip, only she would help him with his shopping. Women liked to do those things.

He glanced down. He was still wearing the boots he'd taken from the hunting lodge at Lake Waccamaw. They seemed to have stretched out a tad, but they were still binding his feet. His pants were several inches too short; between hiking through the swamps in them and washing and drying them, the crease was long gone. They looked like something he expected to see on the homeless men who made the Washington parks their home. His shirt was even worse; the cuff on one arm was too tight to button and the other one was non-existent. Between the tatters of cloth that hung from his shoulder, he spotted the duct tape still fastened across his wound.

Brenda cleared her throat, taking him back into the present. "Do me a favor? Downstairs in the kitchen, there's a cooler. I think it would be wise to pack some drinks, maybe some food, to get us to DC. That way, other than filling up the gas tank, we won't have to stop."

"Good idea." He rose, picked up a candle and started toward the door.

"Oh," she said, "I'll show you the back stairs."

She started to brush past him and then stopped. She took a few steps past the door and opened the gun cabinet. She pulled out a rifle and ammunition and handed it to Chris.

"What's this?" he asked.

Her brows furrowed. "Don't tell me you've never seen a rifle before."

"Of course I have," he said, his back straightening. "But why are you handing it to me?"

"We're taking it with us."

"Why?"

"Why not?"

"Listen, Brenda, I don't feel right about this. I've never shot a rifle before and anyway, I'm not going to get into a shootout with the police. Nope. Count me out."

"Fine. Have it your way." She carried the rifle and ammunition into the hallway with them. "The front stairs are down there," she motioned, "but there's a narrow set of steps here at the back of the house."

He followed her to a narrow door he would have mistaken for a closet. She stepped inside and beckoned for him to follow her.

He stepped onto a wrought iron spiral staircase. It was narrow, but its sides touched all four walls.

"This used to be a dumb waiter," she said, making her way down in the dark. "But when Daddy was a little boy, his parents replaced it with this staircase. My sister and I used to love using it. We pretended we lived in a castle…"

Whether she stopped talking or her voice simply faded, Chris didn't know. The candle did a poor job of illuminating the narrow steps and the circular movement disoriented him. He almost slipped off a broken tread; reaching down, he realized the bolts were dangerously loose. He stepped past it and continued circling. He was relieved when he reached the bottom, where the door opened into the kitchen.

Brenda propped the rifle against the wall, placed the box of ammunition on the floor beside it, and crossed to the pantry, where she pulled out a cooler and some empty paper grocery bags.

"Get whatever you think we'll need," she said. "Pantry's full of stuff. I'll go back up, pack my bags, and we'll leave when you're ready."

Chris turned around to watch her. For some reason he couldn't quite put his finger on, he didn't want to be separated from her. But he didn't mention it; it would seem too cowardly. Besides, she wouldn't leave him in the house alone. They were leaving together.

"That's odd," she said, stopping in the hall.

"What is it?"

"Oh, just the cellar door. It's open."

He stepped into the hallway and watched her close it. She latched the metal bar into place and stood for a moment, looking at it. Then she shrugged and turned back toward him.

"It's nothing," she said. "Probably worked its way loose."

"What's in the cellar?"

She laughed but her laughter seemed forced. "Nothing but coal. There's no exterior door down there; none you could use, anyway."

He watched as she retreated into the stairwell, making her way up the spiral staircase in the pitch blackness.

He returned to the kitchen and opened the refrigerator. It was still cold but darkened, so he set the candle on a shelf to illuminate it. It didn't contain much, but it was obvious this was where she was accustomed to eating her meals. A fresh head of lettuce, a cluster of grapes, and other perishable items were sitting on the shelves as if she'd just come home from the grocery. He retrieved one of the paper bags and began filling it.

Then he filled a second bag with snacks from the pantry, items he thought would be easy to eat while barreling up the highway. He carried the two bags to the back door and set them down. Then he returned to the kitchen and filled the cooler with ice, bottled water, and soft drinks. The cooler soon joined the bags.

He stopped in the kitchen and studied the rifle. It was totally impractical, he thought. It was between three and four feet in length. He picked it up and was surprised at its light weight – maybe ten pounds, but he suspected it was lighter than that. He lifted it to his shoulder and peered through two sights. Then he held it in the palms of both hands and turned it over. It was labeled "M1903"; he hoped that didn't denote the year it was made.

He picked up the box of ammunition and carried it with the rifle from the kitchen into the hallway, where it joined the cooler and bags. He just didn't have a good feeling about taking it. Even if they never shot it, it wouldn't look good if they were pulled over.

The candle was only a puddle of wax as he began his ascent up the spiral staircase. His foot groped for the loose step, and he breathed a sigh of relief as he found it and crossed beyond it.

He could see the outline of the door as he approached the second floor. With each step he took, his heart felt heavier, though he was hard-pressed to understand why. He found himself walking more softly, his heavy shoes barely audible against the iron treads.

He had almost reached the top step. Instinctively, he pushed one hand forward to push the door open when a shot rang out.

55

The flash of lightning penetrated the gaps between the shutter slats, sending streams of light across the room. As Chris burst through the bedroom door, he caught a glimpse of Brenda as she fled into the bathroom. The man was standing with his back to the door, lowering his weapon. Before he could pursue her, Chris grabbed a heavy brass lamp from the dresser, ripping the cord out of the wall with one fierce movement. He was approaching the man, his own movements feeling as if he were moving in slow motion.

Just as he reached striking distance, the man pivoted, coming face to face with him. The vivid blue eyes, so soulless and cold, almost disarmed Chris and he felt his grip loosening. Then with one desperate lunge, he railed the lamp at the man, catching him against the side of his head and knocking him off his feet.

Chris heard the pistol clatter to the hardwood floor, but the lightning was gone and the room was left in total blackness.

He turned and ran, bumping against the side of the dresser before finding the door and catapulting himself into the hallway. He crashed into Brenda as she ran down the hall toward the back stairwell.

"Hurry!" he hissed, pushing her forward.

They flew into the stairwell as another shot rang out, ricocheting off the wall with a whizzing sound that almost deafened him.

"Go! Go! Go!" he heard himself shouting, but Brenda was somewhere below him, too far away now for him to sense her in the darkness.

His foot hit the loose step and he started to tumble. He flailed at the air, his hand catching the center pole, and he hung there, half-suspended and half-clinging, until his foot found a sturdy step. He reached to the treads beneath him, finding the offending step and pulling it loose. The tread echoed through the stairwell as it was hurled below.

Then he was running again, the sounds of the man echoing above him, gaining speed and threatening to overtake him.

As he reached the door into the downstairs hall, he heard him cry out and begin to tumble, as if his foot had been caught in the gap from the missing step.

Another flash of lightning cut through the sky, and he glimpsed Brenda hurling the back door open. He was behind her in an instant, grabbing the rifle and the ammunition as they propelled themselves forward into the driving rain.

"The truck!" he exclaimed.

Brenda grabbed his arm, causing his wound to sear in agony. "No keys!" she screamed, her voice almost lost in the wind and rain. She pointed toward the barn.

He grabbed her hand and they ran through the back yard, their feet slipping and sliding in the mud, the ground overtaken with growing streams of water. She almost fell as they neared the barn, and Chris stopped and grabbed her by the waist, pulling her up and pushing her forward.

He caught a glimpse of the man at the back door, searching the darkness and the surrounding terrain.

They reached the barn, pulled the door open and slipped inside. Chris bolted the door behind them.

"Jesus!" he exclaimed, checking to see if he'd been shot again. "Jesus!"

The wind howled against the aged structure, penetrating openings between the boards and sending sheets of rain inward. They backed away from the walls toward the center of the barn.

Chris heard a noise behind him and whipped around to face a beautiful brown horse with a white star. As his heart stopped pounding in his head, his brain registered three horses and four stalls. He pulled Brenda into the empty stall, and they sat on the floor, their chests heaving.

"How do you use this thing?" he asked, holding up the rifle.

Brenda grabbed the box of ammunition. He tried to watch her in the darkness as she dropped in five cartridges, and he hoped he remembered which direction they faced in the chamber.

"I took the safety off."

"What does that mean?"

"Just don't get your face too close when you shoot," she said. "It kicks."

"Yeah. Right."

"After you shoot, pull this bolt back. It ejects the spent shell, and loads the next round."

"Jesus."

"My pistol is in the house."

"That's a good place for it."

"Ya think?"

A bolt of lightning lit up the barn, simultaneous with a crack of thunder. One of the horses reared up, and the others kicked their stalls. The door rattled ever so gently.

Chris stared at it for a moment and then turned to Brenda. From the look on her face, he knew she had seen it also. His gut told him it wasn't caused by the wind.

As the storm grew in intensity, the lightning and thunder increased. Chris stood and peered around the stall door. He found himself in a barn that might have been about twenty-five feet square. At both ends were double doors. Like a hallway from one door to the next was a wide, open area. And on either side were two stalls.

As he peered upward, he could see the ceiling and water streaming in through a couple of holes in the roof. There was no loft, and nowhere to hide.

He stared at the front double doors, focusing on the planks that had weathered and pulled slightly apart. A shadow moved around the doorway, and he held his breath, wondering if it were only his imagination or shadows created by swaying trees.

"I can't let him shoot my horses."

Chris hadn't heard Brenda moving up behind him, and her hoarse whisper caught him by surprise.

"I hate to tell you this," he said, turning to face her, "but I don't know how we can stop him."

She grew silent and they both watched the door. It was unmistakable now; he was moving along the wall almost as if he were checking for a weak spot or a point of entry. It would only be a matter of time before he was upon them.

"I don't suppose you have the keys to your parent's car, do you?" Chris asked.

"You're kidding, right?"

The distance between the barn and the house flashed through his mind, of running from one structure to another, of finding the keys in the dark, of locating Brenda's pistol, of getting into the detached garage, and somehow escaping. It would be an impossible feat.

He stared at the barn's interior. They were trapped. The man knew they were inside, and he could be as patient as he wanted to; knowing at some point they would have to come out—or he would get in.

He was moving around the edge of the building. Chris lost sight of him as he brushed past the first stall, and he pulled Brenda close to him, sheltering her along the inner edge of the stall, waiting for him to move past them. When he did, it was methodical, deliberate, and slow.

He passed their stall and moved toward the opposite end of the barn, toward the back door. It was then that Chris realized the door was not bolted.

He sucked in his breath. He felt Brenda following his eyes, both of them peering at the double doors, waiting for the inevitable moment when they would swing open.

Brenda hurled open the stall door.

"What are you doing?"

"I'm letting the horses out the front door."

Before he could stop her, she was on the other side, flinging open the stall. Then he was helping her, opening the second door while she opened the third. They met at the double doors, both their hands on the bolt.

"You can ride a horse," he said, more of a statement than a question.

"I've been riding my whole life."

"Then you go with them. You can get farther on a horse than you could by foot."

Her eyes searched his. "Come with me."

He swallowed hard. "I can't. I've never ridden a horse. I'd just slow you down."

She opened her mouth to protest, but he placed his finger across her lips. "I have to stay here," he said. "I can stall him while you get away."

Before she could speak, he pushed her toward one of the horses. As she climbed onto it, he threw the bolt and screamed at the horses. They galloped from the barn, racing into the torrential rain.

He caught a glimpse of Brenda, her body flat against the horse's broad body, hanging onto the mane as they disappeared into the swirling rain and darkness.

Then he turned toward the back door, raised the rifle and fired.

The rifle kicked against his face and for a brief moment, he thought his jaw had been broken. He saw stars, and he fought to focus on the far wall. About ten feet off the ground, he noticed a hole that hadn't been there a moment ago.

Well, that's a little high, he thought as he scurried to the closest stall. He dropped to the ground and backed against the side of the stall. His breathing was heavy and labored, and his heart was pounding in his temples. He wondered if the man had followed Brenda, or if the single shot had encouraged him to stay.

While he searched the barn in the darkness, the front double doors swung back and forth with the intense storm.

He suddenly realized he hadn't discharged the spent shell, and he threw the bolt back. The spent shell popped out.

He offered a silent prayer. He had been much braver when Brenda was here, he thought. Now he envisioned her riding away from him, and his heart sank.

The doors swung open again and he sucked in his breath as he spotted the dark outline standing just off-center, staring into the barn.

The man walked deliberately, confidently, crossing the threshold as the rain poured off the brim of his hat. It was his measured footsteps that terrified Chris the most: footsteps that moved with assurance, the footsteps of a professional hit man who knew how to kill.

There was no way out for him now, Chris thought. He would die here in this barn in a location he never knew existed until a few hours ago. Alone, just as he'd lived his life.

But he wouldn't give up without a fight.

He shifted to the other side of the stall, where he had a clearer view of the man.

"Who are you?" he yelled into the darkness.

The man stopped. Chris had the sense that he was visually searching the barn for the location of the voice. "You know who I am, Mr. Sandige," he said calmly. "And you know you can't escape me."

"How did you know my name?"

His head moved slightly in his direction. "I know who you are," he said, "and I know why you're here."

"I'm here because my car ran off the road," Chris yelled back. "I don't know you, and I have nothing to do with anything going on around here."

"Is that so?" The man took a measured step in his direction. "Then how do you know Brenda Carnegie and Nate Landon?"

"I don't—didn't—know Nate. I just met Brenda two days ago. Why did you kill Nate and his wife? Why are you trying to kill Brenda and me?"

"You know why I killed Nate."

"I don't know."

"Nate was about to compromise the operation," he said as smoothly as if he were reading a child a bedtime story. "Peggy Lynn was collateral damage."

As the man continued in his direction, Chris spotted a movement outside the barn. Oh, no, he thought, his pulse quickening, Brenda didn't come back. She couldn't have.

Then he realized there were two people, moving stealthily through the rain, watching the man approach him.

He thought he detected a glint of metal, but it could easily have been his imagination.

He hoped there would be no more flashes of lightning as he raised the rifle to his shoulder. He was still seated on the ground, but judging from his first shot, he decided it was the perfect spot.

With his sudden movement, the man turned and began firing. Chris felt a bullet sear through his thigh and he cried out in pain. He fought to focus on the rifle sights but his vision blurred as he pulled the trigger. The sound was deafening and he was kicked back against the wall as the man shot again.

Chris could hear shouting but he was deafened from the noise of the rifle. He pulled back the bolt and the spent shell popped out. He felt another bullet strike his right shoulder and he shakily raised the rifle as blood spurted across the stock.

The man was bloodied, he thought, or maybe it was his own eyesight that was bloodied. He fired again, and the man went down, and then the people outside the barn were rushing in, shouting. He dropped his rifle into his lap and tried to hang onto consciousness. His brain shouted at him to pick up the rifle, to expend the spent shell, to fire again, but now it was no longer raining and there were no more shouts and the barn was getting darker as the world faded around him.

56

The Carnegie farm was lit up like a football field. Somewhere in the back of his brain, Chris knew the medics were stopping the flow of blood, applying pressure and placing a tourniquet on his leg. He knew from a sentence or a word caught here and there that he'd been shot three times—in the leg and in both arms. He suspected the third shot was the one still wrapped in duct tape.

He wanted nothing more than to sleep, but the medics kept questioning him, asking him what his name was, who was president, and what year it was. He didn't care who he was anymore, could care even less who was president and the year didn't matter. All that mattered was sleep.

They carried him to a nearby gurney, the movement causing pain to sear through his extremities as if his whole body were on fire. He felt the world fade and bubble around him, his eyes no longer focusing.

They wheeled the gurney toward the barn door and stopped to talk to the sheriff's deputies. The rain had lessened now, the brunt of the storm having moved through, but the water was still running off the roof as if a water hose had been turned on and left above the doorway.

He opened and closed his eyes, trying to will himself
into consciousness. Then he realized only a few feet away
from him was another gurney and another person, and he
was staring at him.

"You'll never be safe," the man said. "They'll send
someone else. And they'll keep sending them until you're
dead."

Then the medics were back, wheeling him from the
barn to a waiting ambulance, past vehicles with blue lights
flashing, past uniformed officers and bright lights that lit
up the yard like daylight.

57

Monday morning

Dawn was breaking over the horizon as Alec pulled the cruiser into the traffic circle at Southeastern Regional Medical Center. The rain had stopped several hours earlier and a warm front had moved in. As Alec and Dani stepped out of the car, the gentle winds almost felt balmy.

"Okay," Dani was saying on the radio, "we're here. We'll be right up." She turned to Alec. "They're ready for us to transport Joseph Gabucci to the jail."

"What about his injuries?"

"Shot five times. He's lucky to be alive... But they're not life threatening injuries, and there's no need for him to stay here."

"Yeah. I'll feel better when he's behind bars... The Czar wants to talk to us; there'll be a routine inquiry, since we both fired our weapons."

"They were able to remove all the bullets—"

"—yes. They'll figure out which one of us hit him, and where... You know the drill."

"I don't," Dani said with a sly smile. "This is my first shooting."

"Let's hope it's your last."

They reached the hospital doors and Dani stopped before entering. "Listen, Alec."

"Yes?"

"About the other day, my request to be transferred…"

"Oh. Yeah."

"I'm sorry. I've reconsidered everything, and I was wrong."

"Yeah?"

"Yeah. I'm going to speak to Sheriff Czarnecki this morning, and tell him I want to remain your partner."

"Really?"

"Really."

"Well, we do—"

"—work really well together."

"Yeah."

"Yeah."

"We finish—"

"—each other's sentences. I know."

They entered the hospital, waved at the ladies behind the Information Desk, and continued on to the elevator. "Dani, I'd like to make a stop before we go to Gabucci's room."

"The baby?"

"Yeah."

"I figured as much."

The elevator doors opened and they stepped in. Alec pushed the button for the maternity ward, and Dani reached across him and pushed a separate button. "I'll meet you at his room," she said.

The baby was so tiny, Alec thought as he stood behind the window and looked at her. She still lay in the incubator, the oxygen tube taped to her nose and IV fluids pumping into her tiny body.

"She's going to be okay," a soft voice said.

He turned to face the nurse.

She smiled at him demurely. "She's responding well. There's so much that can be done for her... and I hear that a fund is being established, and all sorts of folks are coming forward to donate money for her—her upbringing, her education—"

"It won't ever take away the pain of losing her parents."

"No. Nothing can bring them back. But this little girl won't lack for love. I can tell you that... Jerry Landon has been here every day, about twenty hours a day, it seems. And lots of folks stop by to see her."

"Good. I'm happy to hear it."

He turned and looked back at the little girl. She stirred and tried to place her fist into her mouth.

"See those beautiful pink booties and cap she's wearing?" The nurse had moved alongside Alec and was admiring the baby as if she were her own. "A gift. A nice man came in late last night, said he'd knit them for her. Aren't they beautiful?"

Alec nodded.

"Her name's Annabel."

"Annabel."

"It suits her, don't you think?"

"Yes," Alec said. "It suits her."

The nurse leaned toward him, and he turned to face her. Her eyes were wide, a light blue-green with a thin ring of black along the edges that only served to emphasize their color. "My name's Sandy."

Alec instinctively held out his hand. "I'm—"

"Alec Brodie. I know." She shook his hand. A lock of her blond hair fell across her brow.

After they performed the obligatory shake, he remained with her hand in his. She didn't seem to be in a hurry to disengage herself from him, either.

"I have tickets to a dinner theatre," she said, "over in Whiteville. It's community theatre; one of the employees here at the hospital is playing in it."

Alec nodded, unsure what to say.

"Would you like to go with me?"

"Yes," he said immediately. "Yes, I would."

A few minutes later, he was stepping off the elevator with a phone number in his pocket, plans for the coming week, and a lighter step. It was going to be a beautiful day.

58

The limousine driver sat in the car, planning the route to Capitol Hill. Chris stood a short distance away and watched as his car was loaded onto a flatbed truck. He was wearing a new pair of casual slacks, having retrieved them from his luggage at the hotel, along with the pair of tennis shoes he'd intended to wear in Florida. It was a good thing the pants were loose; one thigh had been bandaged heavily after the bullet had been removed. They might have provided him with a crutch to help him walk, but both arms were bandaged as well—one at the shoulder and one around the upper arm.

His ragged shirt, abused pants, and the hunter's boots were in the wastebasket at the hotel. His two suitcases and briefcase were in the limousine's trunk.

The service manager approached him with a clipboard.

"I hate to ask you to sign this," he said, eyeing his arms.

"Just hold it up for me," Chris said, taking the pen and scratching his name in the vicinity of the signature line. "Will that do?"

"Yes, sir." The service manager tore off the top copy. "Where—?"

"My back pocket, please."

He folded the paper and tucked it into his pocket beside his wallet. The wallet was no longer waterlogged, but Chris knew as soon as it was practical, he would be replacing it.

"Oh," he said suddenly, "my cell phone. It's in the back seat of my car."

The service manager climbed onto the flatbed and retrieved the phone. It was ringing, but stopped before Chris could answer it. There would be plenty of time to answer calls, he thought as he envisioned the long road trip ahead.

A car pulled alongside him and Alec Brodie and Dani Malleck stepped out.

"Mr. Sandige," Alec said as he approached.

"Lieutenant," Chris said, "I can't thank you enough. You saved my life."

Alec nodded.

"What happens now?"

"Lieutenant Malleck and myself heard Gabucci confess to killing Nate and Peggy Lynn. And Lumberton P.D. found the Lexus that had been spotted at Lake Waccamaw. Lots of interesting things found in the trunk."

"I'll bet."

"You'll be coming back to Lumberton," Alec continued. "We'll need you to testify."

"I understand. You know how to reach me."

"Yes; we do." His eyes narrowed. "You still don't have any idea where Ms. Carnegie would have been headed?"

Chris shook his head. "But now that you know she didn't kill Nate and Peggy Lynn—"

"She's still wanted. She's considered an accomplice because she was there, at the scene of the crime—"

"But she can explain that."

"I'll bet she can," he said. Chris thought his tone sounded more than a little sarcastic. "That's why we need to speak to her… And there are other crimes involved—a shell company, money laundering… She has a lot of questions to answer."

Chris nodded.

"But your story checks out," Alec said. "And we've spoken to Congressman Willo. We'll be in touch." He glanced at the limousine. "That your ride?"

"Yep. That's it."

Dani and Alec walked him to the car. With the aid of the limousine driver, they helped him into the back seat.

"You going to be alright?"

Chris nodded. "I'm on pain pills now; I'm not feeling a thing. I hope to sleep most of the way home."

The driver closed the door and climbed into the front seat. "Are you ready, sir?"

Chris nodded. "I'm ready."

The driver pulled the car through the parking lot, giving Chris one last look at Lieutenants Alec Brodie and Dani Malleck. His Lincoln was being secured in the flatbed; with any luck, he and his car would arrive in D.C. before nightfall.

As they drove along the service road, the sun was rising higher. Though it was November, it almost looked like a spring day. The rain was gone, the winds had passed through, and there was no evidence of the ice storm that had brought him south on Interstate 95.

All three of the horses had come back to the Carnegie farm before the ambulance had taken him away. They'd been secured and Animal Control was expected there today to make sure they were cared for. But there had been no trace of Brenda Carnegie.

He wondered if Brenda would be waiting for him when he arrived home, if she might at this very moment be driving northward… or if she was on her way out of the country.

The phone rang and he answered it.

"Chris!"

He recognized the intern's voice immediately. "Yes."

"Where are you? We've been trying to reach you all weekend!"

The limousine stopped at a traffic light and Chris peered around him. "I've been on vacation," he said.

"Well, you're gonna have to come back right away. We've got stuff happening here… There's a subcommittee meeting that's just been scheduled this week. Some experts will be testifying about the depletion of oil reserves, and they're looking into relationships between members of Congress and oil cartels…"

"Is Willo implicated?"

"Not yet, but it could only be a matter of time before Congress—and the media—start asking questions."

"I'm on my way."

Chris clicked off the cell phone and placed it in his lap. The light changed and the limo turned onto the entrance ramp to Interstate 95. He glanced across the roadway at Robeson Community College, where a tan dog played at the edge of the parking lot with two other strays. As the car picked up speed, he turned and looked through the rear window at the embankment where he'd run off the road beside a green and white sign that said simply, *Exit 22.*

A Note From The Author

The shell corporation that Brenda Carnegie registered in the Cayman Islands is a growing tactic used by United States corporations to avoid taxes, oversight, and sometimes corporate and criminal law. The U.S. Government Accountability Office reported in the year 2004 that only 39% of United States corporations paid taxes on their income and profits. This amounts to only 14.4% of the total tax burden in the United States. This figure is expected to continue dropping as the middle class shoulders more of the tax burden.

One of the ways in which corporations are avoiding taxes is to start shell corporations outside United States jurisdiction. The islands in the Caribbean, including the Bahamas, Cayman Islands, Bermuda and others, are popular locations. It's estimated the United States could be losing more than $100,000,000,000 *per year* due to these shell corporations in income taxes alone, not counting the Social Security and Medicare tax burdens to which off-shore corporations are exempt. There is currently legislation in the House and Senate that would limit or eliminate a lot of the tax loopholes and breaks off-shore companies have enjoyed, but as of this writing, the legislation has not been passed.

The scam Brenda was involved in with regard to using a shell corporation to make it appear as if oil was moving through more than one processor is a variation of schemes that have actually been used in the past by various industries. Sometimes these schemes are made possible by deregulation and lessening oversight of specific industries, as was the case with Enron. Enron's scheme, nicknamed "Death Star", used shell companies to make it appear as if they were transferring electricity from one location to another to relieve congestion. Their scheme ultimately led to the California energy crisis. Enron also used a scheme they called "Ricochet", in which they bought power in-state, "sold" it to an out-of-state intermediary (which was only an Enron-run shell company), and then "re-purchased" it at an inflated price as "imported electricity", all in order to increase company profits.

Bank regulations have tightened, especially after 9/11, so the wiring of money as described in Chapter 45 should, in reality, trigger numerous controls. Most banks do not have a specific schedule for audits as shown in this book, but rely on ad hoc audits to avoid the possibility of an employee such as Nate Landon participating in such a scheme. Many banks with American-sounding names are now owned and controlled by entities outside of the United States, so it is possible to transfer money within this country and have it ultimately end up outside our borders.

In Chapter 25, a mysterious young woman appears at *The Triple R Hunt Club*. Her name is Sheila Carpenter, and she was engaged in an adventure that was unrelated to Brenda's. Her adventure is the subject of my third suspense, *Ricochet*, which was released prior to *Exit 22*.

At the end of the book, Christopher Sandige was set to embark on his own adventure involving oil and politics. This is the subject of another book I am currently writing, which has no relation to Brenda Carnegie's scams but spins off in its own, unique direction.

p.m.terrell is the pen name for Patricia McClelland Terrell. She is the internationally acclaimed author of the suspense/thrillers *Ricochet*, *The China Conspiracy*, and *Kickback*, all published by Drake Valley Press, as well as the historical adventure/suspense, *Songbirds are Free*. She is also the author of *Take the Mystery out of Promoting Your Book* (published by Palari Publishing) and several nonfiction computer books, including *Creating the Perfect Database* (Scott-Foresman), *The Dynamics of WordPerfect* and *The Dynamics of Reflex* (Dow Jones-Irwin), and *Mememto WordPerfect* (Edimicro, Paris.)

Ms. Terrell is the co-founder, along with Officer Mark Kearney of the Waynesboro, Virginia Police Department, of the Book 'Em Foundation, a partnership between authors and law enforcement agencies dedicated to raising public awareness of the correlation that exists between high crime rates and high illiteracy rates, increasing literacy, and reducing crime. Their web site is www.bookemfoundation.org.

Ms. Terrell is also proud to serve on the Robeson County Friends of the Library Board of Directors (www.robesoncountylibrary.com) and on the Board of the Robeson County Arts Council (www.robesonarts.org). Both organizations are committed to supporting the arts, science, history and heritage of Robeson County, North Carolina.

Ms. Terrell is the founder of McClelland Enterprises, Inc., one of the first companies in the Washington, DC area devoted to PC training in the workforce, and Continental Software Development Corporation, which provides applications development, website design, and computer consulting services throughout the United States and its territories. Her clients have included the U.S. Secret Service, CIA and Department of Defense, as well as various local law enforcement agencies.

She is also a staunch supporter of Crime Stoppers, Crime Solvers, and Crime Lines, which offer rewards and anonymity to individuals reporting information on criminal activity. She is proud to have served as the first female President of the Chesterfield County/ Colonial Heights (Virginia) Crime Solvers Board of Directors (2003-2004) and as the Treasurer for the Virginia Crime Stoppers Association.

Visit her website at www.pmterrell.com for more information.